The Financial Expert

Indian Thought Publications

Other works by Narayan in this imprint

Novels

Swami and Friends

The Bachelor of Arts

The Dark Room

The English Teacher

Mr. Sampath – The Printer of Malgudi

Waiting for the Mahatma

The Guide

The Man-eater of Malgudi

The Vendor of Sweets

The Painter of Signs

A Tiger for Malgudi

Talkative Man

The World of Nagaraj

Grandmother's Tale

Short Stories

Malgudi Days

Under the Banyan Tree and Other Stories

Autobiography

My Days

The Financial Expert

R.K. Narayan

INDIAN THOUGHT PUBLICATIONS

INDIAN THOUGHT PUBLICATIONS

New No.38, Thanikachalam Road,
T. Nagar, Chennai - 600 017

© Legal Heirs of R. K. NARAYAN

The Financial Expert

ISBN: 978-81-85986-05-0

First published in Great Britain in 1952 Methuen & Co. Ltd.
Reissued in 1979 by William Heinemann Ltd.
First published in the U.S. by Michigan State University Press 1953
German edition by Nymphenburger
French edition by Plon
Dutch edition by Uitgeverji V/h c., de Boer

First Indian Edition 1958
35th Reprint 2012

Printed in India at
BHAVISH GRAPHICS
New No.6, McNichols Road,
Chetput, Chennai - 600031.

To the
Memory of a very dear friend
Kittu R. Purna

PART ONE

FROM time immemorial people seemed to have been calling him "Margayya". No one knew, except his father and mother, who were only dimly recollected by a few cronies in his ancestral village, that he had been named after the enchanting god Krishna. Everyone called him Margayya and thought that he had been called so at his naming ceremony. He himself must have forgotten his original name: he had gradually got into the habit of signing his name "Margayya" even in legal documents. And what did it mean? It was purely derivative: "Marga" meant "The Way" and "Ayya" was an honorific suffix: taken together it denoted one who showed the way. He showed the way out to those in financial trouble. And in all those villages that lay within a hundred-mile radius of Malgudi, was there anyone who could honestly declare that he was not in financial difficulties? The emergence of Margayya was an unexpected and incalculable offshoot of a co-operator's zeal. This statement will be better understood if we watch him in his setting a little more closely.

One of the proudest buildings in Malgudi was the Central Co-operative Land Mortgage Bank, which was built in the year 1914 and named after a famous Registrar of Co-operative Societies, Sir ———, who had been knighted for his devotion to Co-operation after he had, in fact, lost his voice explaining co-operative principles to peasants in the village at one end and to the officials in charge of the files at the Secretariat end. It was said that he died while serving on a Rural Indebtedness Sub-committee. After his death it was discovered that he had left all his savings for the construction of the bank. He now watched, from within a teak frame suspended on the central landing, all

1

the comings and goings, and he was said to be responsible for occasional poltergeist phenomena, the rattling of paper-weights, flying ledgers, and sounds like the brisk opening of folios, the banging of fists on a table, and so on—evidenced by successive night watchmen. This could be easily understood, for the ghost of the Registrar had many reasons to feel sad and frustrated. All the principles of co-operation for which he had sacrificed his life were dissolving under his eyes, if he could look beyond the portals of the bank itself, right across the little stretch of lawn under the banyan tree, in whose shade Margayya sat and transacted his business. There was always a semi-circle of peasants sitting round him, and by their attitude and expression one might easily guess that they were suppliants. Margayya, though very much their junior (he was just forty-two), commanded the respect of those who sat before him. He was to them a wizard who enabled them to draw unlimited loans from the co-operative bank. If the purpose of the co-operative movement was the promotion of thrift and the elimination of middlemen, those two were just the objects that were defeated here under the banyan tree: Margayya didn't believe in advocating thrift: his living depended upon helping people to take loans from the bank opposite and from each other.

His tin box, a grey, discoloured, knobby affair, which was small enough to be carried under his arm, contained practically his entire equipment: a bottle of ink, a pen and a blotter, a small register whose pages carried an assortment of names and figures, and above all—the most important item—loan application forms of the co-operative bank. These last named were his greatest asset in life, and half his time was occupied in acquiring them. He had his own agency at work to provide him with these forms. When a customer came, the very first question Margayya asked was, " Have you secured the application form? "

" No."

"Then go into that building and bring one—try and get one or two spare forms as well." It was not always possible to secure more than one form, for the clerks there were very strict and perverse. They had no special reason to decline to give as many forms as were required except the impulse to refuse anything that is persistently asked for. All the same, Margayya managed to gather quite a lot of forms and kept them handy. They were taken out for use on special occasions. Sometimes a villager arrived who did not have a form and who could not succeed in acquiring one by asking for it in the bank. On such occasions Margayya charged a fee for the blank form itself, and then another for filling in the relevant details.

The clerks of the bank had their own methods of worrying the villagers. A villager who wanted to know his account had to ask for it at the counter and invariably the accounts clerk snapped back, "Where is your pass-book?" A pass-book was a thing the villager could never keep his hand on. If it was not out of sight it was certain to be out of date. This placed the villager fully at the mercy of the clerk, who would say: "You will have to wait till I get through all the work I have now on hand. I'm not being paid to look after only your business here." And then the peasant would have to hang about for a day or two before getting an answer to his question, which would only be after placating the clerk with an offering in cash or kind.

It was under such circumstances that Margayya's help proved invaluable. He kept more or less parallel accounts of at least fifty of the members of the bank. What its red-tape obstructed, he cleared up by his own contrivance. He carried most of the figures in his head. He had only to sight a customer (for instance Mallanna of Koppal, as it now happened to be) to say at once: "Oh! you have come back for a new loan, I suppose. If you pay seventy-five rupees more, you can again take three hundred rupees within a week! The bye-law allows a new loan when fifty per cent is paid up."

"How can I burden myself with a further loan of three hundred, Margayya? It's unthinkable."

3

Now would begin all the persuasiveness that was Margayya's stock-in-trade. He asked point blank, " What difference is it going to make? Are you not already paying a monthly instalment of seventeen rupees eight annas? Are you or are you not? "

" Yes . . . I'm paying. God knows how much I have to——"

" I don't want all that," Margayya said, cutting him short. " I am not concerned with all that—how you pay or what you do. You may perhaps pledge your life or your wife's sarees. It is none of my concern : all that I want to know is whether you are paying an instalment now or not."

" Yes, master, I do pay."

" You will continue to pay the same thing, that is all. Call me a dog if they ask you for even one anna more. You fool, don't you see the difference? You pay seventeen rupees eight annas now for nothing, but under my present plan you will pay the same seventeen rupees eight annas but with another three hundred rupees in your purse. Don't you see the difference? "

" But what's the use of three hundred rupees, master? "

" Oh! I see, you don't see a use for it. All right, don't come to me again. I have no use for nincompoops like you. You are the sort of fellow who won't——" He elaborated a bawdy joke about him and his capacity, which made the atmosphere under the tree genial all round. The other villagers sitting around laughed. But Margayya assumed a stern look, and pretended to pass on to the next question in hand. He sat poring over some papers, with his spectacles uneasily poised over his nose. Those spectacles were a recent acquisition, the first indication that he was on the wrong side of forty. He resisted them as long as he could —he hated the idea of growing old, but ' long-sight ' does not wait for approval or welcome. You cannot hoodwink yourself or anyone else too long about it—the strain of holding a piece of paper at arm's length while reading stretches the nerves of the forearm and invites comments from others. Margayya's wife laughed aloud one day and

4

asked: "Why don't you buy a pair of glasses like other young men of your age? Otherwise you will sprain your hand." He acted upon this advice and obtained a pair of glasses mounted in silver from the V.N. Stores in the Market. He and the proprietor of the shop had been playmates once, and Margayya took the glasses on trial, and forgot to go that way again. He was accosted about it on the road occasionally by the rotund optician, who was snubbed by Margayya: "Haven't you the elementary courtesy to know the time and place for such reminders?"

"Sorry, sorry," the other hastened to apologize, "I didn't intend to hurt or insult you."

"What greater insult can a man face than this sort of thing? What will an onlooker think? I am busy from morning to night—no time even for a cup of coffee in the afternoon! All right, it doesn't matter. Will you send someone to my house? I'm not able to use those glasses either. I wanted to come and exchange them if possible, but——" he trailed off into indefiniteness, and the optician went away once again and soon ceased to bother about it. It was one of his many bad debts, and very soon he changed his commodity; gradually his show-case began to display powder-puffs, scents, chocolate bars—and the silver-rimmed glasses sat securely on Margayya's nose.

He now took off his spectacles and folded the sides as if disposing once and for all of the problem of Mallanna. He looked away at a man on his right and remarked: "You may have to wait for a week more before I can take up your affair."

"Brother, this is urgent, my daughter's marriage is coming off next month."

"Your daughter's marriage! I have to find you the money for it, but the moment my service is done, you will forget me. You will not need your Margayya any more." The other made several deprecating noises, as a protestation of his loyalty. He was a villager called Kanda who had come walking from his village fifteen miles away. He owned about twenty acres of land and a house and cattle, but all of it was tied up in mortgages—most through Margayya's advice and assistance. He was a gambler and drank heavily, and he always asked for money on the pretext of having to marry his daughters, of whom he had a good number. Margayya preferred not to know what happened to all the money, but helped him to borrow as much as he wanted. "The only course now left is for you to take a joint-loan, but the difficulty will be to find someone as a partner." He looked round at the gathering before him and asked, "All of you are members of the Co-operative Society. Can't someone help a fellow-creature?" Most of them shook their heads. One of them remarked, "How can you ask for our joint-signature? It's risky to do it even for one's own brother."

"It's most risky between brothers," added Margayya. "But I'm not suggesting it for brothers now. I am only suggesting it between human beings." They all laughed and understood that he was referring to an elder brother of his with whom he was known to be on throat-cutting terms. He prepared to deliver a speech: "Here is a great man, a big man, you cannot find a more important man round about Somanur. He has lands, cattle, yes, he's a big man in every way. No doubt, he has certain habits: no use shutting our eyes to it; but I guarantee he will get over them. He must have a joint loan because he needs at least five hundred rupees immediately to see him through his daughter's marriage. You know how it is with the dowry system——" Everybody made a sympathetic noise and shook their heads. "Very bad, very bad. Why should we criticize what our ancestors have brought into existence?" someone said.

"Why not?" another protested.

"Some people are ruined by the dowry."

"Why do you say some people?" Margayya asked. "Why am I here? Three daughters were born to my father. Five cart-loads of paddy came to us every half year, from the fields. We just heaped them up on the floor of the hall, we had five halls to our house; but where has it all gone? To the three daughters. By the time my father found husbands for them there was nothing left for us to eat at home! "

"But is it not said that a man who begets a son is blessed in three lives, because he gives away the greatest treasure on earth? " said someone.

"And how much more blessed is he that gives away three daughters? He is blessed no doubt, but he also becomes a bankrupt," Margayya said.

The talk thus went on and on, round and round, always touching practical politics again at some point or other. Margayya put his spectacles on, looked fixedly at Mallanna, and said: "Come and sit near me." The villager moved up. Margayya told the gathering, "We have to talk privately." And they all looked away and pretended not to hear, although all their attention was concentrated on the whispering that now started between the two. Margayya said: "It's going to be impossible for Kanda to get a joint-loan, but he ought to be ready to accept whatever is available. I know you can help him and help yourself— you will lose nothing. In fact, you will gain a little interest. You will clear half your present loan by paying seventy-five rupees and apply for a fresh one. Since you don't want it, give it to Kanda. He will pay you seven and a half per cent. You give the four and a half per cent to that father-in-law " (Margayya always referred to the Co-operative Bank with a fresh sobriquet) "and take the three per cent yourself. He will pay back the instalments to you. I will collect and give them to you." Mallanna took time to grasp all the intricacies of this proposition, and then asked: "Suppose he doesn't? " Margayya looked horrified at this doubt. "What is there to be afraid of when I am here? " At this one of the men who were supposed to be out of earshot remarked: "Ah, what is possible in this world without mutual trust? " Margayya added, "Listen to him. He knows the world."

7

The result of all this talk was that Mallanna agreed to the proposal. Margayya grew busy filling up a loan application form with all the details of Mallanna's heritage, etc. He read it out aloud, seized hold of Mallanna's left thumb, pressed it on a small ink pad he carried in his box and pressed it again on the application form and endorsed it. He took out of the box seventy-five rupees in cash, and handed them to Mallanna with: "Why should I trust you with this without a scrap of paper? Now credit this to your account and halve your loan; and then present that application."

"If they refuse to take it?"

"Why should they refuse? They have got to accept it. You are a shareholder, and they have got to accept your application. It's not their grand-father's money that they are giving you but your own. Bye-law——" He quoted the bye-law, and encouraged by it, the other got up and moved on.

It is impossible to describe more clearly than this Margayya's activity under the tree. He advanced a little loan (for interest) so that the little loan might wedge out another loan from the Co-operative Bank; which in its turn was passed on to someone in need for a higher interest. Margayya kept himself as the centre of all the complex transaction, and made all the parties concerned pay him for his services, the bank opposite him being involved in it willynilly. It was as strenuous a job as any other in the town and he felt that he deserved the difficult income he ground out of a couple of hundred rupees in his box, sitting there morning till evening. When the evening sun hit him on the nape of the neck he pulled down the lid of his box and locked it up, and his gathering understood that the financial wizard was closing his office for the day.

Margayya deposited the box under a bench in the front
room of his house. His little son immediately came running out from the kitchen with a shout: " *Appa!——* " and
gripped his hand, asking: " What have you brought
today? " Margayya hoisted him up on his shoulder:
" Well, tomorrow I will buy you a new engine, a small
engine." The child was pleased to hear it. He asked, " How
small will the engine be? Will it be so tiny? " He indicated
with his thumb and first finger a minute size. " All right,"
said Margayya and put him down. This was almost a daily
ritual. The boy revelled in visions of miniature articles—
a tiny engine, tiny cows, tiny table, tiny everything, of the
maximum size of a mustard seed. Margayya put him
down and briskly removed his upper cloth and shirt, picked
up a towel that was hanging from a nail on the wall, and
moved to the backyard. Beyond a small clump of banana
trees, which waved their huge fan-like leaves in the darkness, there was a single well of crumbling masonry, with
a pulley over its cross-bar. Margayya paused for a moment
to admire the starry sky. Down below at his feet the earth
was damp and marshy. All the drain water of two houses
flowed into the banana beds. It was a common backyard
for his house and the one next door, which was his
brother's. It was really a single house, but a partition wall
divided it into two from the street to the backyard.

No. 14 D, Vinayaka Street had been a famous land-mark,
for it was the earliest house to be built in that area. Margayya's father was considered a hero for settling there in a
lonely place where there was supposed to be no security
for life or property. Moreover it was built on the fringe
of a cremation ground, and often the glow of a burning
pyre lit up its walls. After the death of the old man the
brothers fell out, their wives fell out, and their children
fell out. They could not tolerate the idea of even breathing
the same air or being enclosed by the same walls. They
got involved in litigation and partitioned everything that

their father had left. Everything that could be cut in two with an axe or scissors or a knife was divided between them, and the other things were catalogued, numbered and then shared out. But one thing that could neither be numbered nor cut up was the backyard of the house with its single well. They could do nothing about it. It fell to Margayya's share, and he would willingly have seen his brother's family perish without water by closing it to them, but public opinion prevented the exercise of his right. People insisted that the well should remain common property, and so the dividing wall came up to it, and stopped there, the well acting as a blockade between the two brothers, but accessible from either side.

Now Margayya looked about for the small brass pot. He could not see it anywhere.

" Hey, little man! " he called out, " where is the well-pot? " He liked to call his son out constantly. When he came home, he could not bear to be away from him even for a moment. He felt uneasy and irritated when the child did not answer his call. He saw the youngster stooping over the lamp, trying to thrust a piece of paper into the chimney. He watched him from the doorway. He suppressed the inclination to call him away and warn him. The child thrust a piece of paper into the lamp, and when it burned brightly he recoiled at the sudden spurt of fire. But when it blackened and burnt out he drew near the lamp again, gingerly putting his finger near the metal plate on the top. Before Margayya could stop him, he had touched it. He let out a shriek. Margayya was beside him in a moment. His shriek brought in Margayya's wife, who had gone to a neighbouring shop. She came rushing into the house with cries of "What is it? What is it? What has happened? " Margayya felt embarrassed, like a man caught shirking a duty. He told his wife curtly, "Why do you shout so much, as if a great calamity had befallen this household—so that your sister-in-law in the neighbourhood may think how active we are, I suppose! "

" Sister-in-law—how proud you are of your relatives! "

Her further remarks could not be continued because of the howling set up by the child, whose burnt finger still remained unattended. At this the mother snatched him up from her husband's arms, and hugged him close to her, hurting him more, whereupon he shouted in a new key. Margayya tried to tear him out of his wife's arms, crying: "Quick, get that ointment. Where is it? You can keep nothing in its place."

"You need not shout!" the wife answered, running about and rummaging in the cupboard. She grumbled: "You can't look after him even for a second without letting him hurt himself."

"You need not get hysterical about it, gentle lady, I had gone for a moment to the well."

"Everyone gets tap-water in this town. We alone——" she began, attacking on a new front.

"All right, all right," he said, curbing her, and turning his attention to the finger. "You must never, never go near fire again, do you understand?"

"Will you buy me a little elephant tomorrow?" the child asked, his cheeks still wet with tears. By now they had discovered a little wooden crucible containing some black ointment in the cupboard, hidden behind a small basket containing loose cotton (which Margayya's wife twisted into wicks for the lamp in God's niche). She applied the ointment to the injured finger, and set the child roaring in a higher key. This time he said, "I want a big peppermint."

At night when the lights were put out and the sounds of Vinayaka Street had quietened, Margayya said to his wife, lying on the other side of their sleeping child: "Do you know—poor boy! I could have prevented Balu from hurting himself. I just stood there and watched. I wanted to see what he would do alone by himself." His wife made a noise of deprecation: "It is as I suspected. You were at the bottom of the whole trouble. I don't know ... I don't

know . . . that boy is terribly mischievous . . . and you are
. . . you are . . ." She could not find the right word for it.
Her instinct was full of foreboding, and she left the sentence unfinished. After a long pause she added: " It's
impossible to manage him during the afternoons. He
constantly runs out of the house into the street. I don't
have a moment's peace or rest."

" Don't get cantankerous about such a small child," said
Margayya, who disliked all these adverse remarks about
his son. It seemed to him such a pity that that small
bundle of man curled beside him like a tiny pillow should
be so talked about. His wife retorted: " Yes, I wish you
could stay at home and look after him instead of coming
in the evening and dandling him for a moment after he has
exhausted all his tricks."

" Yes, gladly, provided you agree to go out and arrange
loans for all those village idiots."

The child levied an exacting penalty on his parents the
next day for the little patch of burn on his finger. He held
his finger upright and would not let anyone come near
him. He refused to be put into a new shirt, refused food,
refused to walk, and insisted on being carried about by his
mother or father. Margayya examined the hurt finger and
said: " It looks all right, there seems to be nothing wrong
there."

" Don't say so," screamed the boy in his own childish
slang. " I'm hurt. I want a peppermint." Margayya was
engaged all the morning in nursing his finger and plying
him with peppermints. His wife remarked: " He'll be ill
with peppermints before you are done with him."

" Why don't you look after him, then? " he asked.

" I won't go to mother," screamed the boy. " I will be
with you."

Margayya had some odd jobs to do while at home in the
mornings. He went to the nearby Urban Stores and bought
sugar or butter, he cut up the firewood into smaller sizes

if his wife complained about it, or he opened his tin box and refreshed his memory by poring over the pages of his red-bound account book. But today the boy would not let him do anything except fuss over him.

The child kept Margayya at home for over an hour beyond his usual time. He could leave for the Co-operative Bank only at mid-day, stealing out when, oblivious of his surroundings, the little fellow's attention was engaged in splashing about a bucket of water in the backyard. When the water was exhausted he looked all round and let out such an angry shout for his father that the people on the other side of the wall remarked to each other: "This is the worst of begetting sons late in life! They pet them and spoil them and make them little monsters." The lady on the other side of the wall could well say this because she was the mother of ten.

§

Margayya looked up as a shadow fell on his note-book. He saw a uniformed servant standing before him. It was Arul Doss, the head peon of the Co-operative Bank, an old Christian who had grown up with the institution. He had wrinkles round his eyes, and a white moustache and mild eyes. Margayya looked up at him and wondered what to do—whether to treat him as a hostile visitor or as a friend. Instinctively he recoiled from anyone coming out of that building, where he knew he was being viewed as a public enemy. He hesitated for a moment, then looked up silently at the figure before him. "Sit down, won't you, Arul Doss?" Arul Doss shot a glance over his shoulder at the office.

"He will not like it if he sees me dallying here. He, I mean the Secretary, asks you to come——" said Arul.

"Me!" Margayya could hardly believe his ears. "The Secretary! What have I to do with your Secretary?"

"I don't know at all, but he said, 'Go and tell Margayya to come here for a moment.'"

On hearing this, Margayya became indignant. " Go and tell them I am not their paid—paid——" he was about to say " servant ", but he remembered in time, even in his mental stress, that the man standing before him was literally both paid and a servant, and thought it would be injudicious to say so now. So he left off the sentence abruptly and asked: " Do they pay me to appear before them when they want me? "

" I don't know," said this very loyal Co-operative man. " He told me to tell you. The Secretary is no ordinary person, you know," he added. " He receives a salary of over five hundred rupees a month, an amount which you and I will probably not see even after a hundred years of service." Now Margayya's blood was stirred. Many angry memories welled up in him of all the indignities that he had suffered at the hands of his brother, who cut him off with half a house, while he himself passed for a man of means, a respectable citizen. Margayya felt that the world treated him with contempt because he had no money. People thought they could order him about. He said to Arul Doss: " Arul Doss, I don't know about you; you can speak for yourself. But you need not speak for me. You may not see a hundred rupees even after a hundred years of service, but I think I shall do so very soon—and who knows, if your Secretary seeks any improvement of his position, he can come to me."

Arul Doss took a few moments to understand, then swayed with laughter. Tears rolled down his cheeks. " Well, I have been a servant in this department for twenty-nine years, but I've never heard a crazier proposal. All right, all right." He was convulsed with laughter as he turned to go. Margayya looked at his back helplessly. He cast his eyes down and surveyed himself : perhaps he cut a ridiculous figure, with his *dhoti* going brown for lack of laundering and with his shirt collar frayed, and those awful silver spectacles. " I hate these spectacles. I wish I could do without them." But age, age—who could help long-sight? " If I wore gold spectacles, perhaps they would take me seriously and not order me about. Who is this Secretary to call me through the peon? I won't be ridiculed. I'm at least as good as they." He called out: "Look here, Arul Doss." With a beaming face, Arul Doss turned round. "Tell your Secretary that if he is a Secretary, I'm really the proprietor of a bank, and that he can come here and meet me if he has any business——"

"Shall I repeat those very words?" Arul Doss asked, ready to burst out laughing again.

"Absolutely," Margayya said. "And another thing, if you find yourself thrown out of there, you can come to me for a job. I like you, you seem to be a hard-working, loyal fellow." Further parleys were cut off because a couple of villagers came round for consultation, and started forming a semi-circle in front of Margayya. Though Arul Doss still lingered for a further joke, Margayya turned away abruptly, remarking: "All right, you may go now."

§

"Please," said a peasant, "be careful, sir. That Arul Doss is a bad fellow."

"I'm also a bad fellow," snapped Margayya.

"It's not that. They say that the Secretary just does what this fellow says. If we go in to get just one single form, he charges us two annas each time. Is that also a Government rule?" asked the peasant.

"Go away, you fools," Margayya said. "You are people who have no self-respect. As long as you are share-holders, you are masters of that bank. They are your paid servants."

"Ah, is that so?" asked the peasant. And the group looked up at each other with amazement. Another man, who had a long blanket wrapped round his shoulder, a big cloth turban crowning his head, and wore shorts and was bare-foot, said: "We may be masters as you say, but who is going to obey us? If we go in, we have to do as they say. Otherwise, they won't give us money."

" Whose money are they giving away?" asked Margayya.
" It is your own."

" Margayya, we don't want all that. Why should we talk
of other people? "

" True, true," said one or two others approvingly.

Encouraged by this, the peasant said: " We should not
talk about others unnecessarily." He lowered his voice and
said: " If they hear it they may——"

Margayya's blood rushed to his head: " You get away
from here," he thundered. " I don't want to have anything
to do with people without self-respect, who don't know
their importance and strength. What better words can we
expect from someone like you who wraps himself in that
coarse blanket at this time of the day? What better stuff
can we expect from a head weighed down by so many folds
of a dirty turban? " The peasant was somewhat cowed by
Margayya's manner. He mumbled: " I didn't mean to
offend you, sir. If I did, would I be here? "

" That's all right. No further unnecessary talk. If you
have any business, tell me. Otherwise get out of here.
Before dusk I have to attend to so many people. You are
not the only one who has business with me."

" I want a small loan, sir," began the peasant. " I want
to know how much more I have to pay to clear the balance
loan."

" Why don't you go in there and ask your Arul Doss? "

" Oh, they are all very bad, unhelpful people, sir; that's
why I never like to go there, but come to you first. Why
do we come to you, sir, of all persons in this big city? It's
because you know our joys and sorrows and our troubles,
our difficulties and——"

" All right, all right," Margayya said, cutting him short,
yet greatly mollified by his manner. " I know what you are
trying to say. Don't I? " He looked round at his clients.
And they shook their heads approvingly, making appropriate sounds with their tongues, in order to please him.

After all these bouts he settled down to business. He had a busy day: filling up forms, writing applications, writing even petitions unconnected with money business for one or two clients, talking, arguing, and calculating. He was nearly hoarse by the time the sun's rays touched him on the nape of his neck, and the shadows of the banyan tree fell on the drive leading to the Co-operative Bank. He started to close his office. He put back his writing pad, neatly folded up some pieces of paper on which he had noted figures, scrutinized again the little register, counted some cash, and checked some receipts. He arranged all these back in the small tin box, laid a few sheets of loan application forms flat on top of them so as to prevent their creasing, restored to its corner the ink bottle, and laid beside it the red wooden pen. Everything in its place. He hated, more than anything else, having to fumble for his papers or stationery; and a disordered box was as hateful to him as the thought of Arul Doss. His mind was oppressed with thoughts of Arul Doss. He felt insulted and sore. What right had he or anyone to insult or browbeat him? What had he done that they themselves did not do? He would teach this Arul Doss a lesson—no matter at what cost . . .

At this moment he heard a step approaching, and looking up saw a man, wearing a brown suit, standing before him. His hands were in his pockets, and behind him at a respectable distance stood Arul Doss. The man looked very smart, with a hat on his head; a very tidy young man who looked "as if he had just come from Europe," Margayya reflected. Looking at him, he felt himself to be such a contrast with his brown *dhoti*, torn shirt, and the absurd little tuft under the black cap. "No wonder they treat me as they do," he said to himself. "Perhaps I should have exercised greater care in my speech. God knows what that Arul Doss has reported . . . I should not have spoken. This fellow looks as if he could do anything." Margayya looked at Arul Doss, and shuddered, noting the wicked gleam in his eye. He soon recovered his self-possession: "I am not a baby to worry about these things. What can anybody do

17

to me? " He resolutely fixed his gaze on the hard knobs on his box, gave its contents a final pat, and was about to draw down the lid when the other man suddenly stooped, thrust his hand inside and picked out a handful of papers, demanding: " How did you come by these ? These are our application forms ! "

Margayya checked the indignation that was rising within him: " Put them back, will you? What right have you to put your hand into my box? You look like an educated man. Don't you know that ordinary simple law? " In his indignation he lost for a moment all fear. Arul Doss came forward and said, " Take care how you speak. He is our Secretary. He will hand you over to the police."

"Stop your nonsense, you earth-worm! Things have come to this, have they, when every earth-worm pretends that it is a cobra and tries to sway its hood ... I will nip off your head as well as your tail, if you start any of your tricks with me. Take care. Get out of my way."

Arul Doss was cowed. He withdrew a little, but he was not to be dismissed so easily. He began: "He is our Secretary——"

"That's all right. It's written all over him," yelled Margayya. "What else can he be? He can speak for himself, can't he? You keep away, you miserable ten-rupee earner. I want none of your impertinence here. If you want an old piece of cloth, torn or used, come to me." The Secretary seemed to watch all this with detachment. Arul Doss fretted inwardly, tried to be officious, but had to withdraw because the Secretary himself ordered him away. "You go over there," he said, indicating a spot far off. Arul Doss moved reluctantly away. Margayya felt triumphant, and turned his attention to the man before him. " Secretary, you will put back that paper or I will call the police now."

"Yes, I want to call the police myself. You are in possession of something that belongs to our office."

" No, it belongs to the shareholders."

" Are you a shareholder? "

18

"Yes, more than that——"

"Nonsense. Don't make false statements. You'll get into trouble. Reports have come to me of your activities. Here is my warning. If you are seen here again, you will find yourself in prison. Go——" He nodded to Arul Doss to come nearer, and held out to him the loan application forms. Arul Doss avidly seized them and carried them off like a trophy. The Secretary abruptly turned round and walked back to the porch of the building, where his car was waiting.

§

Presently Margayya bundled up his belongings and started homewards. With his box under his arm and his head bowed in thought, he wandered down the Market Road. He paused for a moment at the entrance of the Regal Hair-Cutting Saloon, in whose doorway a huge looking-glass was kept. He saw to his dismay that he was still wearing his spectacles. He pulled them off quickly, folded up their sides and put them into his pocket. He didn't feel flattered at the sight of his own reflection. "I look like a wayside barber with this little miserable box under my arm. People probably expect me to open the lid and take out soap and a brush. No wonder the Secretary feels he can treat me as he likes. If I looked like him, would he have dared to snatch the papers from my box? I can't look like him. I am destined to look like a wayside barber, and that is my fate. I'm only fit for the company of those blanket-wrapped rustics." He was thoroughly vexed with himself and his lot.

He moved to the side of the road, as cyclists rang their bells and dodged him; jutka men shouted at him, and pedestrians collided against him. His mind was occupied with thoughts of his own miserableness. He felt himself shrinking. Two students emerged laughing and talking from the Bombay Anand Bhavan, their lips red with betel leaves. They stared at Margayya. "They are laughing at me," he thought. "Perhaps they want to ask me to go with them to their rooms and give them a hair-cut!" He kept glancing over his shoulder at them, and caught them turning and glancing at him too, with a grin on their faces. Somebody driving by in a car of the latest model seemed to look at him for a fleeting second and Margayya fancied that he caught a glimpse of contempt in his eyes. . . . Now at the western end of Market Road he saw the V.N. Stores, with its owner standing at the door. "He may put his hand into my pocket and snatch the glasses or compel me to give him a shave." He side-stepped into Kabir Lane, and, feeling ashamed of the little box that he carried under his arm, wished he could fling it away, but his sense of possession would not let him. As he passed through the narrow Kabir Lane, with small houses abutting the road, people seemed to stare at him as if to say: "Barber, come early tomorrow morning: you must be ready here before I go for my bath." He hurried off. He reached Vinayak Street, raced up the steps of his house and flung the box unceremoniously under the bench. His wife was washing the child on the back verandah. At the sound of his arrival the little fellow let out a yell of joy, through the towel.

"What's happened to make you come back so early?" asked Margayya's wife.

"Early! Why, can't I come home when I please? I am nobody's slave." She had tried to tidy herself up in the evening after the day's work. "She looks . . ." He noticed how plebeian she looked, with her faded jacket, her patched, discoloured saree and her anaemic eyes. "How can anyone treat me respectfully when my wife is so indifferent-looking?" His son came up and clung to his hand: "Father, what have you brought me today?" He picked him up on his arm. "Can't you put him into a cleaner shirt?" he asked.

"He has only four," his wife answered. "And he has already soiled three today. I have been telling you to buy some clothes."

20

"Don't start all that now. I am in no mood for lectures."
His wife bit her lips and made a wry face. The child let
out a howl for no reason whatever. She felt annoyed and
said: "He is always like this. He is all right till you come
home. But the moment you step in, he wouldn't even
finish washing his face."

"Where should I go if you don't want me to return
home? "

"Nobody said such a thing," she replied sullenly. The
little boy shouted, put his hand into his father's coat-
pocket and pulled out his reading glasses, and insisted
upon putting them over his own nose. His mother cried:
"Give those glasses back or I'll . . ." She raised her arm,
at which he started yelling so much that they could not
hear each other's remarks. Margayya carried him off to
a shop and bought him sweets, leaving his wife behind,
fretting with rage.

In the quiet of midnight, Margayya spoke to his wife
seriously: "Do you know why we get on each other's
nerves and quarrel? "

"Yes," she said at last. "Now let me sleep." And
turned over. Margayya stretched out his hand and shook
her by the shoulder. "Wake up. I have much to tell you."

"Can't you wait till the morning? " she asked.

"No." He spoke to her of the day's events. She sat up
in bed. "Who is that secretary? What right has he to
threaten you? "

"He has every right because he has more money,
authority, dress, looks—above all, more money. It's money
which gives people all this. Money alone is important in
this world. Everything else will come to us naturally if we
have money in our purse."

She said: "You shouldn't have been so rude to Arul
Doss. You should not have said that you'd employ the
secretary. That's not the way to speak to people earning
five hundred rupees a month."

"Let him get five thousand, what do I care? I can also earn a thousand or five thousand, and then these fellows will have to look out." Much of his self-assurance was returning in the presence of his wife. All the despair and inferiority that he had been feeling was gradually leaving him. He felt more self-confident and aggressive. He felt he could hold out his hand and grab as much of the good things of life as he wanted. He felt himself being puffed up with hope and plans and self-assurance. He said, " Even you will learn to behave with me when I have money. Your rudeness now is understandable. For isn't there a famous saying: 'He that hath not is spurned even by his wife; even the mother that bore him spurns him '? It was a very wise man who said it. Well, you will see. I'll not carry about that barber's box any more, and I'll not be seen in this torn *dhoti*. I will become respectable like anyone else. That secretary will have to call me 'Mister' and stand up when I enter. No more torn mats and dirty, greasy sarees for you. Our boy will have a cycle, he will have a suit and go to a convent in a car. And those people " (he indicated the next house) " will have to wonder and burst their hearts with envy. He will have to come to me on his knees and wait for advice. I have finished with those villagers."

§

He became like one possessed. He was agitated, as if he had made a startling discovery. He couldn't yet afford to keep away from the place where he worked. He went there as usual, but he had taken care to tidy himself up as much as possible. He wore a lace-edged *dhoti* which he normally kept folded in his box. It was of fine texture, but much yellowed now. He had always kept it in his box with a piece of camphor, and he now smelt like an incense-holder as he emerged from his small room, clad in this gorgeous *dhoti*. It had been given to him, as it now seemed a century and a half ago, on the day of his wedding when he was sitting beside his wife on a flower-decked swing, surrounded by a lot of women-folk joking and singing and teasing the newly-weds, after the feast at night. He sighed at the thought of those days. How they had fussed about him and tried to satisfy his smallest request and keep him pleased in every way. How eminent he had felt then! People seemed to feel honoured when he spoke to them. He had only to turn his head even slightly for someone or other to come rushing up and inquire what his wishes were. He had thought that that would continue for ever. What a totally false view of life one acquired on one's wedding day! It reminded him of his brother. How he bargained with the bride's people over the dowry! He used to be so fond of him. His brother's face stood out prominently from among the wedding group in Margayya's memory, as he sat in the corner, beyond the sacrificial smoke, in their village home. Margayya sighed at the memory of it; they had got on quite nicely, but their wives couldn't. "If women got on smoothly ..." Half the trouble in this world is due to women who cannot tolerate each other.

§

His wife was amused to see him so gaudily dressed. "What's the matter?" she asked. "Are you going to a wedding party?" "This is the only good one I have. They will never see me in that again," he said, indicating his discarded *dhoti*. "Keep it and give it to Arul Doss. He may come for it." He was pleased with his own venom aimed at the distant Arul Doss. This quiet pleasure pricked his veins and thrilled his body. He put on a new shirt which he had stitched two years ago but had not had the heart to wear—always reserving it for some future occasion. The child too seemed to be quite pleased to see his father in a new dress. He clapped his hands in joy and left him in peace, concentrating his attention on a piece of elephant made of lacquer-painted wood. Margayya had

23

elaborately tied up his *dhoti*, with folds going up, in the dignified Poona style, instead of the Southern fashion, looked down upon by people of other provinces. He explained to his wife: "You see, if we are treated with contempt by people it is our fault. Our style of tying *dhoti* and our style of dressing—it is all so silly! No wonder." He talked like a man who had just arrived from a far-off land, he spoke with such detachment and superiority. His wife was somewhat taken aback. She treated him with the utmost consideration when she served him his frugal meal. Usually he would have to ask, "Food ready? Food ready?" several times and then pick up his plate and sit down and wait indefinitely as she kept blowing the fire. If he said: "Hurry up, please." She would retort: "With my breath gone, blowing on this wet firewood, have you the heart . . ." etc. But today she said: "Your plate is there, food is ready." She served him quietly, with a sort of docile agreeableness. "I got this brinjal from the back garden," she said. "You didn't know I had a garden." "No. Nice stuff," he murmured agreeably. Even the little fellow ate his food quietly, only once letting out a shout when he thought his mother wouldn't serve him his *ghee*. On that occasion he threw a handful of rice in his mother's face. She just ignored it, instead of flying at him, and the episode ended there. At the end of the meal Margayya picked up his plate as usual to wash and restore it to its corner in the kitchen. But she at once said: "Oh, don't, I will attend to it." He got up grandly and washed his hands, wiping them on a towel readily brought to his side by his wife. She gave him a few scented nuts and a betel leaf and saw him off at the door as he went down the street. He had opened his little box and picked up a few papers, which he carried in his hand. It looked better. He walked with the feeling that a new existence was opening before him.

His clients were somewhat surprised to see him in his

new dress. He didn't squat under the tree, but remained standing.

"Why are you standing, Margayya?"

"Because I am not sitting," Margayya replied.

"Why not?"

"Because I like to stand—that's all," he replied.

He handed a filled-up application to someone and said: "Give it in there, and come away." He told another: "Well, you will get your money today. Give me back my advance." He carried on his business without sitting down. One of the men looked up and down and asked: "Going to a marriage party?"

"Yes," replied Margayya. "Every day is a day of marriage for me. Do you think I like a change of wife each day?" He cracked his usual jokes. He placed his paper on the ledge of a wall and wrote. He had brought with him, hidden in his pocket, the little ink-bottle wrapped in paper, and his pen. As he bowed his head and wrote he muttered: "I just want to help people to get over their money troubles. I do it as a sort of service, but let no one imagine I have no better business."

"What else do you do, sir?" asked a very innocent man.

"Well, I have to do the same service for myself too, you see. I have to do something to earn money."

"You get interest on all the amounts you give us."

"Yes, yes, but that's hardly enough to pay for my snuff," he said grandly, taking out a small box and inhaling a pinch. It sent a stinging sensation up his nostrils into his brain, and he felt his forehead throbbing with excitement. It made him feel so energetic that he felt like thumping a table and arguing. He said aggressively: "I want to do so much for you fellows, do you know why?" They shook their heads bewildered. "Not because of the petty interest you give me—that's nothing for me. It is because I want you all to get over your money worries and improve your lives. You must all adopt civilized ways. That's why I am trying to help you to get money from that bastard office." He pointed at the Co-operative Bank. They all turned and

25

looked at it. Arul Doss was seen approaching. "He is coming," they all said in one voice. Arul Doss approached them somewhat diffidently. His gait was halting and slow. He stopped quite far away, and pretended to look for a carriage or something on the road. Margayya thrust himself forward and watched him aggressively. Arul Doss stole a glance now and then at Margayya. Margayya felt annoyed. The sting of the snuff was still fresh. He cried out: "Arul Doss, what are you looking for? If it is for me, come along, because I am here." Arul Doss seemed happy to seize this opportunity to approach. Margayya said: "Mark my words, this is god-given shade under the tree; if you or your secretary is up to any mischief, I will make you feel sorry for your——" The villagers were overawed by Margayya's manner of handling Arul Doss. Arul Doss had no doubt come spying, but now he felt uncomfortable at Margayya's sallies. If Margayya had been squatting under the tree with his box, he might have had a tale to bear, but now he saw nothing wrong. He had only one worry—that of being called an earth-worm again before so many people. He tried to turn and go, saying, "I just came to see if the Secretary's car had come."

"Has your secretary a car?" Margayya asked patronizingly.

"Haven't you noticed that big red one?"

Margayya snapped his fingers and said: "As if I had no better things to observe. Tell your secretary——" He checked himself, not being sure what his tongue might utter. "Arul Doss, if you are in need of an old *dhoti* or shirt, go and ask my wife. She will give it to you." Arul Doss's face beamed with happiness.

"Oh, surely, surely," he said. He approached nearer to Margayya and whispered. Margayya raised his hand to his face and put his head back. The other's breath smelt of onion. Margayya asked: "Do you nibble raw onion in the morning?" Arul Doss ignored the question and whispered: "You must not think that I myself tried to bother you yesterday. It's all that fellow's orders." He

26

pointed towards his office. "He is a vicious creature! You won't think that I . . . You can carry on here as you like, sir, Don't worry about anything." He turned and abruptly walked back. Margayya looked after him and commented to his circle: "That's the worst blackguard under the sun —both of them are. This fellow carries tales to him and then he comes and behaves like a great governor here. What do I care? If a man thinks that he is governor let him show off at home, not here, for I don't care for governors."

§

As he went through the town that day he was obsessed with thoughts of money. His mind rang with the words he had said to the villagers: "I'm only trying to help you to get out of your money worries." He began to believe it himself. He viewed himself as a saviour of mankind. "If I hadn't secured three hundred rupees for so-and-so, he would be rotting in the street at this moment. So-and-so married off his daughter, educated his son, retained his house."

His mind began to catalogue all the good things money had done as far as he could remember. He shuddered to think how people could ever do without it. If money was absent men came near being beasts. He saw at the Market Fountain a white sheet covering some object stretched on the pavement. It was about six in the evening, and the street was lit up with a blaze of sunlight from the West. Pedestrians, donkeys and jutkas were transformed with the gold of the setting sun. Margayya stood dazzled by the sight. A ragged fellow with matted hair thrust before him a mud tray and said, pointing at the sheet-covered object on the ground, "An orphan's body, sir. Have pity, help us to bury him." Margayya threw a look at the covered body, shuddered and parted with a copper, as so many others had done. There was a good collection on the tray.

27

Margayya averted his face and tried to pass quickly. Farther on yet another man came up with a mud tray whining: " Orphan body——"

" Get off, already given," said Margayya sternly, and passed on. There was money on this tray too. Margayya was filled with disgust. He knew what it meant. A group of people seized upon an unclaimed dead body, undertook to give it a burial and collected a lot of money for it. He knew that they celebrated it as a festive occasion. When they saw a destitute dying on the roadside they cried to themselves: " Aha! A fine day ahead." They left their occupations, seized the body, carried it to a public place, put it down on the pavement, placed a few flowers on it, bought a few mud trays from the potter, and assailed the passers-by. They collected enough money at the end of the day to give a gorgeous funeral to the body. They even haggled with the grave-digger and were left with so much money at the end of it all that they drank and made merry for three or four days and gave up temporarily their normal jobs, such as scavenging, load-carrying, and stone-quarrying. It made Margayya reflective. People did anything for money. Money was men's greatest need, like air or food. People went to horrifying lengths for its sake, like collecting rent on a dead body: yet this didn't strike Margayya in his present mood as so horrible as something to be marvelled at. It left him admiring the power and dynamism of money, its capacity to make people do strange deeds. He saw a toddy tapper going a hundred feet up a cocoanut tree and he reflected: "Morning to night he wears a loin cloth and goes up tree after tree for fifty years or more just for the eight annas he gets per tree." He saw offices and shops opened and people sweating and fatiguing themselves, all for money. Margayya concluded that they wanted money because they wanted fellows like the Secretary of the Co-operative Bank to bow to them, or to have a fellow like Arul Doss speak to them with courtesy, or so that they might wear unpatched *dhoties* and be treated seriously. Margayya sat down for a moment on a park bench. The Municipality had made a very tiny park at the angle where the Market Road branched off to Lawley Extension. They had put up a cement bench and grown a clump of strong ferns, fencing them off with a railing. He passed through the stile and sat down on the bench. Cars were being driven towards Lawley Extension. Huge cars. He watched them greedily. " Must have a car as soon as possible," he said to himself. " Nothing is impossible in ·this world." A cool breeze was blowing. The sun had set. Lights were lit up here and there. " If I have money, I need not dodge that spectacle dealer. I need not cringe before that stores man. I could give those medicines to my wife. The doctor would look at her with more interest, and she might look like other women. That son of mine, that Balu—I could give him everything." His mind gloated over visions of his son. He would grow into an aristocrat. He would study, not in a Corporation School, but in the convent, and hobnob with the sons of the District Collector or the Superintendent of Police or Mangal Seth, the biggest mill-owner in the town. He would promise him a car all for himself when he came to the College. He could go to America and obtain degrees, and then marry perhaps a judge's daughter. His own wife might demand all the dowry she wanted. He would not interfere, leaving it for the women to manage as they liked. He would buy another bungalow in Lawley Road for his son, and then his vision went on to the next generation of aristocrats.

At this moment he saw a man coming from Lawley Extension: a cadaverous man, burnt by the sun, wrapped in a long piece of white cloth, his forehead painted with red marks and his head clean shaved, with a tuft of hair on top. A tall, gaunt man, he was the priest of the temple in their street. An idea struck Margayya at the sight of him. He was a wise man, well-versed in ancient studies, and he might be able to give advice. Margayya clapped his hands till the gaunt man turned and advanced towards him.

"Ah! Margayya! What are you doing here?"

"Just came for a little fresh air. The air is so cool here, unlike our Vinayaka Street."

"Oh, these are all aristocratic parts, with gardens, and fresh air. Our Vinayaka Mudali Street! It's like an oven in summer."

"And what a lot of mosquitoes!" Margayya added.

"I couldn't sleep the whole night," the priest said.

"Why should they make such a row in our ears? Let them suck the blood if they want, but it's their humming that is so unwelcome," said Margayya.

They spoke of weather and mosquitoes and fresh air and the diseases prevalent in the town for about half an hour. The priest lived in a sort of timelessness and seemed to be in no hurry. The stars were shining in the sky. Margayya asked: "How was it you were coming this way?"

"I had gone to perform a *Puja* in a house in Lawley Extension. You know the Municipal Chairman's house: they are very particular that I alone should perform these things. They won't tolerate anyone else. So every evening I do it there and then rush back to our temple, where the devotees will be waiting. A man can't be in two places at the same time."

"Truly said. I will walk back with you to the temple, if you are going there."

"I have to go to another place on the way and then on to the temple. Just a minute's delay there, that's all. Do come with me. There's nothing so good as company on the road. I've to walk miles and miles from morning to night."

They walked back towards the Market Road. The priest led him into some unnamed lanes behind the Market. He stopped in front of a house and said: "If you will wait here, I will be back in a moment." He went in. Margayya sat up on the pyol. There was a gutter below him. "This is worse than our Vinayak Street," Margayya reflected. The place was occupied by a class of handloom weavers. All along the lane they had set up weaving frames with yarns dyed in blue and hung out to dry on them. Somebody came out of the house and said to Margayya: "Won't you come in?" Margayya felt pleased at this attention and followed him in. There was a very small front hall in the house piled up with weaving frames, stacks of woven sarees in different colours, and several rolls of bedding belonging to the members of the household. At one corner they had put up a small wooden pedestal on which a couple of figures of Gods and one or two framed pictures were hanging. An incense stick was burning. His friend the priest sat before the pedestal, with his eyes shut, muttering something. The master of the house with his wife and children stood devoutly at a distance. There were four children. One or the other of them was being constantly told: "Don't bite your nails before God." And they were so much overwhelmed by the general atmosphere that they constantly put their finger tips to their lips and withdrew them quickly as if they had touched a frying pan. Margayya was very much impressed with their seriousness, and wondered at the same time what his Balu would have done under these circumstances. "He'd have insisted upon doing what he pleased—and not only bitten his own nails but other people's as well. He would have upset all this holy water and camphor flame," Margayya reflected, with gratification. It seemed to him a most enchanting self-assertiveness on the part of his child. It gave him a touch of superiority to all these children, who wouldn't bite their nails when ordered not to. He felt a desire to go home and spoil his son. "I left so early in the day," he reflected. He suddenly asked himself, "Why am I knocking around with this priest instead of going home?" An old lady, probably the grandmother of the house, sat before the God with a small child on her lap. Only the child's eyes were visible, gleaming in the sacred lamps. It was entirely wrapped in a blanket. Margayya guessed that it must be very sick. They were all fussing over it. "How old is that child?" Margayya wondered, unable to get a full glimpse of it. Somehow this worried him. "If Balu were in his position would he have consented to be chained up like this? Some children are too dull——"

It was nearly nine o'clock when they came out. Margayya followed the priest mutely through the streets. The town had almost gone to sleep. The streets were silent.

"It's so late!" he murmured.

"What is late?" asked the priest.

"We are so late."

"Late for what?"

Margayya fumbled for a reply. He said clumsily: "You said you'd be kept there only a short time. I thought you would be kept only a short time—that's why——"

"In holy business can we be glancing at a wrist watch all the time? That child has been crippled with a dreadful disease from childhood. It is now much better. It is some wasting disease——"

"Do you perform *Pujas* for his sake?"

"Yes, every Friday. It is the *Puja* that enabled young Markandeya to win over *Yama*, the God of Death."

"O!" Margayya exclaimed, interested but not willing to show his ignorance.

"Every child knows that story."

"Yes, of course, of course," Margayya said non-committally. He felt he ought to say something more and added: "Those people," indicating over his shoulder a vast throng of wise ancestors, "those people knew what was good for us."

"Not the people you mean, but those who were there even before them," corrected the priest in a debating spirit.

"All right," Margayya agreed meekly.

The priest asked him further on: "What do you gather from the story of Markandeya?"

Margayya blinked, and felt like a schoolboy. He said ceremoniously: "How can I say? It's for a learned person like you to enlighten us on these matters."

"All right. Who was Markandeya?" asked the man persistently.

Margayya began to feel desperate. He feared that the

other might not rest till he had exposed his ignorance. He felt he ought to put a stop to it at once, and said: "It's a long time since I heard that story. My grandmother used to tell it. I should like to hear it again."

"Ask then. If you don't know a thing, there is no shame in asking and learning about it," moralized the priest. He then narrated the story of Markandeya, the boy devotee of God Shiva, destined to die the moment he completed his sixteenth year. When the moment came, the emissaries of *Yama* (the God of Death) arrived in order to bind and carry off his life, but he was performing the *Puja*—and the dark emissaries could not approach him at all! Markandeya remained sixteen to all eternity, and thus defeated death. "That particular *Puja* had that efficacy—and it's that very *Puja* I am performing on behalf of the child, who is much better for it."

"Will the child live?" asked Margayya, his interest completely roused.

"How can I say? It's our duty to perform a *Puja*; the result cannot be our concern. It's *Karma*."

"Yes, yes," agreed Margayya, somewhat baffled.

They now reached the little temple at the end of Vinayak Mudali Street. There under a cracked dome was an inner shrine containing an image of Hanuman, the God of Power, the son of Wind. According to tradition this God had pressed one foot on the very spot where the shrine now stood, sprang across space and ocean and landed in Lanka (Ceylon), there to destroy Ravana, a king with ten heads and twenty hands, who was oppressing mankind and had abducted Rama's wife Seetha.

The priest was part and parcel of the temple. There was a small wooden shack within its narrow corridors, where he ate his food and slept. He looked after the shrine, polished and oiled the tall bronze lamps and worshipped here.

Margayya hesitated at the entrance. It seemed already very late. "I'll go now," he said.

"Why don't you come in and see the God, having come

33

so far?" asked the priest. Margayya hesitated. He was afraid to ignore the priest's suggestion. He feared that that might displease God. As he hesitated, the priest drove home the point: "You stopped me there at the park to say something. You have been with me ever since and you have not spoken anything about it." Margayya felt caught. He found himself behaving more and more like a school boy. He remembered his old teacher, back there in his village, an old man with a white rim around his black pupils that gave him the look of a cat peering in the dark, whose hands shook when he gripped the cane, but who nevertheless put it to sound use, especially on Margayya's back, particularly when he behaved as he behaved now, blinking when he ought to be opening his lips and letting the words out. Later in life Margayya remedied it by not allowing any pause in his speech, but the disease recurred now and then. This was such a moment. He wanted to talk to the priest and seek his advice, but he felt reluctant to utter the first word. As he stood there at the portals of the temple he feared for a second the old whacking from a cane. But the priest only said: "Come in."

"Isn't it late?"

"For what?"

Margayya once again blinked. He mutely followed the priest into the shrine. The main portion of the image went up into the shadows, partly illuminated by a flickering oil lamp. The priest briskly swept into a basket some broken cocoanut, plantains, and coins, left on the doorstep by devotees. He held up a plantain and a piece of cocoanut for Margayya. "Probably you are hungry. Eat these. I will give you a tumbler of milk." He went into his shack and came out bearing a tumbler of milk.

Margayya squatted on the floor, leaning against the high rugged wall of the corridor. The town had fallen asleep. Vinayak Mudali Street was at the very end of the town, and no one moved about at this hour. Even the street dogs, which created such a furore every night, seemed to have fallen asleep. A couple of cocoanut trees waved against the

34

stars in the sky. The only noise in the world now seemed to be the crunching of cocoanut between Margayya's jaws. It was like the sound of wooden wheels running over a sandy bed. Margayya felt abashed, and tried to eat noiselessly. A bit of cocoanut went the wrong way, and he was seized with a fit of coughing, which racked his whole frame. He panted and gasped as he tried to explain: "It . . . It . . . It . . . ." The priest seemed to watch with amusement, and he felt indignant. "What right has this man to keep me here at this hour and amuse himself at my expense?"

The priest said: "Drink that milk, it will make you all right."

"He asks me to drink milk as if I were a baby. Next, I think, he will force it between my lips." He suddenly grew very assertive and said resolutely: "I don't like milk . . . I have never liked it." He pushed away the tumbler resolutely. The priest said: "Don't push away a tumbler of milk with the back of your hand." Margayya was no longer going to be treated and lectured like a schoolboy. He said: "I know. But who doesn't?"

"And yet," said the priest with amused contempt, "you push away milk with the back of your hand as if it were a tumbler of ditch water."

"No, no," said Margayya semi-apologetically. "I didn't push it with the back of my hand. I just tried to put away the tumbler so that you might take it."

Ignoring this explanation and looking away, far away, the priest said: "Milk is one of the forms of Goddess Lakshmi, the Goddess of Wealth. When you reject it or treat it indifferently, it means you reject her. She is a Goddess who always stays on the tip of her toes all the time, ever ready to turn and run away. There are ways of wooing and keeping her. When she graces a house with her presence, the master of the house becomes distinguished, famous and wealthy." Margayya reverently touched the tumbler and very respectfully drank the milk, taking care not to spill even a drop.

"That is better," said the old man. "There was once upon a time——" He narrated from Mahabharata the story of Kubera, the wealthiest man in creation, who undertook a long arduous penance as atonement for spilling a drop of milk on the floor of his palace. When the story ended and a pause ensued, Margayya felt he could no longer keep back his request. He felt somewhat shy as he said: "I want to acquire wealth. Can you show me a way? I will do anything you suggest."

"Anything?" asked the priest emphatically. Margayya suddenly grew nervous and discreet. "Of course, anything reasonable." Perhaps the man would tell him to walk upside down or some such thing. "You know what I mean." Margayya added pathetically.

"No, I don't know what you mean," said the old man point-blank. "Wealth does not come the way of people who adopt half-hearted measures. It comes only to those who pray for it single-mindedly with no other thought."

Margayya began to tremble slightly at this statement. "Perhaps he is a sorcerer, or a black magician or an alchemist." He threw a frightened look at him and then at the shack in which he usually dwelt. "Perhaps he has hidden human bodies in that shack, and extracts from the corpses some black ointment, with which he acquires extraordinary powers."

Margayya wanted to get up and run away. In the starlight the man looked eerie, his hollow voice reverberating through the silent night. Margayya's mind was seized with fears. "Perhaps he will ask me to cut off my son's head." He imagined Balu being drugged and taken into the shack. "It's midnight or probably dawn. Let me go home."

He got up abruptly. The old man did not stop him. He merely said: "Yes, go home. It is very late. Probably your wife will be anxious." Margayya felt tremendously relieved that after all he was permitted to leave. He got up, prostrated before the God's image, scrambled to his feet hurriedly, lest the other, sitting immobile where he had

36

left him, should call him back. He hurried off through the silent street. Far off a night constable's whistle was heard. " I hope he will not take me for a' thief." He was wearing his wedding *dhoti*, carrying his account papers under his arm; the whole thing struck him at this hour as being extremely ridiculous.

He stood before his door unable to make up his mind to knock. It might rouse his wife or his son. But unless his wife was roused . . . And how could he explain his late coming? " Something has happened to me—everything seems to be going wrong. That Arul Doss has perhaps cast a spell: can't be sure what everybody is up to——" The world seemed to be a very risky place to live in, peopled by creatures with dark powers. As he stood there undecided, his wife threw back the bolt and let him in. She hadn't put out the kerosene lamp. She looked at him sourly and asked: " What have you been doing so late? " Once inside his home all his old assertiveness returned. He was the master in his house, with nobody to question him. He ignored her and quickly went into the smaller room to undress and change. He washed himself briskly at the well. His son was sleeping near the doorway of the smaller room on a rush mat. He threw a loving look at him, with a feeling that but for a quick decision on his part the little fellow might have been in that shack put to no end of tortures. His wife was very sleepy as she waited for him in the kitchen. He found that she had spread out two leaves. " What? You have not had your dinner yet! " he said, feeling pleased that she had waited for him.

" How could I without knowing what had happened? In future, if you are going to be late——"

" I must ask your permission, I suppose," he said arrogantly.

They consumed their midnight dinner in silence. They went to bed in silence. He lay on the mat beside his son. She went down into her room, and lay on a carpet on

37

which she had already snatched a few hours of sleep before he arrived. Margayya lay in bed unable to shut his eyes. He lay looking at the ceiling, which was dark with smoke; cobwebs dangled from the tiles like tapestry. "She ought to clean it and not expect me to have to see such things," he said to himself angrily. He got up and blew out the kerosene lamp and lay down. He slept badly, constantly harassed by nightmares composed of the priest, the secretary, and Arul Doss. One recurring dream was of his son stepping into the shack in the temple, with the priest standing behind the door, and all his efforts to keep him back proved futile. The young fellow was constantly tiptoeing away towards the shack. It bothered Margayya so much that he let out a cry: "*Aiyo! Aiyo!*" which woke up the child, who jumped out of bed with a piercing scream; which in turn roused his mother sleeping in the other room, and she sprang up howling: "Oh, what has happened! What has happened!" It was about half an hour before the dawn. All this commotion awakened Margayya himself. He cried: "Who is there? Who is there?" "Someone was moving about." "Someone made a noise." The uproar increased. "Where are the matches?" Margayya demanded suddenly, and cursed in the dark. "Who asked you to blow out the light?" his wife said. He sprang up and ran towards the backyard thinking that the intruder must have run in that direction. The little boy cried, "Oh, father, father, don't go . . . Don't go . . ." His mother clutched him to her bosom. He struggled and wildly kicked for no reason whatever. The people of the next house woke up and muttered: "Something always goes wrong in that house. Even at midnight one has no peace, if they are in the neighbourhood."

§

Margayya was sitting before his small box, examining the accounts written in his red book. His son came up to sit on his lap. Margayya said: "Go and play, don't disturb me now," and tried to keep him off. "This is my play, I won't go," said the child, pushing towards him again and climbing resolutely on his lap. Margayya had to peep over his head in order to look at the register before him; Balu's hair constantly tickled his nostrils and he felt irritated. He cried: "Balu, won't you leave me alone. I will buy you a nice——"

"What?" asked the child.

"A nice little elephant."

"All right, buy it now, come on."

"No, no, not now. . . . I'm working now," he said, pointing at the small register. Balu shot out his little leg and kicked away the register petulantly, and in the process the ink-well upset beside it and emptied on the page. Then the child stamped his heel on the ink and it splashed over Margayya's face and spoiled the entire book. Margayya felt maddened at the sight of it. He simply gripped the boy by his shoulder, lifted him as he would lift an unwanted cat, and almost flung him into a corner. Needless to say it made the child cry so loudly that his mother came running out of the kitchen, her eyes streaming with tears owing to the smoke there. "What has happened? What has happened?" she cried, rushing towards the child, who, undaunted, was again making a dash for his father as he stooped over the wreckage trying to retrieve his damaged account book. "Look what he has done," he cried excitedly. "This monkey!"

"*You* are a monkey!" cried the boy, hugging his father's knee as he was blotting the spilled ink.

"If you don't leave me, I'll—I'll——" he was too angry. "I'll give you over to the temple priest . . . He'll flay your skin."

"He will give me plantains," corrected the boy. He turned aside and suddenly pounced on the book, grabbed it and dashed off. His father ran after him with war cries. The boy dodged him here and there, going into this corner and darting into that. His tears had by now dried, he was enjoying the chase, and with hysterical laughter he was running hither and thither clutching the precious red note book in his hand. It was a small space within which he ran, but somehow Margayya was unable to seize him. Margayya panted with the effort. He cried: "If you don't stop, I'll flay you."

"What is the matter with you? What has come over you?" asked the wife.

"I'm all right," Margayya replied proudly. "You'll see what I'll do to that little monkey, that devil you have begotten." His wife gave some appropriate reply, and tried to help in the chase. She pretended to look away and suddenly darted across to seize the boy. He was too swift even for her calculations. She only collided against her husband, which irritated him more; and it allowed the child to dash into the street with his prize, with his father at his heels. He cried impatiently to his wife, "Get out of the way—you——" at which she turned and went back to the kitchen murmuring: "What do I care? I only let the rice overboil watching this tomfoolery." The boy dashed down the front steps, with his father following him. Margayya was blind to all his surroundings—all he could see was the little boy with his curly hair, and the small red-bound book which was in his hand. Some passers-by in Vinayak Mudali Street stopped to watch the scene. Margayya cried shamelessly: "Hold him! Hold him!" At which they tried to encircle the boy. It was evident that by now he had become completely intoxicated with the chase. Presently he found that he was being outnumbered and cornered. As a circle of hunters hemmed in, he did an entirely unexpected thing—he turned back as if coming into his father's arms, and as he was just about to grasp him, darted sideways to the edge of the gutter and flung the red book into it. The gutter ran in front of the houses; roaring waters went down the drain, God knew where. It was well known that any object which fell into it was lost for ever, it sank and went out of sight, sank deeper and deeper into a black mass, and was hopelessly gone. The gutter was wide as a channel. Once in a while, especially before the elections, the Municipal officials came down and walked along the edge, peering into its dark current and saying something among themselves as to its being a problem and so on But there they left it until the next election. It was a stock cynicism for people to say when they saw anyone inspecting the drains: " They are only looking for the election votes there! " At other times the gutter continued its existence unhampered, providing the cloud of mosquitoes and the stench that characterized existence in Vinayak Mudali Street.

Presently a big crowd stood on the edge of the drain looking at its inky, swirling waters. People sympathized with Margayya. Wild, inaccurate reports of what had fallen into it were circulated. Margayya heard people tell each other: " A box was dropped into it." " That child threw away a gold chain into it." Everyone looked at Balu with interest. He seemed to have become a hero for the moment. He felt abashed at this prominence and hung his head. The sun was shining on them fiercely, though it was just nine-thirty in the morning. Margayya looked red with anger and exertion. His son's face was also flushed. The little boy crossed his arms behind him and stood on the edge of the gutter watching it with fascination. There was no trace of the book left anywhere. Margayya's blood boiled as he watched the unconcern of the boy, who, true to the type in that street, wore only a shirt covering the upper half of his body. Two pedlars carrying green vegetables, a cyclist who jumped off on seeing the crowd, a few schoolchildren, a curd-seller, and a few others formed the group which now watched the gutter, with varying comments passing between them. A man was saying: " Some people are so fond that they give their children everything they ask for." On hearing this Margayya felt so enraged that he lifted the edge of the shirt the little boy was wearing and slapped him fiercely across his uncovered seat. The boy cried aloud: " Oh! " and turned round on his father. It started a fresh scene. Someone

41

dragged away the child, saying: " Save the child from this ruffian." Another said: " He would have pushed the child into the gutter." A woman with a basket came forward to ask: " Are you a heartless demon? How can you beat such a small child? " She flung down her basket and picked up the child on her arm. Balu copiously sobbed on her shoulder. Another woman tried to take him from her, commenting: " Only those who bear the child for ten months in the womb know how precious it is. Men are always like this." Someone objected to this statement; it turned out to be the man holding the cycle, who retorted with great warmth: " Boys must be chastised; otherwise do you want them to grow up into devils? " Margayya looked at him gratefully. Here at last was a friend in this absolutely hostile world. He swept his arms to address all the women and the gathering: " It's all very well for you to talk. . . . But he has thrown in there an important account book. What am I to do without it? "

" How can a baby know anything about account books and such things? God gives children to those who don't deserve them."

" You should not have kept it within his reach. You must always be prepared for such things where there are children."

A washerwoman, who had come forward, said: " You were childless for twelve years, and prayed to all the Gods and went to Thirupathi: was it only for this? "

" What have I done? " Margayya asked pathetically. He was beginning to feel very foolish. Society was pressing in upon him from all sides—the latest in the shape of this woman who had on her back a bundle of unwashed linen. Vegetable sellers, oil-mongers, passers-by, cart-men, students—everyone seemed to have a right to talk to him as they pleased. Society seemed to overwhelm him on all sides. The lone cyclist was hardly an adequate support on which to lean. Margayya turned and looked for him. He too was gone. He saw his son clinging fast to the waist of the cucumber seller, sobbing and sobbing, and gaining

42

more sympathizers. Margayya knew that the little boy would not let his sympathizers go until they took him to the shop across the road and bought him peppermints.

The crowd turned away and was now following Balu, and Margayya felt relieved that they were leaving him alone. He broke a twig off an avenue tree, and vaguely poked it into the gutter and ran the stick from end to end. He only succeeded in raising a stench. A schoolmaster who passed that way advised: " Call a scavenger and ask him to look for it. He'll have the proper thing with him for poking here. Don't try to do everything yourself." Margayya obediently dropped the stick into the drain, reflecting, " No one will let me do what I like." He turned to go back into his house. He climbed the steps with bowed head, because his brother's entire family was ranged along the wall on the other side. He quickly passed in. When he was gone they commented: " Something is always agitating that household and creating a row." Margayya went straight into the kitchen, where his wife was cooking, ignorant of all that had happened, and told her: " The folk in the next house seem to have no better business than to hang about to see what is going on here . . . Do they ever find the time to cook, eat or sleep? " This was a routine question needing no reply from his wife. She merely asked: " Where is the child? " " Probably rolling in the gutter," he answered wearily. " What has come over you? " she asked. " You don't seem to be in your senses since last night."

" I'm not. And if you try to imply that I have been drinking or spending the night in a brothel, I leave you free to think so——"

§

The loss of the little book produced endless complications for Margayya. He could hardly transact any business without it, and he had to conceal the loss from his customers, who he feared might take advantage of it. He had to keep out of the tree shade, remain standing or moving about, and give out figures from his head—it was all most irksome. It was an important day; he had to collect money from three or four men to whom he had advanced cash.

"Where is the book, master?" asked Kali, one of his old customers. Margayya said: "I'm rebinding it. You know it must look tidy. But it is really not necessary for me. I have everything I want here," he added, tapping his forehead. Kali had not been here for some weeks now and so looked with suspicion at this man standing beyond the gate, without his box, without his book. "Perhaps," thought Margayya, "Arul Doss has been speaking to him." Kali was like a tiger which suddenly meets the ring-master, without the ring, or the whip in his hand.

"Why are you not in your place?" he asked.

"Oh! I'm tired of sitting and sitting—some sort of lumbago here," Margayya said. He sat down on the short compound wall. A country cart passed along, and it threw up dust. Margayya sneezed. "You see, you should not sit there," moralized the other. "I should not, that's why I'm looking for an office hereabouts with chairs and tables. When eminent people like you arrive, you will be seated in chairs," he said. "I must also look to your convenience, don't you see?"

"Of course," said the other. "But that banyan shade was quite good, sir. So much fresh air. I always like it."

"I don't," replied Margayya. "It's all very well for a man like you, who comes out to lounge and have a nap in the afternoon. But for a businessman it is not good. The uproar those birds make! I can hardly hear my own voice! And then their droppings! And those ants down below. I used to suffer agony when I was sitting there."

"Where is your box, sir?" asked Kali, noticing its absence.

"Sent it for re-painting: it's a lucky box, my dear fellow. I don't like to throw it away . . . It's not looking quite tidy. I've sent it for painting. I have it more as a keep-sake."

"Yes, whatever article has grown up with us must be kept all our life . . . In our village there was a fellow who had a hoe with a broken handle——"

"I know all that," Margayya cut in, snubbing him just for the sake of effect. "When he changed the handle, his harvest suffered, didn't it?"

"How do you know, sir?" asked Kali, overawed.

"I know everything that goes on in people's minds; otherwise, I should not have taken to this banking business. . . . Now I know what is going on in your mind. You have got in your purse, which you have tucked at the waist, money drawn from the bank."

"No, no, sir," he protested. "Is it so easy to get money out of them?"

"Listen! Your loan application was considered and passed on Monday last. You must have in your purse now two hundred and seventy-nine rupees and four annas; that is, you have given eight annas to the clerk, and four annas as a tip to Arul Doss. Is it, or is it not a fact?" He cast a seaching look at Kali, who had wrapped himself in a large sheet. There were a hundred corners over his person where he might tuck a whole treasure. Kali met his gaze, and turned to go. It was the dull hour of the afternoon when his other clients had gone into the bank or were dozing in the shade. They would all come a little later. Margayya was glad it was so, because he wanted to tackle this difficult man alone. Others would not be able to take a lesson from him. Kali was attempting to retreat. He looked up at the sky and said: "Looks like three o'clock. They have asked me to call in at three again. You know how it is, if we go in even a minute late. They make it an excuse——" Margayya looked at him. If he let him go out of sight, he would pass into the bank and then out of it by the back door.

He said firmly: "You give me the fifty rupees I advanced, with interest." The other looked puzzled.

"Fifty! With interest! What is it you are talking about, Margayya?" At other times, if anyone said such a thing,

45

Margayya would open the pages of his red-bound book and flourish it. He thought of his son. Why did the boy do such a thing? He had left the book alone all these days! Kali stopped, looked at him haughtily and said: "I never like to be called a liar! You may settle my account to-morrow, the first thing ... Let me see what it is, and I will settle it the first thing tomorrow, to the last pie." He moved away. Margayya stood helplessly. He watched him with sorrow. He could not even throw after him any curse and threats (brilliant ones that occurred to him, as usual, a little too late). "Margayya, you have been made a fool of. They have made a frightful fool of you." "They haven't ... I should have told him ... You son of a guttersnipe ... Don't I know what your father was! He went to jail for snatching a chain from a child's neck! You come of a family which would steal a match stick rather than ask for it ... I shouldn't have associated with you, but I'll get at you one day, don't worry. I can——" But it was no use arguing with himself in this manner. The man was gone, while Margayya stood watching him dumbly. He recollected that he had helped him get loans four times—when his life and honour, as he said, were at stake. "And this is what I get." He was filled with self-pity. He thought of the account book. Suppose he announced a reward to any scavenger who might salvage it? Even if it was salvaged what was the use? How was it to be touched again and read!

He had to wait at the gate, away from the line of vision of the secretary's room, sitting on the short parapet, and keep an eye on all his old customers who might go in and come out of the building Without giving himself too much away, he was able to tackle a few of his old customers, and they didn't prove as tricky as Kali. He was able to salvage the bulk of his investments within the next fifteen days, which amounted to just two hundred rupees.

§

Margayya stepped into the temple, driven there by a vague sense of desperation. He told himself several times over that he was going to see the God and not the priest. But he did not believe it himself—nor did the priest let him view only the God and go away. As soon as he entered the portals of the temple the priest's voice came to him from an unknown, unobserved place, behind the image in the dark inner sanctum. " Oh, Margayya, welcome to this God's home." Margayya was startled as if a voice from Heaven had suddenly assailed him. He trembled. The last worshipper had prostrated before the image and was leaving. Margayya prostrated on the ground before the inner sanctuary. A couple of feeble oil lamps were alight; a mixed smell of burning oil, flowers, and incense hung in the air. That was a combination of scent which always gave Margayya a feeling of elation. He shut his eyes. For a moment he felt that he was in a world free from all worrying problems. It was in many ways a noble world, where everything ran smoothly—no Arul Doss or Co-operative Society Secretary, no villagers with their complex finances, no son to snatch away an account book and drop it in a gutter. Life was a terrible affair. The faint, acrid smell of oil seemed to detach him from all worries for a moment. He shut his eyes and let himself float in that luxurious sensation, with the tip of his nose pressed against the flag-stones of the corridor. It was still warm with the heat of the day's sun. Its smell of dust was overpowering—the dust carried by the feet of hundreds of devotees and worshippers or blown in by the wind from Vinayak Mudali Street. When Margayya withdrew from the feeling of ecstasy and lifted his head, he saw the feet of the priest near his face. He looked up. The priest said: "Margayya's mind is deeply engrossed in God ... if a man's piety is to be measured by the length of time he lies prostrate before God. Get up Margayya. God has seen your heart already." Margayya got to his feet. He smiled at him and felt some explana-

47

tion was due. He began awkwardly: "You see, you see
. . I felt I should visit God at least once a week———"

"Yes, you were here only last evening, have you forgotten it already? "

"Not at all, not at all," Margayya replied. "I wonder
what the time is."

"In this house there is no need for us to look at a watch.
If it is dark, it is night. If it's sunny, it's day: that's all
we know. This is not a bank, you see." At the word 'bank'
Margayya gulped suddenly. He thought it referred to
him. He said: "I don't have a watch either."

"But you ought to." said the priest. "A bank keeps a
watch to see how fast interest is accumulating."

"My bank is finished. This is all I have," said Margayya, taking out of his pocket a small packet of currency
notes—all that he was able to salvage from his banking
operations. "Just two hundred rupees—what is it worth? "

"Two hundred rupees," replied the priest. "Come in,
I will give you some milk and fruit! "

"What again! " asked Margayya.

"Yes, again, and again! " answered the priest. "Is there
anything strange about it? Don't we have to eat everyday,
again and again? " Margayya was cowed. He explained:
"It's not that. I was wondering what the time might be."

"It's not yet tomorrow, that's all I know," replied the
priest. "If it is really late for you, you can go." He turned
and moved down the corridor and passed out of sight.
Margayya stood still for a few moments. He looked at the
image of the God and threw it a vague nod. His wife might
once again start a lot of bother and pull a long face and
think he'd been visiting a brothel. "Funny creature, so
jealous at my age! " he reflected. "I can tell her I've been
out on important business. What makes her think I have
sweethearts! " Ever since he could remember she had
had always shown a sort of uneasiness about Margayya.
"Who'd consent to be a sweetheart to me! " he said. "A
fellow with the name 'Margayya,' which seems almost a
branding with hot iron." He remembered how a year or

48

so ago she raised quite a lot of bother when he mentioned that a woman had come to him as a client under the tree. She looked sullen for two days until he convinced her that he had only been joking.

He found himself obeying the priest without a single thought of his own. At a look from this gaunt man, he peeled four plantains and swallowed them in quick succession, and he drank a huge vessel of milk, treating the matter with as much reverence as he could muster. When the priest said approvingly, "That's very good indeed. That's an excellent performance," he felt proud of the certificate. The priest added, "You have been hungry without knowing it."

"Yes, but when one's mind is full of worries, one does not notice," he said, feeling that the time had come for him to say something. The stars were out. A cool breeze was blowing, and night seemed quiet; the nourishment he had taken filled him with a sense of harmony, and so when the priest said: "Margayya! What is ailing you? You can speak out," he felt that he could no longer hesitate and fumble; that all barriers between himself and the world had been swept away and that he stood alone; that he alone mattered. He had a right to demand the goods of life and get them, like an eminent guest in a wedding house—a guest who belongs to the bridegroom's party, with the bride dancing attendance, ever waiting for the slightest nod or sign to run to his side and do some pleasing act . . . He swelled with his own importance . . . When he inhaled the fresh night air it seemed to increase his stature so much that the earth and the sky were only just big enough to hold him . . . He began to talk in a grand manner . . . the priest with his eyes glinting in the starlight listened without speaking a word . . . He looked like a sloth-cub in the darkness as he humped into a ball with his chin on his knees, his lank face thrust forward . . . Margayya catalogued all his demands. He was like a Departmental Officer indenting for his stationery—a superior baize cover for his office table, a crystal paper-weight, a shining mirror-

49

like paper-knife, and so on. There was no reason why he should be given the inferior things. Let the stores department beware, he would throw it out of the window if they sent in the miserable stuff they put on their fourth clerk's tables. He would just throw it out, that's all . . . He would be a man of consequence, let them beware: let the Gods beware—they that provided a man with a home, and cars, servants, the admiration of his fellow-men, and good clothes. After letting him run on as long as he liked, the priest opened his mouth and said: "That means you should propitiate Goddess Lakshmi, the Goddess of Wealth. When she throws a glance and it falls on someone, he becomes rich, he becomes prosperous, he is treated by the world as an eminent man, his words are treated as something of importance. All this you seem to want."

"Yes," said Margayya authoritatively. "Why not?" He took out of his pocket his little snuff box and tapped its lid. He flicked it open and took a deep pinch. The priest said: "Go on, go on, no harm in it. A devotee of Goddess Lakshmi need care for nothing, not even the fact that he is in a temple where a certain decorum is to be observed. It's only a question of self-assurance. He has so much authority in his face, so much money in his purse, so many to do his bidding that he cares for nothing really in the world. It's only the protégé of Goddess Saraswathi* who has to mind such things. But when Saraswathi favours a man, the other Goddess withdraws her favours. There is always a rivalry between the two—between the patronage of the spouse of Vishnu and the spouse of Brahma. Some persons have the good fortune to be claimed by both, some on the contrary have the misfortune to be abandoned by both. Evidently you are one of those for whom both are fighting at the moment." Margayya felt immensely powerful and important. He had never known that anybody cared for him . . . and now to think that two Goddesses were fighting to confer their favours on him! He lifted his eyes, glanced at the brilliant

* Saraswathi is the deity presiding over knowledge and enlightenment.

stars in Heaven as if there, between the luminous walls, he would get a glimpse of the crowned Goddesses tearing at each other.

"Why should they care for me?" he asked innocently.

The priest replied: "How can we question? How can we question the fancies of Gods? They are just there, that's all . . . it's beyond our powers to understand."

Intoxicated by this, Margayya said: "A man whom the Goddess of Wealth favours need not worry much. He can buy all the knowledge he requires. He can afford to buy all the gifts that Goddess Saraswathi holds in her palm."

The priest let out a quiet chuckle at Margayya's very reckless statement. Margayya asked: "Why do you laugh?" Already a note of authority was coming into his voice. The priest said: "Yes, this is what every man who attains wealth thinks. You are moving along the right line. Let me see your horoscope. Bring it tomorrow." Tomorrow! It seemed such a long way off. "Can't you say something today?" Margayya asked pathetically, feeling that he was being hurled back to the earth. The priest said: "About the same time as today, meet me with your horoscope."

"Yet another night out and all the trouble with my wife," Margayya thought immediately.

The priest saw him off at the door and shut the temp gate.

§

The moment his wife opened the door Margayya demanded: "Where is my horoscope?"

"Horoscope?" his wife said dreamily. "What's happened that you want it so urgently at this hour?" She looked him up and down suspiciously and, feeling probably that it was not the right time to drag him into a talk, turned and went back to bed.

51

It was eight o'clock when Margayya got up. He would probably have slept on till eleven, but for the fact that Balu sat on his chest and hammered his head with his lacquered wooden elephant. When he opened his eyes, Balu let out a shout of joy, put his arms round his neck, and pretended to lift him out of bed. Margayya looked at him benignly. "This boy must grow up like a prince. The Goddess willing, he'll certainly . . ." He sprang up from bed. In a quarter of an hour he was ready, bathed, wearing a clean dress, and his forehead smeared with red vermilion and a splash of sacred ash. He seemed to be in such a great hurry that his wife, although she had resolved to ignore his recent eccentric ways, was constrained to ask, "What is agitating you so much?"

"Is coffee ready?" he asked.

She laughed cynically. "Coffee! The milk vendor created a scene here last evening demanding his dues. It was such a disgrace with the people in the next house watching."

"They seem to have nothing better to do," he said irrelevantly, his mind going off at a tangent.

"Anybody will watch when there is something to watch," she said.

"So, no coffee?" he asked with a touch of despair. It seemed terribly hard for him to start the day without a cup of coffee. It produced a sort of vacuum, a hollow sensation. He braved it out saying: "That's right. Why should we want coffee? As if our ancestors——" She added: "There is no milk even for the child." Margayya threw a sad look at Balu. Balu seemed happy to be missing his milk. He said: "Let us drive away that milkman. It will be so nice."

"Why, aren't you hungry?" Margayya asked.

"Yes, I'm hungry. Give me biscuits."

Margayya said: "Wait a little, young man. I'll fill a whole shelf with biscuits and chocolates and fruit."

"All for me?" the boy asked eagerly.

"Yes, absolutely, provided you don't bother me, but

leave me alone now," Margayya said. He went into their little room and pulled out a wooden chest. It was filled with letters in their old envelopes of nearly thirty years ago: there you could find letters written by Margayya's father from a village; Margayya's father-in-law writing to his new son-in-law; a letter from an uncle saying that there was a nice girl to be married and proposing her for Margayya, enclosing horoscopes. There were several letters containing saffron-tipped horoscopes on old stiff paper. There were unknown names of girls—either proposed to Margayya or to his brother, with their horoscopes; and many acrimonious letters that passed between him and his brother before the partition. Every letter he picked up stirred a cloud of dust. Little Balu stole up and stood at his shoulder as he squatted on the ground. Margayya turned round and said: "Balu, you must promise not to put your hand out."

"Why?"

Margayya handed him over to his wife with: "Take this fellow away. If you let him come near me again——"

She snatched him up as he protested and shouted and carried him away, muttering: "This is only a trick to send me off. You don't like me to see what you are doing, I suppose. I don't know what you are up to! So mysterious!"

"Women can't hold their tongues, that's why," Margayya replied. Little Balu made a good deal of noise in the other room and Margayya muttered: "She has completely spoilt him, beyond remedy; I must take him out of her hands and put him to school. That's the only way; otherwise he will be a terrible scoundrel." As he rummaged in the contents of the box his mind kept ringing with his wife's weak protests and grumblings: "Seems to be bent upon worrying me—she's getting queer!" he said to himself. He took up every envelope, gazed on its post-mark, examined the letters, became engrossed for a while in by-gone family politics, and finally came upon a couple of horoscopes tucked into an envelope addressed to his father. A

53

short note by his father-in-law said: "I'm returning to you the originals of the horoscopes of Sowbhagyavathi (ever-auspicious) Meenakshi, and your son Chiranjeevi (eternally-living) Krishna. Your daughter-in-law is keeping well. Any day you ask us to fix the nuptial ceremony I shall bring her over." Margayya (he hadn't yet attained that name) felt a sudden tenderness for his wife. She seemed to become all at once a young bashful virgin bride.

"Meena!" he cried. "Here are the horoscopes." She came up, still bearing her son on her arm. Margayya flourished the horoscopes. "I've found them." He clung to them as if he had secured the plan of approach to a buried treasure. "What is it?" she asked. He held up the letter and cried: "This is a letter from your father about our nuptials." She blushed slightly, and turned away: "What has come over you that you are unearthing all this stuff?" Little Balu would not let her finish her sentence. He started wriggling in her arm, and showed an inclination to dash for his father's horoscope. "Take him away," cried Margayya. "Otherwise we shall find all this in the gutter before our house—so much for this son of ours."

Presently she came without their son to ask: "What exactly are you planning?" Her face was full of perplexity. "Don't worry," he said, looking up at her. He still felt the tenderness that he had felt for her as a virginal bride. He told her: "Don't worry. I've not been hunting out my horoscope in order to search for a wife." He laughed. She found it difficult to enjoy the joke with him. It was too puzzling. She merely said: "By all means look for a wife. I shan't mind." He was disappointed that she sounded so indifferent: he was proud to feel that she guarded him jealously. However, he bantered her about it without telling anything. He could not exactly say in all seriousness what he was trying to do. "You will know all about it very soon." When he started out that day, she asked rather nervously: "Will you be late again today?"

"Yes," he said. "What if I am late? I'm only out on business, be assured."

54

His son said: "I will come with you too," and ran down the steps and clung to him. Margayya could not shake him off easily. He carried him up to the end of the street and lectured him all the way on how he should behave in order to qualify for biscuits and chocolates. The lecture seemed to affect him since he became quite docile when Margayya put him back at his house and left.

§

That night, in his shack, the priest scrutinized the horoscope with the aid of an oil lamp. He spread it out and pored over it for a long while in silence. He said: "Saturn! Saturn! This God is moving on to that house. He may do you good if you propitiate him. Why don't you go and pray in that other temple where they've installed the Planetary Deities? Go there with an offering of honey." "Where can I get honey?" Margayya asked, looking worried. He suddenly realized that he had never bought honey in his life. It was just one of those things that one always had at home, when the household was managed by one's parents. Now he recollected that ever since he became an independent family head he had managed to get along without honey. Now the testing time seemed to have come. The priest burst into one of his frightening chuckles. He remarked: "Margayya shows the whole world how to increase their cash—but honey! He stands defeated before honey, is that it?" "I will manage it," Margayya said haughtily. "I was only saying——" The priest arbitrarily cut short all further reference to the subject. "On Saturday go to the temple and go round its corridor thrice. Do you know that Saturn is the most powerful entity in the world? And if he is gratified he can make you a ruler of this world or he can just drown you in an ocean of misery. Nobody can escape him. Better keep him in good humour." "All right; I will do as you say," Margayya said, with quiet obedience in his voice. He felt as if Saturn were around him, and might give him a twist and lift him up to plunge him into the ocean of misery if he did not behave properly.

It was four o'clock when the priest had finished giving him instructions—a course of prayers and activities. He recited a short verse and commanded Margayya to copy it down in Sanskrit, and side by side take down its meaning in Tamil. He saw him off at the door and said: "You need not see me again, unless you want to. Follow these rules."

"Will they produce results?"

"Who can say?" the priest answered. "Results are not in our hands."

"Then why should we do all this?"

"Very well, don't; nobody compels you to."

Margayya felt completely crushed under all this metaphysical explanation. He bowed his head in humility. The priest closed one door, held his hand on the other, and said: "The *Shastras* lay down such and such rituals for such and such ends. Between a man who performs them and one who doesn't, the chances are greater for the former. That's all I can say. The results are . . . you may have results or you may not . . . or you may have results and wish that you had failed——"

"What is your experience with this *Mantra*?"

"Me!" He chuckled once again. "I'm a *sanyasi*; I have no use for it . . . Don't do it unless you wish to," said the priest and shut the door. Margayya stood hesitating in the road with the stanza in his pocket, and all the spiritual prescriptions written down. He looked despairingly at the closed door of the temple and turned homeward. He felt it was no use hesitating. He might go on putting questions; the other could answer, yet still the problem would remain unsolved. "Problem? What's the problem?" he suddenly asked. It was a happy state of affairs not to remember what the problem was. The priest had been saying so much incomprehensible stuff that Margayya felt dizzy and fuddled. He stopped in the

56

middle of the road and resolved: "He has told me what to do. I shall do it honestly. Let me not bother about other things."

§

Margayya's wife was overawed by his activities. He told her next day: "Clear up that room for me," indicating the single room in their house in which she slept with her child, and into which all the household trunks and odds and ends were also thrown.

"What are we to do with these things?"

"Throw them out. I want that place for the next forty days."

"Where am I to sleep?"

"What silly questions you keep asking! Is this the time to think of such problems?"

She became docile at his attack and begged: "Can't you tell me exactly what you want to do?"

He told her in a sort of way: he'd been advised not to talk of his method and aim even to his wife. The priest had said: "Even to your wife—there are certain practices which become neutralized the moment they are clothed in words."

She asked: "Is this what people call alchemy, changing base metals?"

"No, it is not," said Margayya, not liking the comparison.

"They say that it is like magic—black magic," she wailed, looking very much frightened.

"Don't get silly notions in your head . . . it is not that . . . the priest is not a man who dabbles in black magic. Don't go talking about it to anyone——"

The little room was cleared and all the odds and ends—broken-down furniture, trunks and boxes, stacks of paper, spare bed-rolls, and pillows and mats were pulled out and heaped in a corner of their little central hall. Balu became ecstatic. He pulled down the things and mixed them up

57

and generally enjoyed the confusion. Their neighbours heard the noise of shifting and thought: "They are doing something in the next house; wonder what it is." They tried to spy on them, but there was a blank wall between them. Margayya had the room washed clean, chased out the rats and cockroaches, and swept off the cobwebs that hung on the wall and corners. It was a very small room, less than eight feet broad, with a single narrow window opening on the street. If the shutter was closed the room became pitch dark. Margayya drew up several pots of water from the well and splashed the water about. He then commanded his wife to decorate the floor with white flour designs, a decoration necessary for all auspicious occasions. He had a string of mango leaves tied across the doorway. He took from a nail in the hall the picture of the Goddess Lakshmi, put up a short pedestal and placed the picture on it: the four-armed Goddess, who presides over wealth, distinction, bravery, enterprise, and all the good things in life. When he carried the picture in, his wife understood something of his plans: "Oh, I see, I now understand."

"That's all right. If you understand, so much the better —but keep it to yourself."

He had two hundred rupees in his possession still, which he had to use up. He gave his wife a list of articles she should supply him with—such as jaggery, turmeric, coloured cooked rice, refined sugar, black-gram cake, sweetened sesamum, curd, spiced rice and various kinds of fruit and honey. He would require these in small quantities morning and evening for offering—and most of them were also to be his diet during the period of *Japa*. He gave his wife a hundred rupees and said: "This is my last coin. You have to manage with it."

"What about the provisions for the house—and the milkman?"

"Oh, do something . . . manage the milkman and the rest for some time and then we will pull through. This is more urgent than anything else."

§

A couple of days later, at the full moon, he began his rites. He sat before the image of Lakshmi. He shut the door, though his son banged on it from time to time. He kept only a slight opening of the window shutter, through which a small ray of light came in but not the curiosity of the neighbours. He wore a loincloth soaked in water. A variety of small articles were spread out before him in little pans. He inscribed a certain Sanskrit syllable on a piece of deer skin and tied it round his neck with a string. He had been in an agony till he found the deer skin. The priest had told him: "You must carve out this on an antelope skin."

"Antelope!" he gasped. Was he a hunter? Where did one go and find the antelope skin? "You search in your house properly and you will find one. Our elders have always possessed them for sitting on and praying," said the priest.

"Very well, I will look for one," said Margayya.

"And then, have you seen any red lotus?"

"Yes, I have," Margayya said apprehensively, wondering what was coming next.

"Where?" asked the priest. Margayya blinked and felt disgusted with himself: "They usually sell them in the street for *Vara Lakshmi* festival."

"Exactly!" said the priest. "But now you will have to go where it is found. Formerly, you could pick up a lotus from any pond nearby—there were perhaps ten spots in a town where you could pick up a lotus in former days, but now . . . our world is going to pieces because we have no more lotus about. It's a great flower—the influence it has on a human being is incalculable." After a dissertation on the lotus, the priest said: "Beyond Sarayu, towards the North, there is a garden where there is a ruined temple with a pond. You will find red lotus there. Get one, burn its petals to a pitch-black, and mix it with ghee."

"*Ghee!* Oh, yes——" Margayya said, feeling that here was at least one article which you could find in the kitchen.

59

Even if the store-man was ill-disposed, one might still win him over in view of the impending change of circumstances.

"It must be ghee made of milk drawn from a smoke-coloured cow!" said the priest.

"Oh!" groaned Margayya, not being able to hide his feelings any more.

"You probably think all this is bluff . . . some fantastic nonsense that I'm inventing."

"Oh, no, I don't feel so for a moment, but only how hard . . . what a lot of——"

"Yes, but that is the way it's done. It's so written in the *Shastras*. You have to do certain things for attaining certain ends. It is not necessary to question why. It'll be a mere waste of energy and you will get no answer. . . . Well, follow my words carefully. Take the blackened lotus petal, mix it with ghee, and put a dot of it on your forehead after the prayer, every day, exactly between your eyebrows."

"Yes," Margayya said weakly. He was feeling more and more in despair of how he was going to fulfil these various injunctions. Red lotus, grey-skinned cow, and antelope . . . "Where am I? . . . what a world this is——" It seemed to him an impossible world. "How am I to get all these?" He groaned within.

"Have trust in yourself and go ahead. . . . He will show you a way. Did you imagine that riches came to people when they sat back and hummed a tune?"

§

A whole day was spent by him in going after the red lotus. It took him through the northern part of the town, past Ellamman Street and the banks of the Sarayu. He forded the river at Nallappa's Mango Grove. A village cart was crossing the river. The man driving it recognized him and shouted: "Oh, Margayya!" He jumped out of the cart, sending up a great splash of water, which struck Margayya in the eyes and face; it also cooled his brow after the exertion of the day. The villager was an old client of his. He said: "What has come over you, sir, that we don't see you? Without you, we are finding it so difficult."

"You can't expect me to be at your beck and call all the time. I have other things to do."

"But you cannot just abandon us——"

"I have other business to look after, my dear fellow. Don't imagine this is my only task. I used to do it more as a sort of help to my fellow-men." They were both standing knee-deep in water.

Margayya said: "Let me ride with you up to the branch road." The villager was only too eager to take him and asked his son, who was in the cart, to get down and walk so as to make room for Margayya.

He asked: "So far out! May I know why you are going this way?"

Margayya said: "You must never ask 'Why' or 'Where' when a person is starting out: that'll always have an adverse influence." He felt he was beginning to talk like the temple priest.

"All right, sir," the villager said obediently. "We have to learn all these things from learned people. Otherwise how can we know?"

The wheels crunched, roared, and bumped along. Margayya wondered if he was expected to reach his lotus by walking and not by riding in a cart. Would that in any way affect the issues and would it violate the injunction laid by the priest? "I don't think there is anything wrong in it. He'd have mentioned it. Anyway, better not raise the question. Perhaps this cart was sent here by God."

He got off at the cross roads, and waited till the cart disappeared down the road. He turned to his left, and cut across a field. The sun was already tilting westward. He looked up and said: "Heaven help me if it gets dark before I discover the lotus; I may not be able to know whether it is red or black or what—and then it'll be fine, having to start the whole business again tomorrow! " He cut across the field and walked half a mile, and came upon a garden, hedged off with brambles and thorn. His legs ached with this unaccustomed tramping, and his feet smarted with the touch of thorns. He passed through the thicket expecting any minute a cobra to dart across and nip at him : " This place must be full of them—supply the entire district with cobras from here." There was a small narrow gap in the hedge and he passed through it into a large wood, semi-dark with sky-topping trees—mango, margosa, and whatnot. The place looked wild and deserted and an evening breeze murmured grimly in the boughs above. Down below fallen leaves were ankle-deep, and he passed through them with his feet sending out a resounding crick-crick. " This is just where cobras live—under a blanket of dry leaves——" Here flower gardens had gone wild—all kinds of creepers, jasmine bushes and nerium growing ten feet high, were intertwined and mixed up. " Some fool has let all this go to waste," he reflected. " In fruit alone one might make ten thousand rupees out of this soil."

He arrived at the pond. Its greenish water had a layer of moss, occasional ripples were thrown out by warts or some other darting water creature, and mosquito larvæ agitated the surface here and there. Margayya felt very lonely. The steps of the pond were broken and slippery; half the bank on his side had fallen into the pond. On the other side there was a small *mantap*, its walls covered with cobweb and smoke. Three blackened stones in a corner indicated that some wayfarers had sojourned and lighted a fire here, it might be last year or a century ago. In the middle of the pond there were lotus flowers—red as the rising sun. They were half closing their petals. " They know better than we do that it's nearing sun-set," Margayya reflected. He stood on the somewhat slippery step thinking of how to reach the lotus. He'd have to wade through the greenish water. He stood ankle deep in it and wondered if he had better take off his clothes and go in. "If this *dhoti* gets dirty, it will not merely be dirty but it'll acquire a permanent green dye, I suppose. And it'll be difficult to go back home wearing it. People might stare and laugh. Better take it off . . . there's no one about." He tucked up his *dhoti* and looked round in order to make sure. "If a man lives here, he will not need a square inch of cloth," he reflected. Far in a corner of the little *mantap* on the other bank he saw someone stirring. He felt a slight shiver of fear passing through him as he peered closer. "Is it a ghost or a maniac?" He withdrew a couple of steps, and shouted: "Hey, who are you?" vaguely remembering that if it were a ghost it would run away on hearing such a challenge. But the answer came back. "I'm Dr. Pal, journalist, correspondent and author." Margayya espied a row of white teeth bared in a grin.

"And what are you doing in this lonely place?"

"Why not?" came back the voice. It was a hard resonant voice, and there was no doubt that it was of this earth.

"Why not what?" asked Margayya.

"Why not here as well as anywhere else?" asked the man, rising and coming out. He was a man of thirty or thereabouts, his face still youthful, with a three-day stubble on his chin; a lank, tall man, with sunken cheeks, and a crop of hair falling on his forehead and nape. He wore a pair of blue shorts and a banian. As he came down the steps Margayya pointed at the lotus and said: "Get it for me. You are wearing only shorts." The other nodded, waded through the water and came back with a lotus flower. He gave it to Margayya. Margayya felt over-whelmed with gratitude. "You are a very good fellow," he said patronizingly. "What are you doing here, all alone in this place?"

"Working of course," the other said.

"Single-handed?"

"Yes, it has to be a single-handed job." Margayya looked at the wilderness round them and said: "No

63

wonder the place is as it is—too much for one man." The
other laughed and said: "I have nothing to do with the
garden. I'm here because I find it a very quiet place, and
there seems to be no one to ask me to get out. Sit down;
you will find it a really nice place—though it looks such a
forest."

Margayya feebly protested: "I've to go before it gets
dark."

" Why? "

" I have a long way to go . . . there may be cobras——"

" Not one here. Sit down, sit down——" Margayya sat
down on the steps. The other sat beside him. A breeze
stirred the leaves and sent a few ripplets rolling and striking against the stone steps. Casuarina trees which loomed
over the little *mantap* murmured. Brilliant sun from the
west made the entire garden glitter.

Margayya held the lotus delicately by the stalk and
looked at it. "Now and then people come here for lotus,"
said the other. Margayya wondered if he was going to ask
him to pay for it. He didn't like the idea. Before he should
entertain any such notion, just to divert his mind,
Margayya asked: "What is your connection with this
place? "

"The same as yours," he replied promptly. "As I said,
I am here because it doesn't seem to bother anyone. I
discovered this by a pure fluke. I'm given to cross-country
hikes . . . I have to in my profession——"

"What is your profession? "

"I'm a journalist. I'm a correspondent for all these
districts of a paper called *Silver Way* published in
Madras."

" A Tamil paper? "

"Yes, of course. It is the most widely circulated paper
in Tamil, with an enormous circulation in F.M.S., Ceylon,
and South Africa. I cover these districts for them, and in
my spare time write my own books."

"Oh, you write books? " Margayya asked, full of
wonder.

"Yes, yes, during my spare time—so difficult to find the leisure for it as a correspondent. All day I must knock about courts and offices and meetings on my cycle in search of news. I don't get much time. That's why I stay here, where I can work without disturbance." Margayya was greatly impressed. He had always thought very highly of newspaper people. "How many books have you written?"

"Four," came the reply; and he added: "Three are here," tapping his forehead. "Only one has been got down on paper——"

"What is it? A story?"

"A story! Oh, no, something more serious than that."

"Oh!" said Margayya, feeling that he had better not make inquiries in a region where he was a stranger. Books and writing were not for him: he was only a business man. Margayya rose to go.

"It's getting late," he murmured.

"I will go with you up to the road," said the other and followed him down to the edge of the pond. Margayya was fascinated by the sight of some more red lotus floating on the water, with their petals already closing. He reflected: "Even if there is a pound of paste to be made, we have enough lotus here—provided I can find the grey cow." His mind started worrying about the next stage of the search. "Where are grey cows to be seen?" Perhaps this author and journalist by his side might be able to help. They walked down the grassy path in silence for a while. Margayya surprised the other with the sudden inquiry: "Have you seen a smoke-coloured cow?"

"Where?" the other asked, stopping suddenly.

"Anywhere . . . I mean . . . do you know where a smoke-coloured cow can be seen?"

"Why?"

Margayya felt embarrassed. He blinked again. "I want its milk—for some special, medicinal purpose."

"Are you an *Ayurvedic* doctor or an aphrodisiac-maker?" the other asked, looking at him. "Trying to make some potent drugs with red lotus and so on. I have seen only *Ayurvedic* doctors coming here in a search of some herb or leaf or lotus and things like that." Margayya felt that because he had no ready answer, and no name to give for his avocation in life, the other would give him no useful tip. He covered the entire topic with a loud, prolonged laugh, at the end of which he found the other completing his remark: " I suppose the milk must always be white, whatever the colour of the cow."

Margayya agreed with this remark, laughed afresh, and changed the subject immediately. " What did you say your books were about? "

" Sociology," said the other.

"Oh! I see," said Margayya, trying to look clever, though completely bewildered by the term. He felt like asking: " What is it? " but felt it might be an undignified inquiry. He just nodded his head and remained silent. The other asked: " You know what sociology is, I suppose? " He was trapping him unnecessarily.

" Of course, in a manner, but you know I'm a businessman; we businessmen have not much time for scholarly activities."

Dr. Pal understood the position and said: " It's a subject that has been much neglected in our country—particularly in our own vernaculars, in our mother-tongue. They've everything in English, but in our mother-tongue —no. What should the thousands of people who know only our language do to learn the subject? "

" Yes, yes, it is very difficult," Margayya agreed. They had now reached a thatched hut. " Come in for a moment and see my home and study," said Dr. Pal.

Margayya protested and said something about its being dark.

" I will escort you back safely," said the other. " Don't worry . . . there are no cobras here." He pushed the door open. A mat was spread on the ground with a greasy pillow on it, and away from it stood a small tin trunk with a bottle of ink and a stack of paper on it. A very small bed-room lamp was kept on the trunk. Dr. Pal pushed away the pillow and said: "Pray sit down, I have not much furniture to offer—this is all. But this is a nice place."

Margayya sat down carefully, holding the lotus so as to protect it from being crushed. The place smelt of straw, which was spread on the floor.

"I do all my writing here. I return here at the end of my day's roving in the town. I sit on this mat all night and write; at dusk I go out to that pond and sit contemplating in the *mantap*—it's a very inspiring place." Margayya felt impressed and overawed, so he asked, as a piece of courtesy, "I suppose that is your book. You send it afterwards for printing?"

"Yes, I hope to," said the other. He picked up the manuscript and handed it to Margayya. Margayya received it with the utmost courtesy. The cover was of brown paper. He turned the last page and saw the number: "Oh, a hundred and fifty pages?" he asked admiringly.

"Yes, I want it to be a short book, so that any person may buy and read it." Margayya turned the pages and a chapter-heading caught his eye: "Philosophy and the Practice of Kissing."

"Oh! Kissing! You have written about kissing too! "

"Yes, of course, it is an important subject."

"Whose kisses?—children or——"

"Oh! Children's kisses are of no account here——" Margayya felt interested, and turned to the title of another chapter: "Basic Principles of Embracing." He turned over the pages and started reading the first sentence of the opening chapter: "Man embraces woman, and woman embraces man——" He felt interested. Briskly turning over the leaves, he came upon the title sheet and read out aloud: "Bed-Life or the Science of Marital Happiness."

"What is this?" Margayya exclaimed. "You said it was——"

"Sociology. Yes, this is a branch of sociology. I have spent many years studying this subject. A thousand years

67

ago Vatsyayana wrote his Kama-Sutra or 'Science of Love'. I have based this whole work on it, plus research done by modern scientists like Havelock Ellis and so on. This subject must be understood by every man and woman. If people understood and practised this science there would be more happiness in the world."

"But it seems to be all about . . . about——" Margayya could not find the right word. He felt too shy. He felt eager to read on, but put it away feeling that further inspection would seem indecorous.

"You can read it if you like," said the other.

Margayya put it away as if avoiding a temptation.

"You will have everything you want in a nutshell there." It seemed as if the other would not let him go. The author added: "I want to have a few illustrations if I can find an artist."

"What, those . . . illustrating those?" gasped Margayya.

"Yes, why not? I want to illustrate some of the parts. I want it to be of practical benefit . . . I want it to serve as a guide book to married couples. My aim is to create happiness in the world."

"Are you married?" Margayya asked, coming to the point.

"Yes . . . otherwise how could I write all that."

"But . . . but . . . you are alone——" Margayya said, looking round.

"Yes . . . I have to be——" He seemed saddened by some domestic memory. Margayya's curiosity could no longer be kept in check: "Where is she?" he asked bluntly.

"God knows," said the other. "I have had to leave her——"

"Why? Why?" Margayya said. "How sad!" He sat brooding.

The other said: "She was an impossible woman . . . a terrible woman who was unfaithful, and tried to ogle every man who appeared before her. A woman with a polyandrous tendency." Margayya was somewhat shocked at the

68

free manner in which he spoke. The other laughed and said: "How scared you look at my talk! Don't fear; I am not yet married. Probably you are already thinking how can this fellow write about the happiness of married life when he himself has been such a failure! Was it not the line of your thought?"

"How did you guess?" Margayya asked. Everyone seemed to guess correctly what went on in his mind—a most dangerous state of affairs it seemed to him. "I never married," the other assured him again. "But I only gave you a sample of what is likely to happen when people are ill-matched."

"True, true," said Margayya.

"Reading this book will be a way of preventing such tragedies," said Dr. Pal.

§

The next few days Margayya was lost to the outside world. He sat in the small room repeating:

> Oh Goddess, who affordest shelter to all
> the fugitive worlds! . . .
> Thy feet, by themselves, are proficient in affording
> immunity from fear and bestowing boons.

He had to repeat it a thousand times each day, sitting before the image of the Goddess. He wore a red-silk *dhoti* and smeared his forehead and body with sacred ash. The cries of the pedlars in the street were submerged in the continuous hum that proceeded from his own throat: his son's continued shout of "*Appa! Appa!*" was heard by him as a distant muffled sound. A little light came through the small opening of the shutter. The room was filled with the scent of incense, camphor, sandal dust, and jasmine. All this mingled perfume uplifted the heart and thoughts of Margayya. He was filled with a feeling of holiness—

engendered by the feel of the red silk at his waist. He was gratified at the thought of his wife's obedience. "She is quite accommodating," he reflected. She got up at five and prepared the jaggery-sweetened rice which had to be offered to the Goddess. As he sat down with his eyes shut, he said to himself : "I have achieved difficult things, grey cow's milk butter, red lotus made into black paste. . . . This time last week I could not believe that I should be able to get together grey cow's milk and red lotus. When the Goddess wants to help a man she sends him where all things are available; and who would have thought that there was a deserted garden——— "

This brought to his mind Dr. Pal and his works . . . He felt an unholy thrill at the memory of Pal's book. It seemed as though his mind would not move from the subject. This man wanted to put in pictures—what a wicked fellow. It'd be most awkward . . . Why was Dr. Pal interested in the subject? Must be an awful rake . . . if he could write all that and was unmarried. . . . Some of the chapter headings came to his mind. He realized with a shock what line his thoughts were pursuing, and he pulled them back to the *verse*; the priest had told him to let his mind rest fully on its meaning while repeating it. He kept saying: "Oh Goddess, who affordest . . ." etc., and un-known to him his thoughts slipped out and romped about —chiefly about the fruits of the penance, he was under-taking: forty days of this—afterwards? He visualized his future. How was wealth going to flow in? When he became rich, suppose he bought from his brother the next house too, tempting him with a handsome cash offer. . . . He realized that this was his major concern in life. He would be a victorious man if he could bring his brother to his knees and make him part with his portion of the house; and then he would knock down the partition wall. . . . Each day it took him eight hours of repetition to com-plete the thousand, and then he reverently put the black paste on his forehead, lit the camphor, called in his wife and child and sprinkled the holy water on them. His jaws ached, his tongue had become dry . . . he felt faint with hunger, since he had to fast completely while praying.

He followed this course for forty days. When he emerged from the little room, he had a beard and moustache and hair on his nape. He had been told not to shave in the course of this penance. He looked venerable. His voice became weak; he could not utter any speech without automatically mixing it up with " Oh, Goddess, who affordest shelter . . .". He looked like an examination student who has emerged from the ordeal, sapped in every way but with his face glowing with triumph. Margayya had lost ten pounds in weight: much of the padding on his waist and jowl had gone.

PART TWO

WHEN he was again seen in the streets, shaven and clean, he looked like a young man. His chin sparkled with the long-delayed shave, and his moustache was trimmed to perfection. He looked so tidy when he went along the street again with his shirt and upper cloth that people stopped and asked: " Where have you been all this time, Margayya? " He had no answer. So he said: " Here. All along. Where should I go? "

" I haven't seen you in your usual place or anywhere."

" Usual place! Oh, there, you mean! That was only a side business for me, more for my own diversion. I'm busy with other plans," he said grandly.

About the time he closed his business he had two hundred rupees in hand, out of which the previous month's household expenses took sixty rupees; the forty-day ritual cost him at least two rupees a day for fruit and flowers and special offerings; then he had to have a feast on the last day and feed four brahmins, and give them each a silver rupee on betel leaves after the meal. About a hundred rupees in all were gone. He found himself grudging this expense and explained to himself : " How can I grudge it! Can't a man spend at least so much for earning the benevolence of a Goddess? " He had a magic syllable carved on leather and tied to his sacred thread. He wished he could know when the beneficial effect would start, when the skies would open and start raining down wealth. He wished he could get an answer to his question.

In his despair he tried to meet the priest. But somehow the priest had not encouraged him to call again. For a day Margayya was seized with the horrible thought that the man had played a practical joke on him. What if he had merely fooled him! Priests were capable of anything. Every word that the priest had uttered seemed to lend support to this suspicion. He had even taken the trouble to avoid him.

Days passed, and his misgivings increased. He seemed to have suddenly lost all plans in life. His purse was getting lighter each day. It was difficult to while away the time. From morning to night he had to think what he should do next. If he stayed at home, it invariably resulted in some clash with his wife, for his son misbehaved so much in his presence that either he or his wife felt impelled to chastize him, and each vehemently protested when the other did it. And then all kinds of controversies started between him and his wife. It was such a strain having always to talk in whispers—lest the people next door should overhear. He sat dejectedly facing Goddess Lakshmi and mentally saying to her: "You have taken my last coin. What have you given me in return? Has the priest been fooling me?" He felt indignant at this thought. "If he has fooled me! God help him, I'll have my fingers round his throat!"

As he lay across the hall on a towel spread on the floor, his mind was busy with these thoughts. In that small house, it was a bother to have the head of the house all the time lying across the floor. Margayya's wife had quite a number of visitors coming in each day. A brinjal-seller who brought in her basket walked across the hall and sat in the back-yard verandah to transact her business; the servant-woman who came in to wash the vessels and scrub the back-yard an hour a day; a fat lady, wife of a lawyer, who dropped in for a chat in the afternoons; and some school children who came running in during the afternoon recess for a drink of water. When Margayya lay across the hall of his house he obstructed their passage to the rear verandah and kitchen where the lady of the house received them. Every time a visitor arrived Margayya had to scramble to his feet and stand aside to let the visitor pass. They went on and asked Margayya's wife privately: "Why is your husband not going out?" The lady felt confused and awkward and gave out some reply, but later questioned him: "What has come over you that you don't go out at all——?"

"Where should I go?"

"Like all the other men, why don't you try to do some work and earn some money?"

"Money is not a pebble in the street to be picked up by just going out."

"Oh, is that so? I didn't know. I thought it was something to be had in the street."

Thus their talk went on, entirely lacking in point. She had no clear idea of what she expected him to do and he had no clear idea of what he should do outside the house. He tried it for a few days. His steps naturally led him to the Co-operative Bank. But it was clear that he had lost his place. His previous clients only tried to avoid him, fearing that he might accost them for their old dues. He had no one to talk to. He went through the town like a lost soul, but although to begin with some people spoke to him, now nobody took any notice of him. He could not go down the Market Road for fear of being stopped by the optician. . . . So after a few days of aimless wandering, he took to staying at home. It delighted only his little son and no one else. Next door they remarked: "What has come over that man? He is hardly to be seen outside. Is he hiding from creditors?" They had also wondered previously why so much scent of incense emanated from the next house. "They must be up to some mischief; perhaps trying black magic on someone they don't like. We must be careful with such people."

As the month came to an end and Margayya had to buy rice and salt for the pantry, he found himself short by ten rupees, and they had to manage without ghee. His wife declared: "I have never been in this plight before." Balu made matters worse by asking: "Mother, I want ghee."

"There is no ghee, my boy. You must eat your food as it is," Margayya replied.

"I won't," said Balu, throwing away the rice and getting up.

"You'll learn to be contented with what you get," Margayya moralized foolishly.

"No. I won't. I want ghee," said the boy rebelliously, kicking away his rice plate.

"If you kick away your rice, I will kick you," Margayya said; at which the boy burst into tears and appealed to his mother. She burst into tears too because it reminded her of the story of Gora Kumbar, a potter, who was devoted to the God Vishnu and took no care of his family. At meal times his little son demanded ghee, without which, just like Balu, he would not eat. The lady went out to borrow ghee from the next house, leaving the child in the care of the father, who was stamping on wet clay all the time. When she was gone, he got into a mystic ecstasy and started dancing, and did not notice the child crawling under his feet . . . and when the mother returned with ghee the child had been stamped into the wet mud. Margayya's wife burst into tears, remembering this story, which she had seen as a drama in her young days. Margayya, bewildered and pained by all the scene, ate his food in silence, but, without ghee and with all this misery, it tasted bitter.

He decided to search out the priest. "I can't keep quiet any more. He will have to tell me what is what—otherwise, I will not let him off lightly."

Margayya sought him out late that night. He pretended to go to the temple very late in the evening for worship, and hung about till the crowd cleared. He heard the priest's voice inside the sanctum. When the crowd dispersed he moved up to the threshold of the sanctum and peered in. There was a new man there.

Margayya asked: "Where is he?"

"Who?"

76

" The other priest——"

" Why? "

Margayya felt annoyed. Why were these priests assuming such impudent and presumptuous manners? But the priest was in the proximity of God, and Margayya was afraid to speak sharply. He controlled his voice and temper and answered: " I have some business with him."

" What business? " asked the priest, tossing flowers on the image without turning in his direction. " Does this man think he is God? " wondered Margayya. " He is so indifferent! "

Probably, he thought, the other priest had told him: " Margayya may be dropping in often, asking for me. If he comes, show him the utmost rudeness and keep him out." It seemed quite possible to his sickly imagination. Margayya opened his lips to say something, but in came some devotees with coconut and camphor, and the priest became busy attending to them. Margayya noted with pain the differential treatment that was being meted out. " It's quite clear that he has been told to snub me . . . see how warm and effusive he is to those people! It is because he hopes to get money out of them. Money is everything, dignity, self-respect. . . . This fellow is behaving towards me like the Co-operative Bank Secretary." In his mind he saw arrayed against him the Secretary, Arul Doss, this man, and the washer-woman who abused him on the day his son destroyed the account book. It seemed such a formidable and horrible world that he wondered how he had managed to exist at all.

The priest now came out bearing a plate with a camphor flame on it, which lit up his face. Margayya noted that he was a very young man. The others put money into the plate after touching the flame. The priest paused near Margayya, who just looked away. " I have paid enough for these godly affairs," thought Margayya. The priest threw a sour look at him and went in. The devotees left. The priest sat down before the image and started reciting some holy verse. Margayya stood on the threshold. The

77

other paused during his recitation and asked: "What are you waiting for?"

"I'm only waiting for your honour to come out and answer my question."

"Am I an astrologer? What's your question?"

"This man is practising studied rudeness on me. He has been taught to . . . this young fellow!" thought Margayya. His anger rose. He became reckless. "Hey, young man, who taught you to speak so rudely?"

The young man looked surprised for a moment, and then raised his voice and resumed his recitation.

Margayya cried: "Stop it and answer me! A very devout man, indeed!"

"You want to stop God's work. Who are you?"

"A youngster like you need not ask unnecessary questions. Learn to give correct answers before you think of putting questions. . . . At your age!"

The youth asked: "What do you want?"

"What I want to know is, where is the old priest. And, if you can, answer without asking why."

"He has gone on a pilgrimage."

"When did he go?"

"About a month ago."

"When will he come back?"

"I don't know."

"Where has he gone?"

"To Benares—from there he is going on foot all along the course of the Ganges, to its very source in the Himalayas."

"Why is he doing all this?"

"I don't know. How can I say?"

Margayya felt indignant. He walked out of the temple without another word He felt he had been cheated. That old priest had played a trick on him, making him waste all his money in performing fantastic things. "Benares! Ganges! Himalayas! How am I to get at him!" He wished he could go to the Himalayas and search him out. For a moment he speculated pleasantly on what might happen to the old man there. He might get drowned in the Ganges, or die of sunstroke on the way, or get frozen in the ice of the Himalayas.

§

Next day he wandered up and down, through the east and the west districts of the town, in search of an idea. He got up in the morning, hoping that some miracle would happen, some chance or fortune be picked up on the door-step. He got up early and opened the door. There were the usual goings on of Vinayak Mudali Street, and nothing more—a curd-seller passing with the pot on her head, a couple of cyclists going to a mill, some children running out to play an early game, and so on. But he saw nothing that was likely to bring him the fruits of his penance. He felt acutely unhappy.

He wandered all over the town in search of an idea. He went up to the northern section and sat on the hot sands of the Sarayu thinking. He sat in the shade of a tree and watched the sky and river. His mind had become blank. He went down the Market Road, looking at every shop. He was searching for an idea. He watched every trade critically. Tailoring? Hair-cutting Saloon? Why not? Any labour had dignity. . . . But all of them would be more troublesome than anything he had known. " Nobody will give me money for nothing. I must give them something in exchange——" He sat on the parapet of the Market Fountain and thought. What was it that people most needed? It must be something that every person could afford. The best business under the sun was either snuff or tooth-powder or both. It had to be something for which every citizen would be compelled to pay a certain small sum each day. He was engrossed in profound economic theories. Snuff . . . his mind gloated over the visions of snuff. . . . The initial outlay would be small, just enough to buy a bundle of tobacco. . . . He knew all about it, for there used to be a snuff maker in front of his house. All his equipment was a few cinders of charcoal, a small iron grate, and a mud pot for frying the tobacco in. Fry and pound the tobacco, add a little lime, and leave the rest to the snuffers themselves. " Margayya's snuff for flavour ". This was worth trying. It was an investment of ten rupees. He must fry the leaves in a place far away from human habitation. Tobacco, while being fried, sent up a choking smoke which kept the neighbourhood coughing and complaining. He wondered how long it would take to realize the profits. A year or less or not at all. Suppose people never touched his snuff and it accumulated in tins up to the ceiling? What could he do with them? He might probably use the stock himself. But he himself had been addicted to the Golden Monkey Brand for years, and he dared not try any other. Or he might manufacture tooth powder. His mother used to make a sort of tooth powder with burnt almond shell and cinnamon bark and alum, and it was said to convert teeth into granite.

Margayya now thought of his mother with gratitude. There was always a big crowd of sufferers waiting for her at the hall of their old house. She was of a charitable disposition. She took the stock out of a large earthen jar, and distributed it liberally. His father used to declare: "You will be reborn in a Heaven of Golden Teeth for this." She did it as a form of charity, and their house was known as the Tooth Powder House. It seemed an ideal business to start now. The world was going to be transformed into one of shining teeth. . . . But a misgiving assailed him. How could he make people buy it rather than the dozen other tooth powders? He didn't know the art of selling tooth powder. He couldn't go about hawking it in the streets. . . . It would be a fine look out if the Secretary of the Co-operative Society caught him at it. Arul Doss would call out " Hey, tooth-powder, come here, give me a packet. Here are three pies." And he would have to gather the coppers like a beggar, with peals of laughter ringing out from the whole world. And the old priest might chuckle from the Himalayas at having reduced him to a picker of copper coins! "No," he told himself, "I'm a businessman. I can only do something on the lines of banking. It's no good thinking of all this." He watched the fountain hissing and squirting, while the traffic flowed past, and sighed, as he had sighed so often before, at the thought of his banyan tree business. He sighed, reflecting: "Here is an adult, sitting on the fountain like a vagrant when he ought to be earning." He feared that if this state of affairs continued he might find himself looking for an orphan's corpse and dashing about with a mud tray in his hand.

"Hallo, friend," cried Dr. Pal from the other side of the fountain. He was coming down the road on his cycle. "I thought I should never see you again—you went away without telling me where you lived. You didn't come again for lotus!" It took time for Margayya to be shaken from his business reverie. "Oh, you!" he cried, not exactly liking being disturbed by this man now. He felt shy of meeting him, associating him with smut. Dr. Pal leaned his cycle on the parapet and came over and sat beside him.

"You didn't come again for lotus," he said.

"Oh, lotus—one was enough for me," said Margayya, putting into his tone all the despair he felt at the whole wasted activity.

"People always go for lotus in a series, never in singles——" said the other obscurely. Margayya laughed, pretending that he read some inner meaning. "Well, what makes you spend your time sitting here?" Pal asked.

Margayya thought: "Why can't people leave me alone?" He didn't like to give the correct explanation. He said: "Someone has promised to come up and meet me here."

"Oh, a business meeting, I suppose."

"Of course," said Margayya. "I have no time for just casual meetings. The time is——" He looked around him.

"Four," said the other, looking at his wrist watch. "You won't mind if I keep you company?"

"Oh, not at all," replied Margayya mortified, but he overcame his mortification enough to add, "I only fear it may hold you up unnecessarily. You may have other business."

"I'm on duty even when I'm sitting here and talking to you. I'll make a story of it for my paper—that's all they want. They won't mind as long as I fulfil my duty."

"Surely, you won't write about me!" Margayya said.

"Why not? I might say Mr. ——. Oh, what's your name please? I've not enquired, although I've been around with you so much."

"Why do you want my name?" Margayya asked defensively.

"Don't worry, I won't publish it. I just want to know as a friend, that's all. Suppose somebody asks me who is that friend with whom I have been talking and I say I don't know, it'd look grotesque. Isn't that so? What is your name?"

"People call me Margayya——"

"Excellent name; initials?"

"No initials——"

"Oh, no initials, that's excellent. Initials indicate town and parentage. . . . But that's for lesser folk who have to announce their antecedents."

"It's not necessary for me. If you say Margayya, every one will know. However, that's not my name."

"Oh, I thought it was."

"How?"

"How? How? The 'how' of things is my trade secret. Otherwise I wouldn't be a writer. My business is to know things—not tell anyone how, you understand."

"Extraordinary fellow," Margayya said.

"Yes, I am," said the other. "I know it. Come along, let us go somewhere and gossip."

"We are doing it here quite well," said Margayya.

"Oh, no. . . . This place is too noisy. I want to talk to you privately. Come on, come on; don't say 'no'!" He was irresistible. Margayya remembered in time to protest: "But I have told you I am waiting here for someone."

"Oh, he will follow us there, don't worry."

82

" Where? "

" Come along to my office. I must show you my office."

They walked along, through the crowd. It seemed to be all the same for Margayya, what he did or where he went. He followed the other blindly. He took him through the eastern end of Market Road, turned into a lane, stopped before a house and knocked on the door. A little boy opened it. " Who is inside? " Pal asked.

" No one," the boy said.

" That's fine! " said Pal. " As I expected. Open my office then, young fellow! "

The young man disappeared and opened a side door and put his head out. " Hold the cycle," commanded Pal. The young man came out with alacrity and took hold of the bicycle. Pal marched in, asking Margayya to follow. He followed him into a very small room stuffed with empty packing cases, piled up to the ceiling. There was a stool in the middle of it with a higher stool before it. On the wall hung a printed sheet: " Silver Way—Chief Representative's Office." There were a few stacks of paper in a corner. " Don't look shocked by the state of my office," said Pal. " This is only a temporary place. I'm moving into a big office and showroom as soon as it is ready."

" Where? " Margayya asked.

" Wherever it may be available. That's all I can say. You know how it is with the present housing conditions! " Margayya did not feel disposed to agree with him. He said: " You can get houses if you honestly try. After all, you want only a room——"

" But nobody will give it to me free, don't you see, and that is the only condition on which our chief office is prepared to accept any accommodation! You see my problem. They want a place in the town to be called their office, but they won't pay any rent for it. I got this because I also write accounts for these businessmen and they have allowed me to hang up my board."

" What do they deal in? Tooth-powder or something like that? " Margayya asked.

"They make cheap soap and export it to Malaya—make a lot of money," he said.

"Must be an easy job," Margayya reflected aloud.

"Most messy, and a terrible gamble."

"But I think there is a lot of money in it," said Margayya. His mind at once went off. He had no clear idea how soap was made. He only remembered some piece of odd knowledge about coconut oil and caustic. Perhaps a hundred rupees invested might soon multiply, provided the soap became popular. Give it a lot of attractive colouring and sell it cheap and people would flock to buy it—Margayya's soap, Margayya's tooth-powder, Margayya's snuff. The choice of his business now seemed to be between these three. He would have to make up his mind about it and start somewhere instead of idling away the day on the fountain parapet. . . . There was silence during these reflections. The other watched him, and then asked: "Have you done with your deep reflections!"

"Some ideas connected with my business came to my mind suddenly."

"Sit down there; it's not nice to remain standing," said Pal.

Margayya sat down. Pal sat down on the higher stool.

"Margayya, listen to me very attentively," he began. "I am speaking to you on a very important matter now."

"Go ahead, I am not deaf. . . . You can speak in whispers if you like, if it is such a great secret," Margayya said.

"If you are thinking of making money or more money or just money, speak out," said Pal almost in a whisper, coming close to his face. His eyes were so serious that Margayya said: "How did you guess?"

"There are only two things that occupy men's minds. I'm a psychologist and I know."

"What are they?" Margayya said.

"Money . . . and Sex. . . . You need not look so shocked. It is the truth. Down with your sham and hypocritical self-deception. Tell me truthfully, is there any moment of the

84

day when you don't think of one or the other? " **Margayya**
did not know how to answer. It seemed a very embarrassing
situation. Pal said: "I'm an academician and I'm only
interested in Truth and how human beings face it."

"I think of plenty of other things too," Margayya said
defensively.

"What are they? "

"About my son and what he is doing."

"What is it but sex? " asked the dialectician. "You
cannot think of your son without thinking of your wife."

"Oh, that will do," said Margayya indignantly. "I don't
like anyone to talk of my wife."

"Why not? " persisted Pal. "Have you considered why
people make such a fuss about their wives? It is all based
on primitive sexual jealousy."

"No—you should not speak lightly about wives. You
know nothing about them. If you are a bachelor, then I
don't know what you are."

"I am a sociologist, and I cannot sugarcoat my words.
I have to speak scientifically."

Margayya was overawed by the man's speech. He did
not quite grasp what he was saying. All the same, he said:
"It is generally understood that you may talk of any subject freely—but you must not make free reference to
another man's wife."

"Nor to one's own wife," added Pal. "I don't think anyone can speak openly about his wife. If he could speak out
openly what she means to him and what she thinks of him
or he of her behind the screen of their house or behind the
screen of their bed chamber, you will know."

"Oh, stop, stop," cried Margayya. "I won't hear any
more of it." He felt ashamed. This "sociologist" or whatever he called himself seemed to be preoccupied with only
one set of ideas. Margayya said: "I wish you would marry
some strong girl and settle down. It will give you other
things to think of."

"I don't want to think of anything else. I feel I am made
by God in order that I may enlighten people in these

85

matters and guide their steps to happiness," asserted Pal. "And do you know it is the most paying, most profitable occupation in the present-day world?"

At this Margayya sat up. This was a sentiment which appealed to him. He said: "What do you mean by that?"

"I'm going to start a sociology clinic, a sort of harmony home, a sort of hospital for creating domestic happiness, a sort of psychological clinic, where people's troubles are set right. . . . I can charge a small fee. Do you know how many people will come in and go out of it each day? I am certain to earn five hundred rupees a day easily. My book 'Bed Life'—you remember you saw it?——"

"Yes."

"That's only a first step in the scheme. . . . When that book is published, I expect to have at least a lakh of copies sold."

"At what price?" asked Margayya.

"Say at about a rupee per copy. You must not price it higher than that. After all, our purpose is to reach the common man."

"You mean to say that you are going to make a lakh of rupees out of it?"

"Yes, what is strange about that? That's only for a start."

One Lakh of Rupees! One Lakh of Rupees! In Margayya's eyes this man began to assume grandeur. This lank fellow, cycling about and gathering news, held within his palm the value of a lakh of rupees. Margayya was filled with admiration. Tooth-powder and snuff and all the rest seemed silly stuff beside this. . . . You could never see a lakh of rupees with these commodities; it would probably go back into the oven again and again, perhaps. But here was a man who spoke of a lakh of rupees as if it were a five rupee note!

"That's only a starting point," Pal added. "There is no reason why it should not go on earning a similar sum year after year. It's a property which ought to bring in a regular rent. There is no limit to your sales. The book will simply

86

be—there will be such a clamour from humanity for this stuff that ultimately every human being will own a copy. The Tamil-speaking area in India gives us a good start; add to it the tens and thousands of people in Siam, Burma, South Africa and so on, and you get the number of copies you should print. And then if it is translated into Hindi, it should reach the whole of India—and the population of India is three hundred and sixty millions according to the last census. If every man parts with a rupee, see where you are."

"Yes," replied Margayya greatly impressed. "I never thought there was such a wide scope for selling books."

"Not for all books. For instance, if I wrote a book of, say, poems or philosophy, nobody would touch it—but a book like 'Bed Life' is a thing that everyone would like to read. Do you know, people like to be told facts, people like to be guided in such matters. Ultimately, as I told you, I shall open a clinic. I want to serve mankind with my knowledge. I don't want to keep it within my closed fists. We must all be helpful to each other. I have worked for years and years studying and writing, just in order that mankind may be helped." He spoke without stopping for breath, and concluded: "Do you know, if I just throw down a hint anywhere that there is such a book as this people will fall over each other to publish it."

"Indeed! "

"Yes, there are offers of ten thousand rupees or more for it. But I won't part with it for ten times that amount."

"Why not? " asked Margayya.

"Because I can do better than that if I keep it. If people come to make a business offer, they will find me very hard, let me assure you, because I know my mind."

"So it will be impossible to get it out of you? " asked Margayya.

"Yes, generally, if anyone comes to me as a businessman."

"Oh! " Margayya said, remembering with despair that he came under that category.

87

The other added: "But let a man come to me as a friend and hold out his hand, the book is his."

"But you will lose you lakh——"

"I wouldn't care. Don't imagine I am so fond of money. I treat money as dirt."

This was a shocking statement to Margayya. He cried: "Oh, don't say such things. You must not." He recollected how the Goddess Lakshmi was such a sensitive creature that if a man removed a tumbler of milk she fled from the spot and withdrew her grace.

"I'm a man who cares for work, human relationships, and service to mankind," said Dr. Pal. "Money comes last in my list."

Margayya felt a desperate idea welling up in him. He could hold it back no longer. It almost burst through his lips, and he asked: "Suppose I say 'give me that for printing and selling,' what would you do?"

In answer, the other went out and came back carrying the bag which had been hanging from his cycle handle. He thrust his hand into the bag, and brought out the manuscript. Without another look at it he dropped it on Margayya's lap as he sat on the stool.

"Are you playing?" asked Margayya, hardly able to believe his eyes. It was bound in a blue wrapper. He vaguely turned its leaves to assure himself that it was the right book. "Principles of Embracing."

"You take it. It's yours. Do whatever you like with it," said Pal magnificently.

"No, no, no," said Margayya. "How can I?"

"It's no longer mine," said the other. "It is a bargain which is closed." He looked resolute. He then held out his hand and said: "Give me what you have in your pocket. I will take it in exchange. It's a bargain. You cannot back out of it."

Margayya said: "I haven't brought any money——"

"Then why have you brought that purse? I see its outline."

Margayya looked down with a sigh. Yes, the damned

stuff was showing. "It's not a purse," he tried to say. But the other said: "Take it out, let me see what it is that looks like a purse, but isn't. Stick to your bargain." Margayya put his hand in and brought out the little purse, which had a silver George V embossed on it. He opened it. Twenty-five rupees were all its contents. He took out a five rupee note and placed it on the outstretched palm of Dr. Pal. The other didn't close his fingers or withdraw his arm. He sternly said: "Stick to your bargain. Empty it."

"This is all I have," pleaded Margayya.

"I'm giving you all that I have for my part."

Margayya said: "I have to buy rice. I have a wife and child."

"Don't be theatrical. Stick to your bargain. Here is something I'm giving you worth at least a lakh of rupees. In return for it, give me your purse. I will take it whether it contains one rupee or one thousand or none. Isn't it a fair bargain?"

"I can't give you my purse. It's a lucky purse. I've had it for countless years now."

"I don't want your purse. Give me only its contents."

"I don't want your book. I don't know how to print or sell a book."

"Go to a printer and he will print it. You tell the public the book is ready and they will come and buy it. There are no further complications. It's the easiest business under the sun. In fact you will hardly be able to meet the demand."

"Then why have you not done it yourself?" asked Margayya.

"Well, I was about to. But just to show you what is a bargain, I've made my offer," he drawled. "If you are really keen on cancelling this bargain, I am ready for it. On second thoughts, I don't see why I should waste my breath on you." He reached for the manuscript on Margayya's lap, saying: "Every man must make his choice in life. This is a cross-roads at which you are standing. Some day you will see another man going away in his Rolls, while you sit on the Market Fountain and brood over my words of this evening. 1 will give you five minutes to think it over. I'll have the entire contents of your purse or none at all." He kept his arm outstretched to receive the manuscript back and fixedly gazed at his wrist watch. His face was grim.

Margayya's face perspired with intense excitement. " I'm losing twenty thousand each minute," he told himself. " Twenty, forty, sixty." He wanted to say: " Give me five minutes more," but his throat had gone dry. No words came. By the time he could get his voice to produce a sound again another ten seconds were gone. Looking at this man, he prayed, " God, why have you put me in the company of this terrible man amidst these wooden boxes! " A yellowish sunlight came in through a top ventilator, and fell on the opposite wall. " He will probably choke me if I don't agree," he ruminated. He wondered if he should scream for help. Somewhere a cycle bell sounded. Wasn't it auspicious, the sounding of a bell? " Three seconds more," said the other. The sound of the bell was the voice of God. God spoke through his own signs. Margayya's decision was made. He suddenly felt lighter and said jocularly: " Three seconds! That's a great deal yet." He added grandly: " Tell me when there is still half a second to go," and pushed away the other's outstretched arm.

§

Margayya carried the manuscript home as if he was trying to secrete a small dead body. He was afraid lest somebody should stop him on the way and look at it. He had begged Pal at least to wrap it in paper. Pal snatched up an old issue of *Silver Way* and wrapped it up. Margayya told himself all along the road: " I must see that the young fellow doesn't get at it." His plan had been to tuck it within the folds of a stack of clothes in his box the moment he reached home. At the front door he saw his wife with his

son on her lap, inducing him to swallow his food by divert-
ing his attention to the stars in the sky and the street below.
" Father! " the little fellow cried joyfully, trying to jump
out of his mother's arms. " Wait, wait," Margayya said,
and passed in swiftly, trying to conceal the bundle under
his arm.

" What is it that you are carrying? " his wife asked as
he went by. " Bread? "

He made no reply but walked straight in, opened his
box and securely locked it up. He then went through his
routine of changing and washing. His wife brought in
the child and gave him into his care.

Balu said: " A monkey came to our house."

" That's very good," Margayya said. " What did it
do? "

" It ate coconut and will come again tomorrow. Father,
why don't you buy me a monkey? "

" Yes, when you are a good boy."

" Balu is a good boy," he replied, certifying to his own
conduct.

Margayya sat in the corridor with his son on his lap.
He felt light and buoyant, expansive, and full of hope that
the good things of life were now within his reach. He
hummed a tune to himself, and played with his son. All
the time his wife was very curious to know what he had
brought in the parcel. She knew by trying to look severe
she would never get the truth out of him. She said something agreeable about the boy: " Do you know what a
change is coming over the little fellow? He is so quiet and
obedient nowadays," she said, coming and standing beside
him.

Margayya replied: " He is the finest youngster except
when he is otherwise," and laughed. The boy looked at
him bewildered and said: " Why do you laugh? "

" I don't know," Margayya said, and all of them laughed
heartily.

The boy, having heard a good report about himself,
wanted to keep it up, and did nothing to exasperate his

91

father. He ate a quiet dinner, lay down on his mat and ordered his father to tell him a story. Margayya strained his memory and began the story of the fox, the crow and the lion, till the boy interrupted him with: "I don't like the fox story. Tell me a flower story."

"I don't know any flower story," Margayya pleaded. At this the boy threatened to kick his legs and cry. Margayya hastily began: "Once upon a time there was a good flower ——" and fumbled and hummed and hawed, wondering how people wrote hundreds of pages of stories; which brought to his mind Dr. Pal and his book—how those people ever could sit down and write so many pages. He admired for a moment their patience, and subsequently corrected himself. He didn't like to admire anyone and so said to himself: "These fellows have no better business; that's why they sit down and fill up sheets, whereas we businessmen have hardly any time left even to compose our letters."

The boy insisted on knowing at this stage: "What flower was it?"

"Lotus," he felt like saying, but checked himself and said: "Some flower—why do you want its name now?" and then blundered through a clumsy, impossible story, till the boy fell asleep out of sheer lack of interest.

After finishing all her work, his wife came up with an endearing smile and sat beside him on the mat. He put his arm round her and drew her nearer, recollecting the chapter on "Principles of Embracing". She nestled close to him. It was as if they had thrown off twenty years and were back in the bridal chamber. He said: "Why don't you buy flowers regularly? I see that you don't care for them nowadays."

"I am an old woman, flowers and such things——"

"But this old man likes to see some flowers in this old lady's hair," he said. They laughed and felt very happy. And then she asked at the correct moment: "What is that bundle you brought with you?"

"Oh, that! You wish to see it?"

"Yes, yes, of course," she said, quite thrilled at the prospect.

He got up, opened his trunk and brought out the packet wrapped in *Silver Way*. He slowly opened the wrapping and took out the manuscript. At the sight of it her face shadowed with disappointment.

"What's this?" she asked.

"It's a book."

"Oh! I thought you had brought me a *saree*; some surprise gift, I thought." There was a note of disappointment in her voice. "Book! Paper," she said contemptuously. "What book is this?"

"You see for yourself," he said, and gave her the packet.

She turned the leaves and was horrified. "What is it all about? It seems to be——" But she could not say anything more. "It seems to be so vulgar!"

"No, no, don't say such a thing," he said. He didn't like to hear any disparaging reference to the book. "It's a scientific book. It's going to bring in a lot of money."

She made a wry face and said: "How can anybody have written about all this? You men have no——"

"What's wrong with it? It's something going on all over the world every moment. It's very important. People should possess correct scientific knowledge, and then all marriages will be happy. I'm going to educate Balu in all these matters the moment he is interested."

"Oh, stop that," she cried, and flung away the book.

He picked it up, bent close to the lamp and started reading it aloud. It was probably too scientific for ordinary mortals. She listened both horrified and fascinated.

§

A few days later, Margayya walked into the Gordon Printery in Market Road. It was a fairly big establishment in Malgudi—every form, letter-head, and bill-book in Malgudi was printed at Gordon's. Its proprietor was a man from Bombay who came and settled down here years ago—a hefty, rose-cheeked man called Madan Lal. He sat at a table, right in the middle of a hall where a dozen people were creating the maximum amount of noise with various machines, which seemed to groan and hiss and splutter. In this general uproar he sat calmly poring over proofs, and opposite his table were ranged two iron chairs. Margayya stood at the entrance. He felt lonely and isolated and unhappy. They might sneer at him and tear up his manuscript. If the Secretary and Arul Doss came down at this moment to see some of their own printing. . . . He overcame this sinking feeling immediately. " 'Self-assurance' is the most important quality to cultivate," he realized. He sounded quite assertive when he asked some-one at the entrance: " Where is your proprietor? "

" Sitting there," the man replied.

" Oh, I didn't notice," Margayya said, and went to him. The man looked up from his papers and asked: " What can I do for you? " He pointed at an iron chair. Margayya sat down, placed his manuscript before him and said with a lot of self-assurance: " I wish to have this book printed. Can you take it on?"

" That I can say only after going through the manuscript."

" Go on, read it."

" I have no time now. You can leave it here."

" Impossible," said Margayya. " I am not prepared to leave it with anyone. You can go through it here while I wait."

" I've other business."

" I've also other business. I have come to you for printing, not for any other business. If you are not prepared to take it on, say so," and he put out his arms towards the manuscript.

" Oh, no, don't lose your patience," the other pleaded. " I was only——" He picked up the manuscript and glanced at the title page: " Ah! " he exclaimed. And then he passed on. Every chapter heading and every page seemed to fascinate him. He kept exclaiming, "Ah!" "Ah!" and Margayya sat before him and watched with complete aloofness. He admired himself for it. "This is the right attitude to cultivate in business. If we show the slightest hesitation or uneasiness others are only too ready to swallow us up." Proof-bearers came up and waited around until Lal should look up. An accountant stood there with an open ledger in his hand, waiting to catch his attention. Lal kept exclaiming, "Ah! Ah!" every few seconds. His staff stood around in a circle. "Get out of the way everyone and give me light," he suddenly shouted. The accountant alone came up and said undaunted: "This is urgent." He placed the fat book on the manuscript; Lal snatched a minute to look into it, and pushed it away. When his accountant showed signs of looking over his shoulder, he said brusquely: "Don't try to see what people are reading. Go away." And the accountant went away. Lal looked for a moment at Margayya and said: "The curiosity some people have! They have a lot of unhealthy curiosity about all sorts of things."

Margayya said: "Are you going to read through the entire manuscript?"

"Yes," said the other. "Otherwise, how can I know whether I can print it or not?"

"Have I to sit here all the time?" asked Margayya.

"Why not? That's what you said you would do. Otherwise you may go out and return."

What was the man proposing? Margayya reflected. Perhaps he had some dark design. No, even if it took a whole day, he would sit there, never go out of sight of those papers. "I will wait here," said Margayya. "Go through it fast."

"Yes, yes," the other cut in impatiently. "Don't disturb me."

Papers continued to come to him. Lal was indifferent. Proofs piled up on his table. Attenders waited around for approval of copy. The accountant came up again and again for his signature on a leather-bound book. Lal

95

snapped at him and signed. And then he pushed the other papers unceremoniously off his table saying: " No one is to come near me till I am through with this piece of work: this is very urgent and important. Don't you see this gentleman waiting? " The machine room foreman came up presently. He hovered about, cleared his throat, and ventured to say: " The School report, sir. The machine is idle."

" Oh! " he replied, then rummaged amongst his papers, snatched a proof, and after the briefest glance at it, flung it at him. " Go ahead."

It was one o'clock in the afternoon when Lal looked up and said: " I'm hungry, and yet I have not finished. Still thirty pages more. I have to go home. You wouldn't leave this with me, I suppose! "

" No," said Margayya resolutely. " How can I? "

" Then come along with me for lunch."

Margayya felt worried. This man from the North—God knew what he ate at home: perhaps beef and pork and strange spices. How could he go and sit with him? He said bluntly: " I have already had my food."

" That's excellent; come along with me."

" No, I have to go home."

" Why should you if you have had your dinner already? "

" I have got some other business."

" Then what do you want me to do. Sit here with this, forgoing my meal, is that it?"

" As you please. You must have read enough of it to know what to tell me."

" Be reasonable, Mister," he appealed. " If you give me a little more time, I will finish it and then I shall be in a position to discuss the matter with you."

" Then go on," Margayya said. " I am not preventing your reading further."

The other hammered on the call bell impatiently till an attendent came up and stood before him: " Go home and tell them I'm not coming for my meal today. Send somebody and get something from the restaurant for two."

Coffee and several plates arrived. Lal pushed away all the papers to make space for the plates and invited Margayya to eat. He kept the manuscript on his lap, his eyes running down the lines; his fingers strayed towards the plates on the table and carried the food to his mouth as if they had an independent life of their own. He looked up for a brief moment at Margayya and said: "Go on, go on, make yourself comfortable."

Margayya had some plates on his side of the table; he hesitated only for a moment, and then said to himself: "Why not?" He was hungry. He had had a sparse meal hours ago. They had put before him many tempting coloured sweets and coffee. "This is indeed lucky," he reflected. "This is good tiffin. It'd have cost me over a rupee." He ate the *jilebis*, and wondered if it would be proper to carry a bit of it home for little Balu. He was racked with a feeling that he was stealing some delicacy which ought to have gone to his child.

"Make yourself comfortable," Lal said hospitably from time to time without lifting his eyes from the manuscript.

Margayya noticed that the other was a voracious eater, and polished off all sorts of oddments in a lump, it didn't matter what. "That's why he is so hefty," Margayya reflected. "He is not a half-fed, half-starving businessman like me. That's why he is able to command so much business and income."

When the plates were removed, Lal wiped his mouth with a handkerchief, looked at Margayya and announced: "I have finished reading the book."

"Well, what do you think you can do?"

"It's an interesting book, no doubt."

"It's a book that must be read by everybody," Margayya added.

"No, no, don't say that; it's not fit for everybody's reading. For instance, if a young unmarried person reads it——"

"He will know a lot of facts beforehand," Margayya

97

said; and this established a greater communion between the two.

Lal said: "Mister, I must consult my lawyer first."

"What has a lawyer to do with it?" Margayya asked. The mention of a lawyer was distasteful to him.

"The trouble is," said the other, "I must know if it comes under the obscenity law. There is such a law, you know. They may put us both in prison."

"It's not obscene. It's a work of sociology."

"Oh, is it? Then there is no trouble. But I'd like to be told that by a lawyer. Will you please come again tomorrow at this time?"

"What for?"

"I will have discussed the matter with my lawyer, and then I shall be able to tell you something. If only you could leave the book with me!"

"That I can't do," said Margayya, sensing another effort on the part of the printer to get at the manuscript. He added for emphasis: "That I can't do, whatever may happen."

"Won't you come with me to the lawyer?"

"When?" asked Margayya, with a profound air of having to consider his engagement diary.

"Sometime tomorrow."

Margayya sat considering. It was no use going to a lawyer. The thought of a lawyer was distasteful to him. The Co-operative Society Secretary was a lawyer. All lawyers were trouble-makers. Moreover, why should he cheapen himself before this man? He said: "Impossible. I have a busy day tomorrow. I can probably drop in just for a few minutes if you like, that is if you are going to tell me definitely yes or no." He added: "I came to you because yours is the biggest establishment. I knew you could do it, although a dozen other printers were ready to take on the job."

"Ours is the best and biggest press," Lal said haughtily. "You will not be able to get this service anywhere else, so much I can assure you."

" What will be your charge? "

" I can tell you all that only after we decide to take on the work."

" Will you require a long time to print the book? " Margayya persisted.

" I will tell you tomorrow," Lal said.

Margayya said: " You are a very cautious man. You don't like to commit yourself to anything."

" That's right," the other said appreciatively, sensing a kindred soul. For among businessmen as among states-men, the greatest dread is to be committed to anything. Being non-committal is the most widely recognized virtue among businessmen and it came to Margayya instinctively as his other qualities came to him. The musician hums the right note at birth, the writer goes to the precise phrase in the face of an experience, whereas for the busi-nessman the greatest gift is to be able to speak so many words which seem to signify something, but don't, which convey a general attitude but are free from commitment.

Next day Margayya tidied himself up more than ever and was at the press at the appointed time. He still carried his manuscript securely wrapped in a paper sheet. The moment he entered the press he had a feeling that all was going to go well. He went straight up to Lal and asked: " Well, what does your lawyer say? "

" We can take it if you agree to a couple of small con-ditions."

" You can speak your mind freely," Margayya said, encouragingly. " In business we either conclude a deal or we don't, but there is no room for mincing words. If you don't want it here, I can take it somewhere else," he added.

" No, no, don't say such a thing, Mister," the other said. " I don't like negative statements to be made in this press."

" I don't like negative statements myself unless I am forced to make them," said Margayya, discovering instinc-tively yet another principle of business life: to have the last word. He concluded that he who spoke last gained most. He was burning with anxiety to know if the other

99

would print the book, for he seemed to be a man who knew his job. Margayya looked about and asked in a business-like manner: "What are the two conditions you mentioned just now?"

"I will take up the printing provided it's done on a basis of partnership."

"What's the partnership for?"

"Well, that will make our work more interesting. Let us publish it together, and share whatever we get. I mean fifty-fifty in everything; expenses as well as returns. Do you agree?"

Margayya took a little time before answering: "I won't say 'Yes' or 'No' before thinking it over deeply. What's your second condition?"

"You must indemnify me against any legal action that anyone may take at any time."

"What do you mean?"

"You must bear the legal responsibility for bringing out this book."

"I see!" said Margayya with deep suspicion. "Why?"

"It's because you are bringing it out."

"If I am bringing it out, you have nothing to do with it except to print it, isn't that so. Then why do you ask for profits? How are you concerned with profits?"

For a moment the other looked a little confused, but soon recovered enough composure to say : "I mean to propose a non-liability partnership."

Margayya was not taken in by the high-sounding phrase. What did it mean? It meant evidently sharing his profits, not his troubles.

He said: "I've done a variety of business. I'm experienced in different kinds of partnership."

"What business were you doing before?" asked Lal.

"Chiefly banking," Margayya said. "You know when a man is a banker he is at once involved in a number of other things too," picturing himself writing a letter for a villager here and arranging a joint-loan for another there.

Lal seemed to appreciate this. He said: "We have a

bank in Gujerat, but you know it also deals in oil-seeds in certain seasons."

"It's inevitable," Margayya said, with an air of profundity.

"It's impossible not to be interested in more than one business," added Lal.

They went on talking far into the day. Once again lunch-time came. Once again they got their tiffin from a hotel and Margayya stuffed himself with sweets and coffee and began to feel quite at home in the press. They kept talking non-committally, warmly, discreetly and with many digressions, till late in the evening, but without concluding anything. Their talk, and counter-talk never ceased, and the manuscript lay between. At about six they dramatically stretched their arms over it, shook hands and concluded the pact, whereby Margayya had the satisfaction of seeing himself a fifty-fifty partner without any investment on his part. He covered the satisfaction he had in the deal with: "I'm not keen on this, but you know you seem to have become such a friend to me that I find it difficult to refuse." He pulled a long face and signed a partnership deed with the utmost resignation. He kept saying: "You have won me over. You are a sharp businessman," a compliment which Lal accepted with the utmost cheerfulness.

"We can never be businessmen unless we give and take on a fifty-fifty basis," Lal kept saying, a proposition heartily endorsed by Margayya, although its arithmetic was somewhat complex and beyond the understanding of ordinary men.

Margayya knocked on his door with great authority. Lal had offered to drive him home in his car. But Margayya declined it definitely. He didn't want him to see his house or street. He explained that after all the hours of sitting in a stuffy atmosphere he would prefer a walk, so as to be fit for work next day.

He knocked on his door with such authority that his wife came hurriedly and opened it. She stood aside to let him pass in. She could not pluck up enough courage to put to him the usual irritating questions. She served him his food and then said in a forced light manner: "This has almost become your usual hour?"

"Yes, it may become even later. I shall have to be very busy."

"Oh!" she said. "Is that book printed?"

"It's not so easy," he replied. "There are many complications." And as she did not annoy him with further questions, he added: "I have almost signed a partnership agreement with a big man." He liked the sentence and the feeling of importance that it gave him. But he didn't like the word 'big' that he had used. Reflecting, he felt he might take the word out and knock it flat lest his wife should think he really meant anyone was bigger than he. He rectified his mistake by adding: "*Big* business-man! *Big!* A North Indian; he thinks he is very clever, but I was able to tweak his nose——"

"Oh!" said his wife, gratified. He seemed to acquire a new stature and importance. He finished his dinner, and when he got up she was ready with a bowl of water for his hands. And then she held a towel out to him.

He was pleased with all these ministrations, thinking, "Yes, she is not a bad sort, except when she gets into a bad mood." He said aloud: "We can live differently hereafter, I think. A lot of money is coming in."

§

The next day he had a very busy time discussing several technical matters, of which he was totally ignorant, with Lal. Lal seemed to assume that Margayya knew what he was talking about. Margayya, true to his principles, did not wish to show his ignorance.

Lal asked: "Shall we print on demy or crown?"

What was demy and what crown? What strange terms were these; to what universe did they belong? Margayya frankly blinked, wondering: "What was this man talking about?" He said grandly: "Each has its own advantage, it's for you to decide; you are a technical man."

Lal said: "You see, demy will give us greater area."

Margayya was hearing the word for the first time in his life. He could not understand to which part of a book or press or sales the word referred. He kept himself alert, deciding not to lose any hint that might fall in the course of the other's talk. He added: "If it means extra area, what other consideration can you have?"

"It's not only that, crown is more handy, and will look less like a gazetteer."

At the mention of gazetteer Margayya made a wry face: "Oh, no, we cannot afford to make it look like a gazetteer."

"In that case we will print it on crown."

"All right," he said, permitting it graciously. "But as a matter of formality I shall be glad to know the difference in cost."

"Not much, about an anna per pound," Lal said.

Pound! Where did pounds come in? He was about to blurt out the question, a survival of his boyhood days in the classroom where, whenever the word pound was mentioned, the immediate question was: "Lb Pound or Shilling Pence Pound?" He almost opened his mouth to ask it, but pressed it back in time, remembering that it was a silly betraying question even in those days: the teacher caned all the boys who asked him that question, for it showed that they had not paid any attention to the sum they were doing. Margayya feared if he raised it the other might tear up their agreement or decide to swindle him with absolute impunity. What did they weigh in the book trade? He could understand nothing of it. He dropped it, hoping on some future occasion that he would know all about it. He had an unfailing hope that whatever there was to be known would be known by him one day. "Only I must keep my eyes open, and in six months I shall be able to tell them what is wrong with them," he thought, with much self-esteem.

Lal observed him for a moment and then said: "Why are you silent? You are not saying anything."

"It is because I have nothing to say," said Margayya.

"So you accept my choice."

"Yes, of course," Margayya said, hoping this would once for all save him from further embarrassment.

But Lal turned up with a new poser for him: "Shall we use ordinary ten-point Roman or another series which I use only for special works? It's also ten-point but on an eleven-point body."

Body? Points? Ten and Eleven? What was it all about? Margayya said: "Ah, that is interesting. . . . I should like to see your eleven-point body." He had grotesque visions of a torso being brought in by four men on a stretcher. When Lal reached out his arm and pulled out a book, he didn't think it had any relation to the question he had asked. He thought Lal was trying to read something. But Lal opened a page, thrust it before him and said: "This is it. How do you like this type?" Margayya gazed at it for fully five minutes and said: "It seems all right to me. What do you say?"

"It's one of our finest types," said Lal. "Do you wish to see our ordinary Roman?"

Now he roughly knew what this meant. "If this is your best, there's not much reason why anything else should be seen," he said with the air of a man who could employ those few minutes to better profit. He added, in order not to allow the other too easy a time, "Only tell me if you have any special reasons from the point of view of costs."

"A difference of a couple of rupees per forme, that's all."

"That's all, is it?" Margayya said. "How many formes will there be?"

Lal glanced through the script and said: "Even if it's going to be page for page, it won't be more than ten formes."

"I don't think we ought to worry about a bare difference

of twenty rupees," Margayya said, feeling happy that he could after all take part in the discussion.

"I agree with you," said Lal. "Now about the style of binding, etc."

"Oh, these details!" Margayya exclaimed. "They should not come as far as me. You ought to decide those things yourself."

"But every item has to go into costs. I don't want you to feel at any time that I have incurred any expense without your knowledge."

"That comes only at the end, doesn't it?" Margayya said.

"Of course, in the first quarter following publication."

And Margayya felt relieved—he had a gnawing fear lest he should have to shell out cash immediately.

"And," said Lal, "my lawyer suggests that we had better call this book 'Domestic Harmony' instead of 'Bed Life'. Have you any objection?"

"Oh, none whatever," said Margayya. "In these matters we must implicitly obey the lawyers."

"Otherwise we shall get into trouble."

"Yes, otherwise we shall get into trouble," echoed Margayya, adding: "We must do everything possible to avoid getting into trouble because a businessman's time is so precious."

"You are an uncanny fellow. You seem to understand everything," Lal said admiringly.

When Balu was six years old Margayya admitted him to the Town Elementary School. Margayya made a great performance of it. He took the young man in a decorated motor with pipes and drums through the Market Road: the traffic was held up for half an hour when Balu's procession passed. Balu sat with the top of his head shaved, with diamonds sparkling on his ear lobes, and a rose garland round his neck, in a taxi with four of his picked friends by his side. Margayya walked in front of the car, and he had

invited a few citizens of the road to go with him as well.
Strangest sight of all, his brother was also with him in the
procession. They seemed to have made it up all of a
sudden. On the eve of the Schooling Ceremony, Margayya
stated: "After all, he is his own uncle, his own blood, my
brother. Unless he blesses the child, of what worth are all
the other blessings he may get?" He grew sentimental at
the thought of his elder brother. "Don't you know that
he brought me up. . . . But for his loving care . . ." He
rambled on thus. His wife caught the same mood and
echoed: "No one prevents them from being friendly with
us."

"There are times when we should set aside all our usual
prejudices and notions—we must not let down ties of
blood," Margayya said pompously. As a result of this
sentiment, at five A.M. they both knocked on the door of
the next house and quietly walked past the astounded stare
of his brother as he held the door open. Margayya's wife
went straight into the kitchen to invite the sister-in-law,
and Margayya stood before his brother in the hall and
said: "All of you are keeping well as usual, I suppose!"
adding: "Balu's schooling ceremony is tomorrow morning. Come and bless him——"

"Oh, yes, oh, yes," his brother said, still somewhat dazed.

"Bring yourself and all the children for a meal," Margayya said, and added, "You must not light the oven in
your own house. Come in for morning coffee. Where is
my sister-in-law?"

His brother said: "There."

Margayya shouted : "Sister-in-law!" familiarly, as he
used to do in his boyhood days. It seemed to take him
back decades when he was a student coming home during
the afternoon recess for rice and butter-milk. He made a
move towards the kitchen, when his wife came in the
opposite direction, with bowed head, showing the respect
due to the elder brother-in-law; she moved off fast, giving
Margayya a swift glance, which he understood. He turned
and followed his wife quietly into the street. Hardly had

they gone up their verandah steps when she whispered:
" She will not come."

" Why not? " Margayya asked.

" She bit her lips so and nodded—the vicious creature.
She wouldn't speak a word to me."

" Why not? "

" Why not? Why not? Don't keep saying that. She is
that sort, that is all."

" She used to be very kind to me in those days." Margayya's sentimentality still lingered in him, as he remembered his schooldays.

" No one prevents you from going and asking her again."

" You invited her properly, I suppose," Margayya said.
She flared up: " I have abased myself sufficiently."

" That's all right, that's all right," Margayya said, scent-
ing danger.

His brother and seven of his children came and presided
over the function. He presented young Balu with a silver
box, and at the sight of it Margayya felt very proud and
moved. He asked his son to prostrate himself before his
uncle ceremoniously and receive his blessings, after which
the boy started out for his school in a procession.

§

Margayya's son had a special standing in the school, for
Margayya was the school secretary. Teachers trembled
before him, and the headmaster stood aside while he
passed. They knew Margayya was a powerful man and also
that he could be a pleasant and kindly man, who listened
to their troubles when they met him at home to discuss
small promotions or redress. He listened to them most
attentively and promised to do his best, but hardly remembered anything of it next moment. This was purely a
defensive mechanism. He simply could not keep in his
head all the requests that people brought to him each day.
The utmost he could do for them was to be pleasant to

them. When they pestered him too much he merely said, " See here, I took up this work as a sort of service for our people, but this is not my only occupation. As a matter of fact I did not want all this business, but it was thrust upon me and they wouldn't take my refusal."

He spoke like the president of a political party after an election campaign, but his place on the school board did not come to him unsought nor was it thrust upon him. On the day he admitted Balu to the school he realized that his son would not have a chance of survival unless he admitted himself also to the school. Within fifteen days of the schooling ceremony he heard reports that Balu was being caned almost every day, was having his ears twisted by all and sundry, and that even the school peon pushed him about rudely. He loved his son and it seemed to him that the school was thoroughly in the wrong. He went there once or twice to rectify matters and was told by the head-master that it was all false and perhaps the boy deserved all that and more. They treated him in an off-handed manner which angered him very much. They almost hinted that he might take his son away. At the end of the term Balu came home with his progress card marked zero. Margayya decided to take charge of the school.

He was a busy businessman who could not afford the time for unprofitable honorary work, but he felt he ought to sacrifice himself for the sake of his son's educational progress. He wanted Balu to grow up into an educated man, graduating from a college and probably going for higher studies to Europe or America. He had immense confidence in himself now. He could undertake any plan with ease; he could shape his son's future as if it were just so much clay in his hand. His son might become a great government official or something of the kind, or indeed anything in ten years, if this cursed school were not in his way. . . . He watched for the next election time. It was a strategy of extraordinary complexity and meant expense too; but he did not grudge it. He felt that no expense was too great for a child's future, and slipped into the place of a member whom he had persuaded to retire. After that one could notice a great improvement in Balu's career. He never lost his place in the class, and the teachers seemed to have adjusted themselves to his way of thinking. In addition Margayya picked up a home tutor for him. He made this selection with great astuteness. He kept an eye on all the teachers, and sounded his son himself as to whom he would like to have as teacher at home, to which Balu promptly replied, " No one."

Margayya said, " You are not to say that. You must have a home teacher. Tell me whom you like most in your school."

After a great deal of persuasion, the boy said " Nathaniel."

Margayya knew him to be a mild Christian gentleman whom all the children loved because he told them numerous stories, let them do what they pleased, never frowned at them even once, and taught them history and such innocuous subjects rather than mathematics. Margayya decided at once to eliminate this gentleman from his list as a home tutor. "It is no good appointing a sheep to guard a tiger cub," he told himself. He suddenly asked: " Who is the teacher that beats the boys most? "

" The science attender," replied the young innocent.

" I don't mean him," Margayya said, "I mean among the teachers."

" But the science attender says he is also a teacher. Do you know, father, he beats any boy who doesn't call him ' Sir! ' "

" He does that, does he! " exclaimed Margayya angrily. " You go and tell him that he is merely a miserable science peon and nothing more, and if he tries to show off I will cut off his tail."

" Has he a tail, father," asked Balu. " Oh, I didn't notice." He burst into a laugh, and laughed so loudly and rolled about so much that his father was forced to say, " Stop that . . . Don't make all that noise." The vision of the science attender with a tail behind only made Balu roll about more and more. He made so much noise that his mother came out of the kitchen to ask, " What is the matter ? "

" Mother," the boy screamed, "father thinks that our science teacher has a tail, the science teacher has a tail . . ." He danced about in sheer joy at this vision, and Margayya could not get anything more out of him. The boy was too wild. He left him alone for the moment but questioned him again later and found that the teacher he most detested was Mr. Murti, the arithmetic and English teacher, an old man who always carried a cane in his hand, shaved his head and covered it with a white turban, and wore a long coat. To Margayya it seemed to be a very satisfactory picture of a teacher. None of your smart young men with bare heads and crop, with their entertaining stories and so forth. He immediately asked Murti to see him at his house and fixed him up at once as Balu's teacher at home and a sort of supervisor for him at school too. His own professional work was taking up more and more of his time each day; he wanted another agency to protect the interests of his son at school.

Murti was only too happy to accept this job since he earned only twenty-five rupees at school and the ten rupees that Margayya arbitrarily offered him was most welcome, as was the perpetual contact he would have with the Secretary of the School Board day in and day out. It enhanced his status at school among his colleagues and also with the headmaster, who, if he wanted to sound the secretary's state of mind over any important question at school, called aside Murti and spoke to him in whispers. All this Murti welcomed, but he also lost something in the bargain, and that was his power over his pupil, Balu. He knew that although Margayya had asked him to handle him as he would any other boy, the plan would not work. He had far too much experience with people who had an only child and a lot of money. They never meant what they said with regard to their children. No one lost his head so completely over a question of discipline as the parent of an only child. Murti did not want to offend the young boy and lose his favour so that one day he might tell his father, "I won't be taught by that teacher." On the other hand he did not want the father to feel that he was not able to handle Balu. So he walked warily. He tried to earn the goodwill and co-operation of the pupil himself so that his job might be easy. He gave him many gifts of sweets and pencils and rubbers if he did a sum well and forbore his mischief, and treated him generally as a friend. The scheme worked, although the boy was on the verge of blackmailing his teacher whenever he set him more sums than he cared to do. But on the whole the relationship was successful and Balu progressed steadily from class to class and reached the Fourth Form.

The teacher and the pupil were like old partners now, seasoned partners who knew each other's strong points and weak points. Margayya stuck to his School Board election after election. He boasted to his friends and relations whenever he found a chance: "Balu is just thirteen you know, and in two years . . ." He gloated over a vision of his son passing into a college. He would give him a separate study in the new house he was planning to build in New Extension. He would buy table lamps with green shades; they said that a green shade was good for the eyes. He would send him to Albert Mission College, although it was at the other end of the town, far away from New Extension. He would buy him a car. People would look at him and say, "Well, there goes Margayya's son. Lucky fellows, these sons of businessmen."

§

Margayya had converted the small room into a study for Balu. Every morning Margayya carried out an inspection of this room in order to see that his son learnt civilized ways and kept his things in their proper places, but he always found the mat not spread out on the floor, but stood up against a corner half-rolled, his books scattered on the floor, and his little desk full of stones, feathers, cigarette foils and empty packets. These were all collected from a small shop made of dealwood planks near by which had recently been set up by a man from Malabar. Margayya felt unhappy when he saw the condition of this room. In his view a study had to be a very orderly place, with books arrayed on one side, and the clothes of the scholar folded and in their place on the wire stretched across the wall. Margayya had secured a small framed picture of the Goddess Saraswathi, the Goddess of Learning and Enlightenment, sitting beside her peacock and playing on the strings of a veena. He hung it in the study and enjoined his son ceremoniously to pray to the Goddess every morning as soon as he got up from bed. He inquired untiringly, " Boy, have you made your prostrations before the Goddess? "

" Yes," the boy answered, and ran in and performed them in a moment, then came back to the hall and just hung about staring at the sky or into the kitchen. Margayya felt angry. He told his son sharply: " God is not like your drill class, to go and dawdle about half-heartedly. You must have your heart in it."

" I prostrated all right, father."

" Yes, but your mind was where? "

" I was thinking of . . . of . . ." He considered for a moment, and added, " My lessons," knowing it would please his father. But it did not seem to have that effect.

" When you prostrate, you must not prostrate so fast."

" How long can I lie on the floor prostrate? " the boy asked sullenly. " I can't be lying there all the time."

" If you grumble so much about your duties to the Goddess, you will never become a learned man, that is all," Margayya warned him.

" I don't care," said the boy, very angry at the thought of an exacting Goddess.

" You will be called a useless donkey by the whole world, remember," Margayya said, his temper rising. " Learn to talk with more reverence about the gods. . . . Do you know where I was, how I started, how I earned the favour of the Goddess by prayer and petition? Do you know why I succeeded? It was because my mind was concentrated on the Goddess. The Goddess is the only one who can——"

The boy cut him short with, "I know it is a different Goddess you worshipped. It is that Goddess Lakshmi. I know all that from mother."

Margayya felt upset by this taunt. He called his wife and asked, "Why have you been talking nonsense to this boy? He is saying all sorts of things."

"What has he been saying?" asked the wife, wiping her wet hands on the end of her saree.

Margayya was at a loss to explain. There was really no basis for his charge. He merely said, "That boy contradicts me." He turned furiously on his son and said, "It is all the same Goddess. There is no difference between Lakshmi and Saraswathi, do you understand?"

The boy was not to be cowed. He simply said, "They are different, I know." He said it with an air of finality. Margayya asked, "How do you know? Who told you?"

"My master."

"Who? Murti? I will speak to that fool. If he is putting obstinate ideas into your head, he is not fit to be your teacher." Then he added, "Tell me as soon as he comes tomorrow or this evening."

"But you won't be at home when he comes," said the boy.

"Let him wait for me. Tell him he must see me," said Margayya.

"All right," said the boy.

Margayya then ordered him out, with, "You can go and do your sums now. Don't waste the precious hours of the morning." Balu ran off with great relief to his study and read a page out of his geography at the top of his voice so that all other sounds in the house were drowned.

He went to school trembling with the joyous anticipation of carrying a piece of unpleasant news to his teacher.

The moment he sighted him he cried, "Sir, sir, my father has asked you to wait for him this evening."

The teacher's face turned pale. "Why? Why?" he stammered nervously. There were some boys watching them, and he said, "Go away, boys, attend to your work, why do you stand and gape," as sternly as he could. He then took Balu aside and said: "Tell me boy, why does your father want me to see him?" "I don't know, sir," Balu replied, enjoying the occasion completely. "I don't know, sir." He shook his head, but his eyes were lively with mischief and suppressed information. The teacher tried to frighten him: "Should you not ask him why he wants to when somebody says he wants to meet somebody else? Must you be taught all these elementary things?"

"Oh, my father cannot be asked all that. He will be very angry if he is questioned like that. Why should I be beaten by him, sir? Do you want me to be beaten by him, sir?"

The teacher took him privately under the tamarind tree and begged: "See here, what exactly happened today, won't you tell me, won't you tell your teacher?"

He sounded melodramatic, and Balu started bargaining, "I couldn't do any sums this morning." The teacher assured him that he would condone the lapse. And then Balu went on to the next bargaining point by which the teacher himself should do the sums and not bother Balu except to the extent of showing him what marks he had obtained for them. When it was granted, Balu demanded: "You promised me *bharfi*; I must have it this afternoon, sir."

"You will surely get a packet from me this afternoon," said the teacher affably. After all this, Balu told him the reason why his father wanted to meet him. The teacher cried: "I say, whatever made you speak thus? Have I ever mentioned to you anything about Lakshmi or anything of the kind?"

"My father asked who told me all that, and so I had to say it was you," said Balu, with obscure logic.

The teacher waited for Margayya's arrival in the evening after finishing the lessons with Balu. Balu went in to demand his dinner. It was past eight when Margayya came home. As the pitpat of his sandals were heard outside the teacher felt acutely uneasy and stood up. Margayya carefully put away his sandals in the corridor and came in. He saw the teacher and asked, "What is the matter, teaching so late!" The teacher went forward officiously, rubbed his hands and said, "Oh, I finished the lessons long ago, and Balu has even gone to sleep. I only waited to see you, sir." he added.

"Oh, now, impossible," said Margayya. He proceeded to put away his upper cloth and take off his shirt. "I come home after a hard day's work and now you try to catch me for some idiotic school business, I suppose. Do you think I have no other business? Go, go, nothing doing now."

"All right, sir," the teacher said turning to go, greatly relieved.

"Is there anything else?" Margayya shouted as the other was going. The teacher thought for a moment and said: "Nothing special, sir," in a most humble tone, which satisfied Margayya. His self-importance was properly fed; and so he said, as a sort of favour to the teacher, "I hope Balu is all right?"

"Oh, yes, sir; he is quite up to the mark although he needs constant watching . . ."

"Well, as a teacher that is what you are expected to do, remember. And any time you see him getting out of hand, don't wait for me. Thrash him. Thrash him well." As a sort of general philosophy, he added, "No boy who has not been thrashed has come to any good. I am going to be extremely busy and won't have much time for anything. Don't take your eye off the boy."

"Yes, sir, I will always do my best; as a teacher my interest is to see him rise in the world as a man of——"

Margayya turned and went away to the back-yard without waiting for him to finish the sentence. His wife picked up a vessel of water and gave it to him. As he poured it over himself and she could be sure he was feeling cooler, she said, "Why do you constantly say 'Thrash' 'Thrash' whenever you speak of the child. It is not good."

Margayya replied, "Oh, you believe it! It is just a formality with teachers, that is all. It keeps them in trim. After all, the fellow takes ten rupees a month and he must keep himself alert; but he dare not even touch our little darling. I would strike off that miserable teacher's head."

It was all very bewildering to his wife. She asked, "If you don't want him to do it why do you tell him to thrash him?"

"That is the way things have to be done in the world, my dear. If you see a policeman ask him to catch the thief, if you see a monkey ask him to go up a tree, and if you see a teacher ask him to thrash his pupil. . . . These are the things they do and it pleases them, they are appropriate. If you want to please me tell me to put up the interest, and I at once feel I am being spoken to by a friend and well-wisher!"

§

There was probably no other person in the whole country who had meditated so much on the question of interest. Margayya's mind was full of it. Night and day he sat and brooded over it. The more he thought of it the more it seemed to him the greatest wonder of creation. It combined in it the mystery of birth and multiplication. Otherwise how could you account for the fact that a hundred rupees in a savings bank became one hundred and twenty in course of time? It was something like the ripening of corn. Every rupee, Margayya felt, contained in it the seed of another rupee and that seed in it another seed and so on and on to infinity. It was something like the firmament, endless stars and within each star and endless firmament and within each one further endless . . . It bordered on mystic perception. It gave him the feeling of being part of an infinite existence. But Margayya was racked with the feeling that these sublime thoughts were coming to him in a totally wrong setting. He disliked the atmosphere of the Gordon Printery. He detested his office and the furniture. Sitting in a chair, dangling one's legs under a table, seemed an extremely irksome process; it was as if you remained half suspended in mid-air. He liked to keep his knees folded and tucked—that alone gave him a feeling of being on solid ground. And then his table and all its equipment seemed to him a most senseless luxury. They were not necessary for the welfare and progress of a business man; they were mere show stuff. And all that calling-bell nonsense. The best way to call was to shout "Boy," and keep shouting till the boy's ear drums split and he came running. All this tinkling calling-bell stuff was a waste of time. You were not a shepherd playing on a flute calling back your flock! Margayya was so much tickled by this comparison that he laughed aloud one day while he sat in his office, and was supposed to be counting the orders for *Domestic Harmony*. The boy came running in at the sound of this laughter, and Margayya flung the call-bell at him and said: "Don't let me see this on my table. I don't want all this tomfoolery." This was the starting point.

The business always seemed to him an alien one. The only interesting thing about it seemed to be the money that was coming in. "But money is not everything," he told himself one day. It was a very strange statement to come from a person like Margayya. But if he had been asked to explain or expand it further he would have said: "Money is very good no doubt, but the whole thing seems to be in a wrong setting." Money was not in its right place here, amidst all the roar of printing machinery, ugly streaming proof sheets, and the childish debits and credits that arose from book sales with booksellers and book buyers, who carried on endless correspondence over trivialities about six and a quarter and twelve and a half per cent and a few annas of postage and so forth. It was all very well if you spoke of those percentages with a value of a hundred rupees at least; but here you were dealing with two rupees per copy and involved yourself in all these hair-splitting percentages. It did not seem to Margayya an adult business; there was really no stuff in it; there was not sufficient adventure in it; there was nothing in it. "Book business is no business at all," he told his wife one evening when he decided to part company with Lal. "It is a business fit for youngsters of Balu's age." The lady had no comment to offer since all business seemed to her equally complex and bewildering. She had to listen with patience as he expanded his theme: "It is a rusty business, sitting there all the time and looking at those silly figures ... Well, to let you into a secret, there is not much of that either; the figures are falling off; sales are not as good as they used to be." And then it hurt his dignity to be called the publisher of *Domestic Harmony*. He would prefer people to forget it if possible. When the profits dwindled he began to view the book in a peculiarly realistic light. "Awful stuff," he told his wife. "Most vulgar and poisonous. It will do a lot of damage to young minds."

"And also to old minds, I think. How can people write brazenly of all those matters?" she asked.

Margayya said, "Did you ever notice how I have managed not to bring a single copy into this house? I don't want our Balu even to know that there is such a book." His wife expressed deep appreciation of this precaution. Margayya felt further impelled to add, "I don't want people to say that Balu enjoys all the money earned through *Domestic Harmony*. I would do anything to avoid it." He felt very heroic when he said that. He seemed to swell with his goodness, nobility and importance, and the clean plans he was able to make for his son.

It was quite a fortnight before he spoke of it to Lal. Lal was thinking that Margayya was attending to his work as usual. Their quarterly statement system worked quite smoothly. There was no chance of any mistake or misunderstanding. Lal himself was a man who believed that in the long run honesty paid in any business. Margayya had complete charge of the sales, and the division of the spoils went on smoothly without a hitch. At tiffin time, Margayya called up his boy and told him: "Go and ask Lal if he will come here for tiffin today. Tell him that there is something I have brought from home." Lal came up. Margayya ceremoniously welcomed him and pointed to the chair opposite. "My wife has sent something special today for my afternoon tiffin, and I thought you might like to taste it."

"I have to go home for lunch," said Lal. "I have told them that I would be there."

"I will send word to them. Boy!" Margayya cried. He took complete charge of the other. "Call the master's servant, and send him up to inform the lady at the house that *Sab* is not coming there for his meal. And then run up and bring . . ." He gave an elaborate list of tiffins to be purchased at the canteen next door. "Ask him to make the best coffee."

"I don't want coffee, mister. Let it be tea. I have taken coffee only for your sake once or twice. I don't want coffee."

"All right, make it tea then; and coffee for me. Hurry up! Why are you still standing and blinking? Hurry up, young fellow." There, consuming their repast, Margayya made his proposal. "Lal, you have done a lot for me. I want to do a good turn to you."

At the mention of this Lal sat up interested. "Good turn," he thought. That sounded suspicious. No one like Margayya would do a good turn except as a sort of investment. Lal wanted to know what the proposal was going to mean. He knew that it must be something connected with *Domestic Harmony*, but he felt he should have all his faculties alert. He said very casually, "Well, mister, we must all be helpful to each other, isn't that so? Otherwise, what is life worth? What is existence worth? If we are always thinking of our profits, we shall not be able to do any good in this world. I am glad you think so much of my little service to you. But pray don't think too much of it. I have done the little I could, although financially it has really meant a loss. If I should put into my books all the time and energy, to say nothing of the materials, that have been put into our job, it would really turn out to be a loss. If I had engaged myself in something else . . . But my mind will not run on these lines : I always like to think at the end of the day that I have done something without thought of profit, and only then do I feel able to go to sleep."

Margayya felt it was time for him to interrupt this peroration. " The same with me. I like to go a step further. Not only lack of profit: I like to feel that I have done something with a little sacrifice for another person's sake. It is not often one gets a chance to do such a thing, but when one does, one is able to sleep with the utmost peace that night."

With their mouths stuffed with sweets and other edibles they spoke for about ten minutes more on sacrifices and the good life. When they came to the coffee there was a lull and Margayya said casually, " Here is the proposal about *Domestic Harmony*. I don't like you to bear the burden any more since you say that you have had a loss. Why don't you let me take it over completely? "

" Why? How can that be? There is our partnership deed . . . My lawyer . . ."

" Oh, let your lawyer alone. We don't need lawyers. Why do you bring in a lawyer when we are discussing something as friends? Is this all the regard you have for our friendship? I am very much hurt, Lal. I wish you had not mentioned a lawyer." He sat looking very sad and broken-hearted at this turn of events.

Lal remained quiet for a few moments. He took a cup of tea and gulped it down. He said : " Why should you feel so much upset at the thought of lawyers? They are not demons. Somehow I don't like to do anything without telling my lawyer about it."

" As for me," said Margayya, " you need not imagine

that I have no use for lawyers. I consult not one but two or three at a time in business matters. I never take a step unless I have had a long and complete consultation with my lawyer . . . But now there is nothing to warrant the calling of a lawyer or the police," he added laughing.

The other could not view the matter with the same ease and still looked very serious.

Margayya said: "I am not calling you here to give you trouble, Lal. I am only informally trying to talk over a matter with you, that is all, but if you are going to be so suspicious I had better not speak of it. You see, I am not a person who cares much for advantages; what seems to me the most important thing in human life is good relationships among all human beings."

This maudlin statement had the desired effect and Lal softened a little, and asked, "What is it that you are trying to say?"

"Merely that you should let me buy up the partnership for *Domestic Harmony*."

"It is impossible," he cried. "I can prove that I have observed all the clauses faithfully. How can we cancel it, mister? What is it that you are suggesting?"

"It is only a suggestion," Margayya said. "Just to save you the bother, that's all; there's nothing more in it, especially since I thought you could employ your time and energies more profitably——"

"Impossible!" Lal cried. "I will not listen to it."

"Oh," Margayya said, and remained thoughtful. Then he added, "Well then, I will make a sporting offer." He tapped his chest dramatically, "Just to prove that all is well here I make this sporting offer to you. Take it if you can. You will then know that I am not trying to gain a mean advantage over you."

"What are you saying, mister?"

"It is this. . . . I will speak if you promise you will not call your lawyer or the police after me!"

"Oh, you are a very sensitive man," Lal said. "I meant no offence."

" You might not, but it is very depressing. . . . You are a business man and I am a business man. Let us talk like two business men. Either we agree or we don't agree. . . . Either give the *Domestic Harmony* solely——"

" Impossible," cried Lal once again. " There is our partnership deed."

" What is the deed worth? Tear it up, I say, and take over the book yourself. I do not want any interest in it. I am prepared to give it to you this very moment, although in a couple of months the marriage season will be on and the demand for the book will go up. I am prepared to surrender it. Are you prepared to accept it? "

" No," said Lal promptly. " I do not like to take advantage of anyone's generosity."

It needed, however, two more days of such talk, rambling, challenging, and bordering on the philosophical, before they could evolve an equitable give-and-take scheme; a scheme which each secretly thought gave him a seventy-five per cent advantage. By it Margayya abandoned for ever his interest in *Domestic Harmony* for a lump sum payment, and he tore up his document dramatically and put it into the waste-paper basket under Lal's table, at which Lal seemed to be much moved. He extended his hand and said: " Among business men once a friend always a friend. Our friendship must always grow. If you have any printing of forms or anything remember us; we are always at your service. This is your press."

He saw Margayya off at the door and Margayya walked down the Market Road with a satisfactory cheque in his pocket.

PART THREE

MARGAYYA went straight to the Town Bank. He refused to transact his business at the counter; he had to do it sitting in a chair in the Manager's room. But he found someone talking to the Manager and he had to wait outside for a moment. It was a crowded hour. Margayya never liked to do his transactions through the counter window. He despised the clerks. It was a sign of prestige for a business-man to get things done in a bank without standing at the little window. That was for the little fellows who had no current account but only a savings bank book. He had the greatest contempt for savings bank operations: putting in money as if into a child's money box and withdrawing no more than fifty rupees a week or some miserable amount, not through cheques but by writing on those pitiful with-drawal forms. . . . Having a current account seemed to him a stamp of superiority, and a man who had two accounts, account number one and account number two, was a person of eminence. He saw waiting at the counters petty mer-chants, office messengers, and a couple of students of the Albert College attempting to cash cheques from their parents.

Hearing their inquiries, Margayya felt: " Why do their parents send these boys cheques which they won't know how to cash? " He thought: " What do these people know of cheques? What do they know of money? They are ignorant folk who do not know the worth of money, and think that it is just something to pass into a shop. Fools! " He pitied them. He felt that he must do something to enlighten their minds. He would not be a banker to them, but a helper, a sort of money doctor who would help people to use their money properly with the respect due to it. He would educate society anew in all these matters. He hoped he would be able to draw away all these people into his own establishment when the time came. The reason why people came here was that they were attracted by the burnished counters, the heavy ledgers, the clerks sitting on high stools and so on, and, of course, the calling bells and pin cushions. Once again show, mere show. Showiness was becoming the real curse of all business these days, he thought. It was not necessary to have anything more than a box for carrying on any business soundly; not necessary to have too many persons or tables or leatherbound ledgers; all that was required was just one head and a small note-book in which to note down figures if they became too com-plicated, and above all a scheme. He knew that he had a scheme somewhere at the back of his mind, a scheme which would place him among the elect in society, which would make people flock to him and look to him for guidance, advice and management. He could not yet say what the scheme would be, but he sensed its presence, being a financial mystic. Whatever it was, it was going to revolu-tionize his life and the life of his fellow-men. He felt he ought to wait on that inspiration with reverence and watchfulness.

A peon came up to say " The Manager is free."

" All right, I'll be coming," said Margayya. He liked to give an impression that he was in no hurry to run into the manager's room at his call. He looked through some papers in his pocket, folded and put them back, and sauntered into the manager's room.

The manager was a very curt, business-like gentleman who had recently been transferred to this branch. " Sit down, please, what can I do for you? " he asked. He was a man soured by constant contact with people who came to ask for overdrafts or loans on insufficient security. The moment he heard a footstep approaching, he first prepared himself to repel any demand. So, according to his custom, he put himself behind a forbidding exterior for a moment, and assumed a monosyllabic attitude.

"I wish to open an account," said Margayya. The manager could not take it in easily at first. He still had his suspicions. This man might be anybody; might have come to open an account or to open the safe . . . His hostility affected Margayya too. He said at once, "You don't seem to want a new client . . . If that is so . . ." He pretended to rise.

"Sit down please," said the other. "We have instructions not to admit too many new accounts, but I should like to know——"

"You would like to know whether I am a bankrupt or what. All right, I am not anxious to have an account here. I want it here because it is quite near to my own business place."

"Where is it?"

"You will know it presently."

"Really? What business?"

Margayya would not answer this question. The more the other pressed for an answer, the more he resisted. "Let me tell you this: it is a very specialized business: my clients are chiefly peasants from the villages. I have a great deal to do with their harvests and advances and so forth." To further inquiries by the manager Margayya refused to give an answer: "I cannot give any details of my business at the moment to you or to anyone. No one will be able to get these things out of me. But let me tell you: I have come here only to deposit my money and use it, not to take money out of you . . . I can quite see what is at the back of your mind. Now tell me whether you would care to have my account here or not. . . ." Now he was taking out his trump, namely, the cheque given to him by Lal. "If you don't want me here, give me cash for it; but if you think I am good enough for you, start an account with this."

"Have you an account anywhere else?"

"I don't answer that question," said Margayya out of sheer financial pugnacity; he could have told him that he had quite a sizable account in Commerce Bank in Race Course Road.

The bank manager felt that here was a man who knew his mind and felt a regard for him. "Of course I will open your account here," he said with sudden warmth. "What does a bank exist for unless to serve its clients?"

"Quite right," Margayya said. "I quite appreciate," he added patronizingly, "your precaution as a banker. Only a businessman can appreciate it in another businessman."

He had a feeling that he had after all found the right place for himself in life—the right destination, the right destination being 10, Market Road. It was a block of four shops, each about twelve feet square, with a narrow corridor running in front which was thrown in as a sort of grace to the tenants. The other three were taken by a tailor whose single machine went on rattling all day and night over the din of clients who came to demand their overdue clothes, and next to it was a board announcing itself as The Tourist Bureau, having a number of small chairs and a few benches, and a fourth shop was a doctor's, who claimed to have practised under a great seer in the Himalayas and to be able to cure any disease with rare herbs. Margayya was pleased with this spot. It was a combination which seemed to him ideal. On the very first day he came there he felt that these were just the men with whom he could live: "They are not people who are likely to interfere with my work. Moreover, it is likely that people who come to the tailor or the doctor or the tourist bureau are just the people who have some surplus cash and who are likely to be interested in my business too."

It was Dr. Pal who put him into this setting. Dr. Pal sought him out one day at his house just as he was bullying his son over his lessons. He walked in saying, "I didn't know your house exactly, but just took a chance and came over. I was just sauntering down the road wondering whom to ask when I heard your voice."

Margayya had a slate in his hand and there was a frown on his face and tears in his son's eyes. He got over his confusion and affected a smile: "Oh, Doctor, Doctor, what have you been doing with yourself?"

The doctor looked at Balu and said, "You have evidently been trying to teach this young man. Don't you know that for parents to teach their off-spring is prohibited in all civilized countries?" He then said to the boy, as if taking charge of him immediately, "Now run off, little man." He turned ceremoniously to Margayya and added, "Of course with your permission." Balu did not wait for any further concession; he swept aside his books and ran out of sight as if a bear were behind him.

Margayya's mind had still not come to rest. He kept looking after his son and mumbled, "You have no idea how indifferent and dull present-day boys are."

"Oh, no, don't tell me that. . . . Remember correctly: do you think you gave an easy time to your father or the teachers? Just think over it honestly."

It was not a line which Margayya was prepared to pursue. He brushed aside the topic, remembering suddenly that he had not been sufficiently hospitable. He burst into sudden activity, and began to fuss elaborately over his visitor. He jumped to his feet, clutched the other's hand, and said, "Oh, oh, Doctor, what a pleasure to meet you after all these years! Where have you been all the time? What have you been doing with yourself? What is the meaning of cutting off old friends as you did?" He unrolled a new mat, and apologized, "You know I have no sofa or chair to offer——"

"Well, I didn't come to be put on to a sofa."

"That is right. I don't like furniture, the type of furniture which does not suit us; we are made to sit erect with our feet dangling——"

"I wonder," said Dr. Pal, "if the prevalence of nervous disorders in the present day might be due to the furniture which has become popular. In ancient days our ancestors squatted on the floor, stretched themselves as much as they liked and lived to be wise old men."

Margayya could not understand whether the man was

joking with him or was in earnest. He called his wife and said, "Get two cups of coffee ready immediately. My old friend has come." While waiting for coffee he said, "Now tell me what you have been doing with yourself, doctor. Where have you been hiding all these days?"

The doctor said, "I had gone for a little training in Tourism."

Margayya was bewildered. This man was specializing in obscure and rare activities. "What is Tourism?" he asked.

"It is a branch of social activity," the doctor said. "The basic idea is that all people on earth should be familiar with all parts of the earth."

"Is it possible?"

"It is not, and that is why there must be a specialist in tourism in every town and city."

"What is Tourism?" Margayya asked innocently once again. .

The doctor viewed him with pity and said, "I will explain to you all about it by and by one day when we meet in my office. . . . Now tell me about yourself."

"No, you tell me about yourself first," Margayya said, with a vague desire to avoid the theme of himself for the moment. There was at the back of his mind a faint fear lest the doctor should ask him to render the accounts of *Domestic Harmony*. He wondered if the man had hunted him down for this and he wished to be on his guard. He had hardly made up his mind as to what he should say if he broached the subject, when, as if reading his thoughts, Pal said, "I came here some time ago, but didn't like to meet you lest you should think I had come after my book."

Margayya sniggered and said somewhat pointlessly, "Oh, isn't it a long time since we met?"

"Yes, ages since. I have been away for a long time. You know I am no longer on that paper. I gave it up. It did not seem to me serious enough work. I always feel that we must do something that contributes to the sum and substance of human experience. Otherwise all our jobs seem to be just futile." 128

"I also am about to start a new business."

"Yes, I heard about it from the town bank manager," said Pal.

The man seemed to know everything that was going on everywhere, thought Margayya with a certain amount of admiration. Margayya's wife brought two tumblers of coffee to the door of the kitchen and made some noise with the vessels in order to attract Margayya's attention. Margayya said from where he sat, "You can come in, it is my friend Dr. Pal. I have spoken to you about him."

She was at once seized with fear whether the man was there in order to discuss another book on the same lines as the previous one. She withdrew a little, and Margayya went over and took the coffee from her hands and carried it to the front room.

The conversation languished while Dr. Pal was relishing the coffee, and then he said, "I heard from the bank manager that you are starting a new business. I just came to tell you that if you want a nice place on Market Road, there is one vacant in our block. There is some demand for it."

They went to 10, Market Road. Margayya liked the building when he saw it. A man who made a lot of money selling blankets had bought up the vacant site near to the Municipal Dispensary and built these rooms. At the moment, the house was of one storey. Eventually he proposed to add a first floor and a second floor. The man himself had his own shop in one of the back lanes of the Market, a very small shop stacked with rough blankets. He was a strong dark man with a circular sandal paste mark on his forehead. He sat there all day chasing the flies. "Flies come here, God knows why," Margayya reflected when he went to meet him with Dr. Pal. They had to stand outside the shop and talk to him as he peeped out of his blanket stacks. At the sight of Pal the other man brought his palms together and saluted. He had evidently great reverence for learned people.

"How are you, sir?" Dr. Pal inquired genially. "This

is one of my greatest friends," he told Margayya in an aside, and added, " You cannot imagine how much he has helped me in my most difficult times."

" Tut, tut," said the other from the depth of his woollen stacks. " This is not the place for you to start all that . . . Don't. Now who is this person you have brought with you? "

" He is a friend of mine who wants to be your tenant. He is opening his business in a couple of days. Am I right? " he asked, turning to Margayya. With a sheet of paper Margayya fanned off the flies that were alighting on his nose. The man in the shop announced apologetically, " Oh, too many flies here——"

" What have flies to do here? " Margayya asked, unable to restrain his question any more.

The other replied, " They have nothing to interest them here, but behind this shop there is a jaggery godown. There is a gap in the roof through which flies pass up and down. It is a great nuisance, and I have written to the municipality to get the jaggery shop moved somewhere else . . . but you know what our municipalities are! "

" He is himself a municipal councillor for this ward," Dr. Pal added, " and yet he finds so much difficulty in getting anything done. He had such trouble to get that vacant plot for himself——"

" I applied for it like any other citizen. Being a municipal councillor doesn't mean that I should forgo the ordinary rights and privileges of a citizen."

The conversation went on with the sun beating down on their heads, and a feeling of still greater warmth was given by the sight of the heavy dark blankets all round. Margayya felt somewhat irritated that he was being made to stand in the sun all the time. He suddenly told himself, " I am a businessman with all my time fully booked, why should I stand here in the sun and listen to this fellow's irrelevancies? " He told his friend somewhat sharply, " Shall we get on with the business? "

Dr. Pal looked at him surprised for a moment and asked

the blanket merchant, " Will you give the vacant shop to this gentleman? "

" Of course! " the other said. " If you want it . . . Give it to him if you choose." Dr. Pal turned to Margayya and said, " Take it." Margayya was unused to such brisk and straightforward transactions. He had always a notion that to get anything done one had to go in a round-about manner and arrive at the point without the knowledge of the other party. Margayya rose to the occasion and asked, " What is the rent? "

" Seventy-five rupees," said the other briefly.

" Seventy-five! Rather high isn't it? " Margayya asked, hoping against hope there would be a reduction from this stern and businesslike man.

" Yes, if it were any other place . . . but here the spot has market value. You can take it if you like. But if you are looking for a cheaper place——" said the blanket man.

" I shouldn't be here," said Margayya finishing his sentence for him. " I am taking it definitely from to-morrow." It pleased him very much to be able to speak up confidently in this manner. If it had been those horrible past days, he would have collapsed at the knees on hearing the amount of the rent.

Dr. Pal said to the blanket-seller: " This man is one of my oldest friends. I like him very much, you know."

" Yes, I know, I know," said the other. " I could guess so, otherwise you would not have brought him here. Here is the key." He held out a brass key for Dr. Pal to take.

He asked Margayya, " What may be your line of business? "

" Well . . . sort of banking," Margayya said without conviction, fearing at the word bank these people would at once visualize shining counters and all the gaudy ornamentation.

" It'd be more simple to call it money-lending," said the other from within the blankets.

" It is not merely lending," Margayya essayed to explain. " It is not so cheap as that; I also try to help people about money whenever they are in difficulties." Margayya started on his oration. " Money is . . ." He paused and, turning to Dr. Pal, said, " You have not told me your friend's name." It was more to put the other in his place.

" Oh, we call him Gura Raj," Dr. Pal said.

Margayya began his sentence again. " Guru Raj, money is the greatest factor in life and the most ill-used. People don't know how to tend it, how to manure it, how to water it, how to make it grow, and when to pluck its flowers and when to pluck its fruits. What most people now do is to try and eat the plant itself——"

The other roared with laughter. " I say, you seem to be a very great thinker. How well you speak, how well you have understood all these matters! You are indeed a rare man. Where have you been carrying on your business all these days? "

" Mine is the sort of business that searches me out. I didn't have to move out of my house at all. But you see, it gives me no rest with so many people always coming in——"

" You must never allow your business transactions to invade your home, that will simply shatter the home-life," said Guru Raj.

" I have a son studying in high school," said Margayya. He liked the feel of the word. Studying in High School. He felt very proud of Balu for the moment, but at the same time he felt a tinge of pity at heart. He had been too severe with him during the day.

" Oh, if children are studying it will simply ruin their time to have visitors at all hours," the other said.

After more such polite and agreeable talk, he said, " All right, sir, I wish you all success. May God help you. You may please to go now. I cannot offer you a seat in this wretched shop. It is my fate to sit here amidst the flies, and why should I bother you with them too? And it is not proper to make you stand. . . . I will come and listen to your talk in your own shop, some day."

It was midday and all the stalls in the market were dull and drowsy. Fruit-sellers were dozing before their heaps. Some loafers were desultorily hanging about. Stray calves were standing idly near a shop in which green plantain leaves were for sale. A seller of betel leaves held out a bundle saying, "Finest betel leaves, sir, flavoured with camphor," applying the usual epithets that betel-sellers employ for recommending their wares. Pal took some, haggled for a moment, and paid the price. He stuffed the bundle of betel leaves into his pocket. He stopped for a minute at the next stall to buy a yard of strung jasmine. "Excuse me," he said. "These are necessary to keep the peace at home, necessary adjuncts for domestic harmony, you know."

"Oh!" Margayya exclaimed, and decided to ignore any special significance he might have put into the words *Domestic Harmony*.

"You are no longer alone?" Margayya asked.

"No."

"Are you married?"

"No."

"Are you going to be married?"

"Not yet."

Margayya was mystified. "Where is your house? Are you still in that garden?"

"No, no. I had to leave it long ago. Someone bought it, and has been farming on a large scale there. He cleared the place of all the weeds and undergrowth, which included me. But he appeared to be a nice man. I have been so far away and so busy. I have a house, I live in an outhouse in Lawley Extension . . . Someone else is in the main building. You must come to my house some day."

They reached Market Road, and at once Margayya was enchanted. He had always visualized that he would get some such place. The Malgudi gutter ran below his shop with a mild rumble, and not so mild smell. But Margayya either did not notice or did not mind it, being used to it in his own home. Margayya's blood was completely the city man's and revelled in crowds, noise and bustle; the moment he looked out and saw the stream of people and traffic flowing up and down the road, he felt that he was in the right place. A poet would perhaps have felt exasperated by the continuous din, but to Margayya it was like a background music to his own thoughts. There was a row of offices and shops opposite, insurance agencies, local representatives of newspapers, hair-cutting saloons, some film distributors, a lawyer's chamber, and a hardware shop, into which hundreds of people were going every day. Margayya calculated that if he could at least filter twenty out of that number for his own purposes, he would be more than well off. In about a year he could pass on to the grade of people who were wealthy and not merely rich. He drew a lot of distinction between the two. A rich man, according to his view, was just one caste below the man of wealth. Riches any hard-working fool could attain by some watchfulness, while acquiring wealth was an extraordinarily specialized job. It came to persons who had on them the grace of the Goddess fully and who could use their wits. He was a specialist in money and his mind always ran on lines of scientific inquiry whenever money came in question. He differentiated with great subtlety between money, riches, wealth, and fortune. It was most important people should not mistake one for the other.

§

Next to the subject of money, the greatest burden on his mind was his son. As he sat in his shop and spoke to his clients, he forgot for the time being the rest of the world, but the moment he was left alone he started thinking of his son: the boy had failed in his matriculation exam, and that embittered him very much. He wondered what he should do with him now. Whenever he thought of it, his heart sank within him. "God has blessed me with everything under the sun; I need not bother about any-

thing else in life, but ... but. ..." He could not tell people,
"My son is only fifteen and he has already passed into
college." The son had passed that stage two years ago.
Two attempts and yet no good. Margayya had engaged
three home tutors, one for every two subjects, and it cost
him quite a lot in salaries. He arranged to have him fed
specially with nutritive food during his examination
periods. He bought a lot of fruit, and compelled his wife
to prepare special food, always saying, "The poor boy is
preparing for his examination. He must have enough
stamina to stand the strain." He forbade his wife to speak
loudly at home. "Have you no consideration for the young
man who is studying?"

He was in agonies on examination days. He escorted
him up to the examination hall in Albert College. Before
parting from him at the sounding of the bell he always
gave him advice: "Don't get frightened; write calmly and
fearlessly ... and don't come away before it is time," but
all this was worth nothing because the boy had nothing
to write after the first half hour, which he spent in
scrawling fantastic designs on his answer book. He hated
the excitement of an examination and was sullenly resent-
ful of the fact that he was being put through a most
unnecessary torment. He abruptly rose from his seat and
went over to a restaurant near by. His father had left with
him a lot of cash in view of the trying times he was going
through. He ate all the available things in the restaurant,
bought a packet of cigarettes, sought a secluded corner
away from the prying eyes of his elders on the bank of
the river behind the college, sat down and smoked the
entire packet, dozed for a while, and returned home at five
in the evening. The moment he was sighted his mother
asked, "Have you written your examination well?"

He made a wry face and said, "Leave me alone." He
hated to be reminded of the examination. But they would
not let him alone. His mother put before him milk, and
fruit, and the special edibles she had made to sustain him
in his ordeal. He made a wry face and said, "Take it away,

I cannot eat anything." At this she made many sounds of sympathy and said that he must get over the strain by feeding himself properly.

It was at this moment that his father returned home, after closing his office early, and hastening away in a jutka. All day as he counted money, his and other people's, a corner of his mind was busy with the examination. "Oh, God, please enlighten my son's mind so that he may answer and get good marks," he secretly prayed. The moment he saw his son he said, " I am sure you have done very well my boy. How have you done? " The boy sat in a corner of the house with a cheerless look on his face. Margayya put it down to extreme strain, and said soothingly, "You stayed in the hall throughout? " That was for him an indication of his son's performance.

Whatever was the son's reply, he got the correct answer very soon, in less than eight weeks, when the results came out. At first Margayya raved, " Balu has done very well, I know. Someone has been working off a grudge." Then he felt like striking his son, but restrained himself for the son was four inches taller as he stood hanging his head with his back to the wall, and Margayya feared that he might retaliate. So he checked himself; and from a corner the mother watched, silently with resignation and fear, the crisis developing between father and son. She had understood long before that the boy was not interested in his studies and that he attached no value to them, but it was no use telling that to her husband. She pursued what seemed to her the best policy and allowed events to shape themselves. She knew that matters were coming to a conclusion now and she was a helpless witness to a terrific struggle between two positive-minded men, for she no longer had any doubt that the son was a grown-up man. She covered her mouth with her fingers, and with her chin on her palms stood there silently watching.

Margayya said, " Every little idiot has passed his S.S.L.C. exam. Are you such a complete fool? "

" Don't abuse me, father," said the boy, whose voice had

recently become gruff. It had lost, as his mother noticed, much of the original softness. The more she saw him, the more she was reminded of her own father in his younger days; exactly the same features, the same gruffness, and the same severity. People had been afraid to speak to her father even when he was in the sweetest temper, for his face had a severity without any relation to his mood. She saw the same expression on the boy's face now. The boy's look was set and grim. His lips were black with cigarettes which she knew he smoked: he often smelt of them when he came home . . . But she kept this secret knowledge to herself since she didn't like to set up her husband against him. She understood that the best way to attain some peace of mind in life was to maintain silence; ultimately, she found that things resolved themselves in the best manner possible or fizzled out. She found that it was only speech which made existence worse every time. Lately, after he had become affluent, she found that her husband showed excessive emphasis, rightly or wrongly, in all matters; she realized that he had come to believe that whatever he did was always right. She did her best not to contradict him: she felt that he strained himself too much in his profession, and that she ought not to add to his burden. So if he sometimes raved over the mismanagement of the household, she just did not try to tell him that it was otherwise. She served him his food silently, and he himself discovered later what was right and what was wrong and confessed it to her. Now more than in any other matter she practised this principle where their son was concerned. She knew it would be no use telling her husband not to bother the son over his studies, that it would be no use asking him to return home at seven-thirty each day to sit down to his books with his home teachers . . . he simply would not return home before nine. It was no use shouting at him for it. It only made one's throat smart and provided a scene for the people next door to witness. She left it all to resolve itself. Once or twice she attempted to tell the son to be more mindful of his father's wishes and orders, but he told her to shut up. She left him alone. And she left her husband alone. She attained thereby great tranquillity in practical everyday life.

Now she watched the trouble brewing between the two as if it all happened behind a glass screen. The father asked in a tone full of wrath: "How am I to hold up my head in public?" The boy looked up detached, as if it were a problem to be personally solved by the father, in which he was not involved. Margayya shouted again: "How am I to hold up my head in public? What will they think of me? What will they say of my son?"

The boy spoke with a quiet firmness, as if expressing what immediately occurred to the mother herself. She felt at once a great admiration for him. He said in a gruff tone: "How is it their concern?"

Margayya wrung his hands in despair and clenched his teeth. What the boy said seemed to be absolutely correct. "You are no son of mine. I cannot tolerate a son who brings such disgrace on the family."

The boy was pained beyond words. "Don't talk nonsense, father," he said.

Margayya was stupefied. He had no idea that the boy could speak so much. Talking till now was only a one-way business, and he had taken it for granted that the boy could say nothing for himself. He raved: "You are talking back to me, are you mad?"

The boy burst into tears and wailed: "If you don't like me, send me out of the house."

Margayya studied him with surprise. He had always thought of Balu as someone who was spoken to and never one who could speak with the same emphasis as himself. He was offended by the boy's aggressive manner. He was moved by the sight of the tears on his face. He was seized with a confusion of feelings. He found his eyes smarting with tears and felt ashamed of it before his son and before that stony-faced woman who stood at the doorway of the kitchen and relentlessly watched. Her eyes seemed to watch unwaveringly, with a fixed stare. So still was she that Margayya feared lest she should be in a cataleptic state. He now turned his wrath on her. "It's all your doing. You have been too lenient. You have spoilt him beyond redemption. You with your——"

The boy checked his tears and interrupted him. "Mother has not spoilt me, nor anyone else. Why should anyone spoil me?"

"There is too much talk in this house. That's what's wrong here," Margayya declared, and closed the incident by going in to change and attend to his other activities. The boy slunk away, out of sight. In that small house it was impossible to escape from one another, and the boy slipped out of the front door. The mother knew he would return, after his father had slept, bringing into the home the smell of cigarette smoke.

Margayya stayed awake almost all night. When the boy sneaked back after his rounds and pushed the door open, it creaked slightly on its hinges and he at once demanded: "Who is there? Who is there?"

Balu answered midly: "It's me, father."

Margayya was pleased with the softening that now seemed to be evident in his tone, but he wished at the same time that the boy had not disgraced him by failing. He said: "You have been out so long?"

"Yes," came the reply.

"Where?" he asked.

There was no further reply. Margayya felt that failing the Matric. seemed to have conferred a new status on his son, and unloosened his tongue. He felt in all this medley a little pride at the fact that his son had acquired so much independence of thought and assertiveness. He somehow felt like keeping him in conversation and asked, with a slight trace of cajolery in his voice: "Was the door left open without the bolt being drawn?"

"Yes," replied the boy from somewhere in the darkness.

"That's very careless of your mother. Does she do it every day?"

There was once again a pause and silence. His wife

139

seemed to have fallen asleep too, for there was no response from her. He somehow did not wish the conversation to lapse. He said as a stop gap: "What'll happen if a thief gets in?" There was no response from the son. After blinking in the dark for a few minutes, Margayya asked: "Boy, are you asleep?" And the boy answered: "Yes, I am." And Margayya, feeling much more at peace with himself at heart for having spoken to him, fell asleep at once, forgetting for a few hours the Matriculation examination and his other worries.

They got into a sort of live and let live philosophy. He hoped that when the schools reopened he could put the boy back at school, prepare him intensively for his examination, and if necessary see some of the examiners and so on. Margayya had a feeling that he had of late neglected his duties in this direction. He had unqualified faith in contacting people and getting things done that way. He could get at anybody through Dr. Pal. That man had brought into his business a lot of people known to him. Margayya's contacts were now improving socially. People were indebted to him nowadays, and would do anything to retain his favour. Margayya hoped that if he exerted himself even slightly in the coming year he would see his son pull through Matriculation without much difficulty. Of course the boy would have to keep up a show of at least studying the books and would have to write down his number correctly in the answer book and not merely scribble and look out of the door. It was extremely necessary that he should at least write one page of his answer and know what were the subjects he ought to study.

Margayya felt that if he could persuade Balu to make at least a minimum of effort for his own sake, his mind would be easier. He proposed it very gently to him about a fortnight later as they sat down to their dinner together. Margayya showed him extreme consideration nowadays; it was born out of fear and some amount of respect. The boy was always taciturn and grim. He recollected that it seemed ages since he had seen any relaxation in his face.

He had a gravity beyond his years. That frightened Margayya. Except the one instance when he saw tears in his eyes on the day of the results, he had always found him sullen. He hoped to soften him by kindness, or, at least, outward kindness, for he still smarted inside at the results of the examination. He looked for a moment at the face of his son and said: "Balu, you must make another attempt. I'll see that you get through the examination without the least difficulty."

Balu stopped eating and asked: "What do you mean, father?"

Margayya sensed danger, but he had started the subject. He could not stop it now under any circumstances. So he said: "I mean the Matriculation examination."

"I will not read again," said the boy definitely, defiantly. "I have already spoken to mother about it."

"H'm." Margayya turned to his wife, who was serving him, and said: "He has spoken to you, has he? What has he said?"

"Just what he has told you now," she answered promptly, and went back to the fire-place to fetch something.

"Why didn't you tell me about it?" Margayya asked, eagerly looking for some lapse on her part to justify him in letting off steam.

She merely replied: "Because I knew he was going to tell you about it himself."

Margayya burst out at her. "What do you mean by discussing all sorts of things with the boy and not telling me anything? These are matters——"

His son interrupted him: "Father, if you hate me and want to make me miserable, you will bother me with examinations and studies. I hate them."

Margayya went on arguing with him all through the meal till the boy threatened to abandon his dinner and walk out of the dining room. Margayya assumed a sullen silence, but the atmosphere ached with tension. Everyone was aware that the silence was going to be broken in a violent manner next moment, as soon as dinner was over.

141

Father and son seemed to be in a race to finish eating first. Balu gobbled up his food and dashed to the back yard. He poured a little water on his hand, wiped it on a towel near by and moved towards the street door. Margayya jumped up from his seat, with his hand unwashed, dashed to the street door and shut and bolted it. Frustrated, the boy stood still. Margayya asked: " Where are you going? I have still much to tell you. I have not finished speaking yet." The boy withdrew a few steps in response.

Meanwhile his mother had brought in a vessel of water; Margayya snatched a moment to wash his hand in the little open yard. He said, " Wait " to his son. He opened his office box and brought from it the boy's S.S.L.C. Register. He had secured it on the previous day from the headmaster of the school. The S.S.L.C. Register is a small calico-bound note-book with columns marked in it, containing a record of a high-school boy's marks, conduct, handwriting, and physical fitness. Margayya had got the register from the headmaster and studied its pages keenly the whole of the previous day. Matters did not now appear to him so hopeless. The headmaster had marked " Fair " both for his hand-writing and drill attendance. Margayya had no idea that his son could shine in anything. So this was an entirely happy surprise. . . . His marks in almost all subjects were in single digits. The highest mark he had obtained was twelve out of a hundred in hygiene, and he had maintained his place as the last in the class without a variation.

One would have expected Margayya to be shocked by this, but the effect was unexpected. He was a fond and optimistic father, and he fastened on the twelve marks for hygiene. It seemed so high after all the diminutive marks the boy had obtained in other subjects. Margayya hoped that perhaps he was destined to be a doctor, and that was why his inclination was so marked for hygiene. What a wonderful opening seemed to be before him as a doctor! Doctor Balu—it would be very nice indeed. If only he could get through the wretched S.S.L.C. barrier, he'd

achieve great things in life. Margayya would see to it that
he did so; Margayya's money and contacts would be worth
nothing if he could not see his son through . . .

He had prepared himself to speak to Balu about all this
gently and persuasively. He hoped to lead up to the subject with encouraging talk, starting with hygiene, and then
to ask him if he wished to be a doctor. What a glorious
life opened before a doctor! He would send him to England to study surgery. He could tell him all that and
encourage him. Margayya had great faith in his own persuasiveness. He sometimes had before him a tough customer who insisted upon withdrawing all his deposits and
winding up the account: a most truculent client. But
Margayya remembered that if he had about an hour with
him, he could always talk him out of it. The deposit would
remain with him, plus any other money that the man
possessed. . . . Now Margayya wanted to employ his capacity for a similar purpose with his son. That's why he had
come armed with the S.S.L.C. Register. He could read out
to him the headmaster's remarks "Fair", etc., and prove
to him how hopeful everything was if only he would agree
to lend his name and spare time to go through the
formality of an examination in the coming year.

At the sight of the note-book the boy asked: "What is
this? Why have you brought it from school?" as if it
were the most repulsive article he had seen in the whole
of his life. His face went a shade darker. It symbolized
for him all the wrongs that he had suffered in his life: it
was a chronicle of all the insults that had been heaped
upon him by an ungracious world—a world of schools,
studies and examinations. What did they mean by all this
terrible torment invented for young men? It had been an
agony for him every time the headmaster called him up
and made him go through the entries and sign below. Such
moments came near his conception of hell. Hell, in his
view, was a place where a torturing God sat up with your
scholastic record in his hand and lectured you on how to
make good and told you what a disgrace you were to

143

society. His bitterness overwhelmed him suddenly, as his father opened a page and started: "Here is your hygiene——"

The boy made a dash for the book, snatched it from his father's hand before he knew what was happening, tore its entire bulk into four pieces (it had been made of thick ledger paper and only his fury gave him the necessary strength to tear it up at one effort), and ran out into the street and threw the pieces into the gutter. And Vinayak Mudali Street gutter closed on it and carried the bits out of sight. Margayya ran up and stood on the edge of the gutter woefully looking into its dark depth. His wife was behind him. He was too stunned to say anything. When he saw the last shred of it gone, he turned to his wife and said: "They will not admit him in any school again, the last chance gone." And then he turned to tackle his son—but the boy had gone.

§

The only sign of prosperity about him now was the bright handle of the umbrella which was hooked to his right forearm whenever he went out. He was a lover of umbrellas, and the moment he could buy anything that caught his fancy, he spent eight rupees and purchased this bright-handled umbrella with "German ribs", in the parlance of the umbrella dealers. Hitherto he had carried for years an old bamboo one, a podgy thing with discoloured cloth which had been patched up over and over again. He protected it like his life for several years. He had his own technique of holding an umbrella which assured it a long lease of life and kept it free from fractures. He never twisted the handle when he held an umbrella over his head. He never lent it to anyone. Margayya, if he saw anyone going out in the rain in imminent danger of catching and perishing of pneumonia, would let him face his fate rather than offer him the protection of his umbrella. He felt furious when people thought that they could ask for an umbrella. "They will be asking for my skin next," he often commented when his wife found fault with him for his attitude. Another argument he advanced was, "Do people ask for each other's wives? Don't they manage to have one for themselves? Why shouldn't each person in the country buy his own umbrella?" "An umbrella does not like to be handled by more than one person in its lifetime," he often declared, and stuck to it. He had to put away his old umbrella in the loft, carefully rolled up, because its ribs had become too rickety and it could not maintain its shape any longer. It began to look like a shot-down crow with broken wings. Though for years he had not noticed it, suddenly one day when he was working under the tree in the Co-operative Bank compound, some-one remarked that he was looking like a wayside umbrella repairer and that he had better throw it away; he felt piqued and threw it in the loft, but he could never bring himself to the point of buying a new one and had more or less resigned himself to basking in the sun until the time came when he could spend eight rupees without calculating whether he was a loser or a gainer in the bargain. That time had come, now that thousands of rupees were passing through his hands—thousands which belonged to others as well as to him.

Except for this umbrella, he gave no outward sign of his affluence. He hated any perceptible signs of improvement. He walked to his office every day. His coat was of spun silk, but he chose a shade that approximated to the one he had worn for years so that no one might notice the difference. He whitewashed the walls of his house inside only, and built a small room upstairs. He bought no furniture except a canvas deckchair at a second-hand shop. On this he lounged and looked at the sky from his courtyard. He told his wife to buy any clothes she liked, but she was more or less in mourning and made no use of the offer. She merely said, "Tell me about Balu. That is what I need, not clothes."

Margayya replied: "Well, I can only offer you what is available. If you are crying for the moon, I can't help you much there."

"I am asking for my son, not crying for the moon," she said.

She was always on the verge of hysteria nowadays. She spoke very little and ate very little; and Margayya felt that at a time when he had a right to have a happy and bright home, he was being denied the privilege unnecessarily. He felt angry with his wife. He felt that it was her sulking which ruined the atmosphere of the home. They had so much accustomed themselves to the disappearance of their son that he ceased to think of it as a primary cause: the more immediate reasons became perceptible. He tried in his own clumsy manner to make her happy. He told her, "Ask for any money you want."

"What shall I do with money?" she said. "I have no use for it."

He disliked her for making such a statement. It was in the nature of a seditious speech. He merely frowned at her and went on with his business. What was that business? When at home he carried about him the day's financial position finely distilled into a statement, and was absorbed in studying the figures. When he wanted relaxation he bought a paper and went through its pages. Nowadays he did not borrow the paper from the newspaper dealer but subscribed for a copy himself. He read with avidity what was happening in the world: the speeches of statesmen, the ravings of radicals, the programme for this and that, war news, and above all the stocks and shares market. He glanced through all this because a certain amount of world information seemed to be an essential part of his equipment when he sat in his office. All kinds of people came in and it was necessary that he should be able to take part in their conversation. To impress his clients, he had to appear as a man of all round wisdom.

He walked to his work every day soon after his morning meal. The house was in suspense till he was seen safely

146

off. He did not believe in employing servants at home and so his wife had to do all the work. He often said, " Why should we burden ourselves with servants when we are like a couple of newly-weds? Ours is not a very big family." The lady accepted it meekly because she knew it would not be much use arguing it out with Margayya. She knew, as he himself did, that he did not employ a cook because he did not like to spend money on one. But he was sure to give some other reason if he was asked. He would in all probability say, " Where is the need to show off? " She knew that he viewed money as something to accumulate and not to be spent on increasing one's luxuries in life. She knew all his idioms even before he uttered them. Sometimes when he saw her sitting at the fireplace, her eyes shrunken and swollen with the kitchen smoke, he felt uneasy and tried to help her with the kitchen work, keeping up the pretence of being newly-weds. He picked up a knife here and a green vegetable there, cut it up in a desultory manner, and vaguely asked, " Is there anything I can do? " She hardly ever answered such a question. She merely said, " Please come in half an hour, and I will serve you your meal." She had become very sullen and reserved nowadays.

She brooded over her son Balu night and day. She lost the taste for food. Margayya behaved wildly whenever he was reminded of their son. " He is not my son," he declared dramatically. " A boy who has an utter disregard for his father's feelings is no son. He is a curse that the Gods have sent down for us. He is not my son." It all sounded very theatrical, but the feeling was also very real. When he remembered the floating bits of calico in the street gutter, he felt sorry that his son was no longer there to be slapped. His fingers itched to strike him. He reflected : " If he had at least disappeared after receiving the slap I aimed, I would not have minded much." He discouraged his wife from mentioning their son again and had grandly ordered that the household must run on as if he had not been born. When he spoke in that tone his wife fully understood that he meant it. His affluence, his bank balance, buoyed him up and made him bear the loss of their son. He lived in a sort of radiance which made it possible for him to put up with anything. When he sat at his desk from early in the day till sunset, he had to talk, counsel, wheedle out, and collect money; in fact go through all the adventures of money-making. At the end of the day as he walked back home his mind was full of the final results, and so there was practically no time for him to brood over Balu.

Late at night when the voices of the city had died down and when the expected sleep came a little late, he speculated on Balu. Perhaps he had drowned himself. There was no news of him, although several days and weeks had passed. His wife accused him at first of being very callous and not doing anything about it. He did not know what was expected of him. He could not go and tell the police. He could not announce a reward for anyone who traced him. He could not. . . . He hated to make a scene about it, and solved the whole thing by confiding in Dr. Pal. Dr. Pal had promised to keep an eye on the matter and tell him if anything turned up. No one could do more than that. Margayya had generally given out that his son had gone on a holiday to Bombay or Madras, and lightly added: "Young boys of his age must certainly go out by themselves and see a bit of the world: I think that's the best education."

"But boys must have a minimum of S.S.L.C.," someone remarked.

Margayya dismissed it as a foolish notion. "What is there in Matriculation? People can learn nothing in schools. I have no faith in our education. Who wants all this nonsense about A squared plus B squared. If a boy does not learn these, so much the better. To be frank, I have got on without learning the A squared and B squared business, and what is wrong with me? Boys must learn things in the rough school of life." Whatever he said sounded authoritative and mature nowadays, and people listened to him with respectful attention. These perorations he delivered as he sat in his office.

§

His office consisted of a medium-sized room with four mattresses spread out on the floor. At the other end of it there was a sloping desk where an accountant sat. He was a lean old man, with a fifteen-day-old silver beard encircling his face at any given time. He was a pensioner, a retired revenue clerk, who wore a close coat and a turban when he came to the office. He was expected to arrive before Margayya. It pleased Margayya very much to see him at his seat, bent over his ledgers. He was instructed not to look up and salute when Margayya came in since it was likely to disturb his calculations and waste his time. Margayya said: "I do not want all this formality of a greeting. I see you every day. If you want to please me, do your work, and get on with it without wasting your time." But when he felt he needed an audience for his perorations he addressed him, and any other clerks who might be there.

§

Margayya sat in one corner of the hall. He had a desk before him made of smooth polished wood which he had bought from the blanket merchant at a second-hand price. Margayya loved to gaze on its smooth, rippled grains— remnants of gorgeous designs that it had acquired as a tree-trunk—hieroglyphics containing the history of the tree. Whenever he gazed on it, he felt as if he were looking at a sea and a sky in some dream world. "But what is the use of gazing on these and day-dreaming?" he told himself, sharply pulling his mind back. He lifted the lid and gazed inside, and there was the reality which he could touch and calculate and increase: a well-bound half-leather ledger, a bottle of red ink, a bottle of black ink, an oblong piece of blotting-paper, and a pen—the red holder of which his fingers had gripped for years now. And beside it was a small bag made of thick drill, into which went all the cash he collected. His clerk did not know what he collected each day. He did not look into the account book which Margayya kept, nor did he count the cash. It was all done by Margayya himself. He did not believe that it was necessary for anyone to share his knowledge of his finances; it was nobody's business but his own. The work that he gave the accountant was copying down the mort-gages that were left with him by the villagers who came round for financial assistance. He not only kept the deeds, but put the old man to the task of copying them down entirely in a big ledger. He alone could say why he wanted this done, but he would not open his mouth about it to anyone. The old man was being paid fifty rupees a month, and he was afraid of being thrown out if he questioned too much. He just did his duty. At about two o'clock Margayya locked his safe box and got up saying, " I'm going out for tiffin—will be back in a minute. Look after the office, and keep anyone who may come here till I return."

Margayya was always used to having a semi-circle of persons sitting before him as in the old days and never interrupted his studies or calculations to look at them or receive their greetings. He was a very busy man whose hours were valuable: as the day progressed it was a race with time, for he had to close his books before sunset.

The owner of the house, the blanket dealer, did not like to waste money on installing electric light. He went on dodging his tenant's appeals day after day. His excuse was that materials were not available in the quantities he needed or at prices he was prepared to pay. He went on say-ing that he had sent a direct order to the General Electric in America, that he had business associates of his blanket-contract days who would supply his wants direct, and that he was looking for a reply with every sailing; and thus he kept his tenants in hope. The plain fact seemed to be that he did not like to waste money. He confided to his friends: "Why should anyone keep his shop or office open after six o'clock? Let him work and earn during the day: that is quite enough. I hear that they are going to introduce a law limiting working hours, when it will be a grave penalty to keep shops or offices open after sunset." The result was that the shops remained without light, and since Margayya did not believe in spending his own money on an oil lamp, he had to rush through his day's work and close the accounts before darkness fell. He worked without wasting a minute.

One or two of his clients, who had waited long enough to catch his attention, cleared their throats and made other small sounds. Margayya suddenly looked up from his desk and told one of them, "Go there," pointing at his accountant, sitting at the other end of the hall: "He will give you the deed back." The other showed no sign of moving, at which he said sharply, "You heard me? If I have got to speak each sentence twice, I shall have to live for two hundred years and be satisfied with a quarter of my present earnings."

"Why do you say such harsh things, master?" the other asked. "Is it because I am asking for my deed back? Is it wrong?"

"It is not wrong. Why should anyone refuse to give a title deed that is yours by right?" He said it in such a tone that the other hesitated and said, "You have been as a father to me in my difficulties and you have helped me as much as you could."

"And yet you have not the grace to trust me with your title. Do you think I am going to make a broth of it and drink it?"

The client rose and said, "I will come again for it tomorrow, sir, just to show that I am in no hurry." He rose and walked out.

Margayya said to the others, "You see that fellow . . .

the ingratitude of some of these folk sometimes makes me want to throw up everything and . . ." The others made sympathetic sounds just to please him. His accountant added from his corner his own comment in his hollow, hungry voice:

" He is afraid he may have further interest to pay if he leaves his papers here. . . . I know these people: they are docile and lamb-like as long as they hold our money, but the moment they return the principal and interest——"

Margayya did not like this: " Don't disturb yourself, Sastri, go on with your work." He hated the hungry, tired tone of his accountant.

" I was only giving you a piece of observation . . . it is getting to be a nuisance, some of these fellows demanding their papers back at short notice," Sastri persisted. At this Margayya realized that it would not be feasible to put his accountant down so easily, and cut him short with, " True, true . . . We must include a condition that they must give us at least three days for returning their papers."

A visitor who felt that he had waited too long asked, " Margayya, don't you recognize me? "

" No," replied Margayya promptly.

" I am Kanda," he said.

" Which? "

" Of Somanur——"

" No, you are not," replied Margayya promptly.

The other laughed, leaned forward almost over the desk, and asked, " Do you still say that I am not Kanda, master? "

Margayya scrutinized him closely and cried, " You old thief, it is you, yes! What has come over you? You look like a man a hundred years old. . . . Why those wrinkles round your nose? Why those folds at the chin and that silver filing all over your face? What is the matter with you and where are your teeth gone? " The other just raised his arms heavenward, lifted up his eyes as much as to say, " Go and put that question to the heavens if you like." Now Margayya wanted to clear his hall of all his visitors.

He felt that here was the man he would like to talk to the whole day. He looked at the others, gave a paper back to someone, and said, " I cannot advance you on this——"

" Sir, please . . ." he began.

" Come tomorrow, we will see. Now leave me, I have many important things to talk over with old Kanda."

He had lost sight of Kanda years ago. Margayya had been very fond of this man, who always said that he preferred fluid cash to stagnant land and that it was more profitable to grow money out of land than corn. Kanda had now come to ask Margayya's advice on how best to get money out of some new lands which had unexpectedly come to him through the death of a relative. These lands were in the region of Mempi, whose slopes were covered with teak and other forests, and at whose feet stretched acres and acres of maize fields, with stalks standing over a man's height. Margayya was carried away by visions of this paradise of blue mountains, forest, and green fields. It was wealth at the very source and not second-hand after it had travelled up to town. The more he listened to Kanda's petition the more he felt that here was raw wealth inviting him to take a hand and help himself. Though it had grown nearly dark, he sat and listened to Kanda as he narrated to him his financial ups and downs.

" I am glad you have come back to me, Kanda. I will pull you out of your difficulties," he said as he rose to go.

Kanda explained, " I cannot get any more loans from the Co-operative Bank; they have expelled me for default, although they auctioned the pledges . . ."

" The crooks," Margayya muttered. " They are crooks, I tell you. I do not know why the government tolerate this institution. . . . They should put in jail all the secretaries of co-operative societies." The picture of the secretary and Arul came back to him with all the old force. Margayya warned him, " Don't go near them again; they will see you ruined before they have done with you. I will look after you," he added protectively, starting to lock up his door. He had sent away his accountant, and with a duplicate key he locked the door of his office. He generously indicated to Kanda the verandah. " Sleep here, Kanda, no one will object. I will see you tomorrow morning and then we will go and inspect your property at Mempi. What time is your bus? "

" The first bus leaves the Market Square at six o'clock."

" The next? "

" It is at eight-thirty. . . . Four buses pass Mempi village every day," he said with a touch of pride.

" So that you may come oftener into town and borrow, I suppose! "

" There is also a railway station, about five or six stones off," Kanda said. " From here you can get the evening train and be down there at about twelve o'clock."

" And get eaten by tigers, I suppose," Margayya added, " before reaching home."

Kanda laughed at this piece of ignorance. " Tigers are in the hills and generally do not come down."

" Even then I prefer to come with you by the morning bus," Margayya said. " We will go by the second bus tomorrow. You can have your food in that hotel there."

Margayya walked home. At his house he found a commotion. His wife's voice could be heard wailing, and a large crowd had gathered at his front door. He quickened his pace on seeing it.

" What is the matter? " he asked someone near by. He hoped the people were not rushing in, in order to loot the house. He had kept a few important documents in the front room and a lot of cash. " Must remove it elsewhere," he thought as he pushed his way through the crowd on the front steps. " Get out of the way," he thundered. " What are you all doing here? " Someone in the crowd said, " Your lady is weeping——"

" I see that. Why? "

They hesitated to speak. He gripped one nearby by his shirt collar and demanded, " What has happened? Can't you speak? " He shook him vigorously till he protested, " Why do you trouble me, Margayya? I won't speak."

Margayya let him go and went in. He saw his wife rolling on the floor and wailing, in a voice he had never heard before. He never knew that she had such a high-pitched voice. There were a number of women sitting round her and holding her.

Margayya rushed towards them crying, "What has happened to her? Meenakshi, what is the matter with you?" She sat up on hearing his voice. Her hair was untied. Her eyes were swollen. She wailed, "Balu . . . Balu . . ." Her voice trailed off and she broke down again. She fell on the floor and rolled in anguish. Margayya felt helpless. He saw his brother and his wife also in the crowd. He knew something must be seriously the matter if these two were there, and their many children sucking their thumbs. His brother's wife was sitting beside Margayya's wife and trying to comfort her. Margayya rushed up and pleaded: "Won't someone tell me what has happened?" His brother pushed his way through the crowd and handed him a card. Margayya's eyes were blurred with the mist of perspiration. His excitement had set his heart racing. He rubbed his eyes and gazed on the card. He couldn't read it. He groaned, and fumbled for his glasses. . . . He could not pull them out of his pocket easily. He gave the card to the one nearest him and cried: "Can't someone read it? Is it an illiterate gathering? What are you all watching for?" And then some person obliged him by reading out: "Your son . . . B . . . Balu . . . is no more——"

"What! What! . . . Who says so?" Margayya cried, losing all control over himself. More perspiration streamed down his eyelids and he wept aloud: "My son! . . . my son! Am I dreaming?" The assembly watched him in grim silence.

His wife was sobbing. She suddenly shot towards Margayya and cried: "It's all your doing. You ruined him."

Margayya was taken aback. There was a confused mixture of emotions now. He did not know what to say. One side of his mind went on piecing together his son's picture as he had last seen him.

"Did I treat him too harshly over the examination results? Or have I been too thoughtless over that cursed school-record——?" He felt angry at the thought of examinations: they were a curse on the youth of the nation, the very greatest menace that the British had brought with them to India. . . . If he could see his son now he would tell him, "Forget all about schools and books: you just do as you like, just be seen about the house—that's sufficient for us." In this din, his wife's accusation reached him but faintly. He retorted: "What are you saying, you poor creature! What are you trying to say?"

"You and your schools!" she arraigned him. "But for your obsession and tyranny——"

"You keep quiet," he said angrily. He turned round to someone and enquired: "Do you know how it happened?"

Several voices chorused: "He fell off a fourth floor of a building in Madras," "He must have been run over in that city," "Probably caught cholera," "We don't know——"

"Who was with him?" asked Magayya. He conducted a ruthless cross-examination.

"How can we know—the card is signed by a friend."

"Friend! Friend!" Margayya cried. "What sort of friend is it? Friend, useless blackguard!" He did not know what he was saying. Nor could he check the rush of his words. He babbled as if under the influence of a drug. He saw the whole house reeling in front of his eyes—the surroundings darkened and he sat down unable to bear the strain. He sat on the floor, with his head between his hands, quietly sobbing. His brother sidled up, put his arm round him, and said: "You must bear it, brother; you must bear it."

"What else can I do?" Margayya asked like a child. He still had on his coat and turban. Through all his grief a ridiculous question (addressed to his brother) kept coming to his mind: "Are we friends now—no longer enemies? What about our feud?" A part of his mind kept wondering how they could live as friends, but the numerous problems connected with this seemed insoluble. "We had got used to this kind of life. Now I suppose we shall have to visit each other and enquire and so on . . ." All that seemed to be impossible to do. He wished to tell him then and there: "Don't let this become an excuse to change our present relationship."

Margayya did his best to suppress all these thoughts, but they kept bothering him till he could say nothing, till he was afraid to open his lips lest he should blurt them out. His brother whispered among other things: "We will send you the night meal from our house."

"No, we don't want any food tonight," Margayya said. "Please send all those people away." He was indignant. Because Balu was dead, why should this crowd imagine that the house was theirs? "Shut and bolt the door," he thundered.

His brother left him, went up to the strangers about the house and appealed to them to leave. He said, with his palms pressed together in deference: "Please leave us. This is the time when the family has to be together."

"No," Margayya thundered with deadly irony in his tone. "How can they leave? How can they afford to ignore all this fun and go? If an entrance be charged——" he began, then stopped, for in his condition he realized that he ought not to complete his sentence, which ran: "We might earn lakhs——" He did not think it was a good statement to make. So he merely said: "Oh, friends and neighbours, the greatest service you could do us is to leave us alone." The neighbours grumbled a little and started moving out. On the fringe of the crowd someone was muttering: "When are they bringing the body?"

Margayya never knew till now that he had so many well-wishers in the city. The next day they proposed to bundle him off to Madras. He seemed to have no choice in the matter. All sorts of persons, including his brother, sat around and said: "It's best that you go to Madras—at least once, and verify things for yourself?"

"What for?" asked Margayya. The others seemed to

be horrified at this question, and looked at him as if to say: " Fancy anyone asking such a silly question! "

" I can't go, I won't go, it is not necessary," Margayya said offensively.

His wife had been transformed. She looked like a stranger, with her face swollen and disfigured with weeping. She glared at him and said: " Have you no heart? "

" Yes, undoubtedly," Margayya said in a mollifying manner. He felt that she had lost her wits completely and required to be handled with tact.

" If you have ordinary human feelings then go and do something . . . at least . . . at least——"

" Yes, I understand. . . . But it's all over."

His brother said: " Is this the time to argue about it all? You must go and do something."

His sister-in-law added her own voice: " It's your duty to go and find out more about it. Perhaps, there is still some chance of——"

" But," wailed Margayya, " where am I to go? Madras is a big world—where on earth am I to go there? " He despairingly turned the post-card between his fingers: " There is no address here, nothing is said of where they have written from, nor who has written it."

" Never mind," they all said with one voice. Margayya felt now, more than ever, most unhappy to have been the father of Balu. The duties of a father seemed to be unshakable. He made yet another attempt to make others see reason: " Look here, if I go to Madras, where am I to go as soon as I get down at the railway station? "

" Is this the time to go into all that? " they asked, looking on him as if he were a curious specimen. This encounter left him no time to brood over his own sorrow. There seemed to be so many demands upon him, following the catastrophe, that it was as much as he could do to keep himself parrying all the blows; it left him no time to think of anything else. When there was a pause and his eyes fell upon a little object, the lacquer-painted wooden elephant that Balu had played with as a child, it sent a sharp stab down his heart; it made him wince, he choked at the throat, and the tears came down in a rush, involuntarily—but he was spared more of that experience by the people around him. He almost regretted that his brother and his family were now back in the fold: they seemed to think up a new proposition for him every minute . . . and his wife, who seemed to be already crazed, apparently fell in with every one of their proposals. One moment they kept saying that he must at once make arrangements to get through the ten-day obsequies for the peace of the departed soul and start right away the performance of those rites; the next, they immediately said that he must go to Madras and try and do what he could.

"You want me to buy a train ticket this moment, and in the same breath ask me to send for the *purohit*——"

At the mention of the word *purohit*, his wife clapped her hands over her ears and wailed afresh: "I never hoped in my worst dreams to hear that word applied to my darling——"

"How can you be so callous as to utter that word so bluntly?" asked his sister-in-law, and another lady scowled at him.

He felt irritated, but practised gentle ways with a deliberate effort, fearing lest anything that he might say should once again bring a rupture between the families and continue it for another decade. He contented himself by saying under his breath: "I don't seem to know what to say now—all the wrong things seem to come uppermost." They did not encourage him to go on with even that reflection, but said, "Do something; don't sit there and chat. This is no time for it."

His brother added: "If you are afraid to go to Madras alone, I will go with you. I know one or two people there."

"Here is this man," Margayya at once reflected, "wangling a free journey to Madras." And the prospect of his brother's constant company for so many days appalled him. Lest the women folk and others should follow up the idea, he hastily said : "Don't worry, I will go myself. I don't want anyone to think that I am reluctant to go."

He suddenly saw it as a beautiful opportunity to escape. His grief was unbearable no doubt, but the atmosphere and the people about him made it worse. He saw himself being entangled with these folk for the rest of his life: that seemed to suit his wife, but he liked to be more independent. His house seemed to have lost all privacy. For the rest of their existence these people perhaps intended to sit around and wail over Balu. At the echo of the word 'Balu' in his mind he let a loud cry escape his lips and he beat his brow. It occurred almost involuntarily, and at once brought his brother and a cousin to his side: "No, no, not that way. If you break down and lose all control, what is to happen to the others? You must be in a position to give them strength and——"

"How? How can I?" sobbed Margayya, moved by their sympathy. "I prayed for him, and promised the Gods his weight in silver rupees if he should be born."

"Did you fulfil that promise?" someone asked, going off at a tangent. "For that is a sacred pledge, you know."

Margayya's wife answered: "Yes, it was done within an hour of his birth."

"Yes, these vows must be fulfilled within the shortest time possible. Otherwise the baby will acquire weight. How much did the child weigh?"

"About three hundred rupees weight at birth. We tramped to Tirupathi," said Margayya, recollecting his pilgrimage with his young wife so many years ago. She had worn a saffron-dyed saree, had carried the infant on her arms and walked behind him, as he went to ten houses and begged for alms. His pride would not let him beg, but it was once again his elder brother who bothered him by explaining: "The God at Thirupathi does not like anyone to visit him as a holiday-maker, just for fun. He wants you to go there as a humble supplicant, in the attitude of a beggar." He had put into it all the weight of scholarship that he had acquired. "That's the symbol.

That's why you are obliged to visit at least ten houses with a begging bowl, stand and cry at the door for alms, and then go on the pilgrimage, on foot if possible. The God does not notice a person who goes to him in a holiday mood."

And Margayya had clutched a brightly-polished pot and, followed by his saffron-clad wife, had gone from door to door: "Give me alms——" People had come out of their houses and dropped a handful of rice into his copper pot.

He suddenly recollected now how amused he had felt when he saw his face in that burnished pot—its convex surface distorted his nose and cheeks; it was so grotesque that he could not help grinning at his reflection, which made it so much more funny that it became impossible for him to maintain the gravity needed for the occasion. He remembered that one or two people had felt scandalized by the way he grinned when they came out to give him alms. His wife had pulled him up, but he held the shining pot to her face and she too burst into a laugh. He remembered how at that time he wished he could also amuse the infant. He remembered how he carried the alms and the sovereigns equal to the weight of the child to the Thirupathi Hills and deposited them all in the treasure box in the shrine . . . He felt he had done a good job, and it had been an enchanting pilgrimage. He sighed and groaned at the memory of his son. Through it all he remembered how he had not been a day too soon in weighing the youngster in silver as he showed a tendency to grow heavier each day.

"That vow was fulfilled all right. Nothing wrong there," he said suddenly.

§

He sat in a third class compartment in the train to Madras. He had become extremely unhappy when leaving home. He told his brother, "Keep an eye on this house,

will you?" He had told his wife, "Don't ruin yourself
with crying. I will go to Madras and do what I can." It
had sounded most futile—what could he do at Madras?
Where could he go at Madras? It was all a very confused
business. He felt unhappy that he was not even in a position to utter a promise. He bundled up a couple of shirts
and dhoties into a small jute bag which had no clamp. It
was to serve as a pillow for him at night. He had not
travelled for years now, and he found it exciting. He wondered how he could leave his office. What was to happen
to the business? Suppose somebody did something and
killed his business? He wished he didn't have to leave at
short notice. He wished he had had a little more time to
arrange his affairs and then leave. But death gives no
notice. They were bundling him about: and finally they
thrust him and his bag into a jutka and sent him down to
meet the six o'clock train to Madras coming from Trichy.

He asked at the ticket window: "Will you please give
me a ticket?"

"What class?" he was asked.

"Class! I am not travelling in a saloon. If there is a
fourth class——" Margayya pushed in his money for a
third class ticket.

There was such a crowd that he had to push himself in
through a window—not an easy task considering the
paunch that he was developing as a properous man. The
compartment was no more than normally crowded in a
railway system which issued tickets "till the fingers
ached". It was a compartment meant to seat twelve—a
conception in an ideal world. Perhaps it technically satisfied the rule—because those who could technically be said
to be seated were twelve. The rest kept themselves in it, in
all manner of ways, with their bundles heaped about.
People sat on each other's laps, hung by each other's necks,
curled themselves on luggage racks overhead, spread their
beds and stretched themselves comfortably in the space
under the seats. One of them was explaining: "This is
the best way of travelling. I have always thought this

better than even the first class. I always come two hours before and spread my bed."

Margayya had extreme difficulty in hanging his legs down because quite a lot of people seemed to be sleeping there, and he could not cross his legs because he had managed to secure only half a seat, and had to dispose of the rest of himself somehow in mid-air. Seeing the manner in which the others had disposed themselves, he felt triumphant that he had at least got this seat—and he congratulated himself on his pluck. The moment he had shot in through the window, the impact of his arrival displaced someone who was already seated. Margayya just let himself down there before the other could recover. He was a villager.

When he did recover he cried: " Get out of my seat! "

"Why don't you learn better manners? " Margayya said in his habitual masterful way with villagers.

" I have been sitting here from Trichinopoly," the other began.

" Well, you must be tired of sitting—a change will do you good," replied Margayya.

The others enjoyed the joke and laughed. Thick tobacco smoke hung in the air. Someone had even opened the lavatory door and forgotten to close it. Margayya cried: " Why does not someone pull to that door? " Everyone agreed with him that it must be done, but no one was prepared to risk leaving his place to do it—and the man nearest the door did not care to put out his arm for the purpose. The train, clattering and jingling, went its way, stopping at every station, where more people tried to force their way in through windows and doors, but those inside formed themselves into a class and were unanimous in keeping them out. At about two o'clock the fever in the compartment seemed to subside: people slept and wriggled in the positions in which they found themselves, and snored. Margayya found a peculiar peace in these crazy circumstances. He had found a place for his neck, though not for the little bundle in his hand, which he closely hugged to his bosom. He was amused to see a seller of glass bangles, sitting right in the middle of the carriage with all his fragile merchandise tied up in a huge cloth bundle by his side, who kept warning everyone: "Be careful, sirs, don't knock on this——" And people were very considerate. There was a little girl who was looking wistfully at the bangles through her half-sleepy eyes. Margayya felt drawn to this man and found out that he was going to a fair at a wayside station on the following day. "The day after tomorrow you will see me return this way without my bundle," he said. "But your purse fully loaded, I suppose," said Margayya. He liked the man as a prospective bearer of money. He suddenly felt that he had kept away too long from the thought of money. It was like a tobacco chewer suddenly realizing that he had been away too long from his pouch. Margayya took a pinch of snuff; at the sight of it a police officer sitting next him held out his fingers and Margayya passed him the box. The officer took a deep pinch, felt grateful and became communicative: "Things are not quite good, yet, you know."

"Yes, yes, of course," replied Margayya; thinking it best to be agreeable with a policeman in plain clothes.

"All kinds of bothers," he said. "People will not leave us in peace——"

Margayya looked about cautiously and said: "Can't you put them in their places?"

"Yes," said the policeman. "That's what keeps me on the move like this. My home is in Madras, but I don't get even a couple of hours a month to spend with my family. I have to be on the move constantly—well, they think I have a nose for . . . for . . . wrong-doers, political, criminal, or whatever——"

"Well, it's a dangerous job, I suppose," Margayya said opening his eyes wide.

The policeman adjusted himself in his seat more comfortably and said : "Well, it all depends how we view it. I have been in it for twenty years and have survived."

"Well, one must do one's duty," said Margayya, generalizing. "As they say in Bhagavad-Gita, God helps those who do their duty."

The other leaned forward and said: "Do you know I had to carry a notice of arrest even to Mahatma Gandhi once? I would rather have prostrated before that man, but I had to arrest him. Such is life!" he philosophized vaguely, sleepily. Margayya noticed his sleepiness and said, "But they ought to give you a second class pass at least."

This tickled the policeman considerably. "I can travel first, if I like, nobody will question me. I am really an officer, you know. But what will be the use? I'm not travelling in order to sleep comfortably—that's why I travel third: my catches are almost all in a third class carriage. Sometimes I have to follow political suspects, sometimes brigands, sometimes murderers—all kinds of things: they can assign me any job—but it is always necessary for me to keep wide awake and stay in a crowd."

The others in the compartment had gone to sleep. Only these two were awake. Margayya confided to him his troubles. "I don't know where to go in Madras, or even what to do."

"Have you got the card with you?" asked the policeman.

Margayya took it out of his pocket. The policeman examined it by the dim, insect-ridden light of the compartment. Looking carefully at the post-mark he said: "It's from Park Town."

Margayya asked: "Where is that?"

The inspector ignored his question, and said, "This hand-writing must be analysed." He turned the card and said: "How long will you stay in Madras?"

"I don't know," Margayya said pathetically, refraining from adding: "They have pushed me out on this journey. I don't know where I'm going: I would not even know Madras when I arrived there."

The police officer took charge of Margayya as soon as they arrived in Madras Egmore Station. He took him to the waiting room and said: "Make yourself at home. There is the platform restaurant. You can rest as much as you like. I will be back. Give me that post-card." He spoke to a platform official about Margayya.

Margayya began to doubt how far he ought to trust the man. Perhaps he would throw him in jail or perhaps he was a brigand himself. He was gradually changing his mind about wanting the man's help. In the cold morning light of Madras, things seemed different and more reassuring; there was a certain hopelessness in the dim-lit compartment, which made him want to confide in someone and enlist his sympathy. But now it all seemed different. He reflected: "Why not run away from here?" Suppose he opened the door on the off-side and cleared out? But the police officer gave him no chance. He said, taking him by the sleeve: "Don't move out of here till I come back. I will see what I can do for you."

"Oh, no, I wouldn't bother you," said Margayya, trying to withdraw. The other paid no heed, but just turned round and went away. "Why should anyone be so considerate to a stranger," Margayya's devious mind kept ringing, "particularly in this city, which is notoriously cold-blooded?"

After food, Margayya stretched himself on a bedstead in the waiting room and slept soundly. He snored so loudly that the people moving about the platform stopped and looked in. Margayya dreamt that he had got down at Mempi, and someone whom he could not recognize pointed up to the sun-lit horizon, and said, "All that is yours." Margayya was struggling to work up the interest rate on this proposition and was involved in a terrible quantity of figures, when the police officer came in again and woke him up. Margayya felt very apologetic for having fallen asleep. He said clumsily, "You see . . . I am sorry——"

"There is nothing to apologize about," said the Inspector. "Well, if you like to have a wash, let us go out."

Margayya got up and went round with him in search of a tap. The Madras heat seemed to prick him in a dozen places. He felt better after he emerged from under the tap. He went back to his room dripping, tidied himself up, and put on a long coat and turban. In the heat of Madras, it was like getting into steel armour and helmet.

The Inspector said: "Well, I have good news for you." He returned the post-card to Margayya and said: "I have spent the whole day tracing the author of that postcard. It's a falsehood he has written." Margayya's mind was still clouded with sleep and calculations of interest. He looked dull and uncomprehending. The Inspector held out his hand for a pinch of snuff. "Give me your snuff. It's very good . . . and I will tell you what you should do. You go back to your wife at once and tell her that your son is alive."

"How do you know?" Margayya asked, still dazed.

"Because we've managed to trace it back to the author. He is a madman in Park Town who keeps writing messages like that to any address that he picks up."

"How did he pick up my address?"

"Well, that's what we shall investigate, if you will stay for another day," said the Inspector.

§

The Inspector took him along to a house in Park Town. It was a very big house in a lane, occupying the space of three or four blocks together. Its outside was painted green and red in alternating strips with oil distemper. Its front verandah was enclosed by iron rods painted yellow: the whole scheme made the house look like a crayon box with its lid open. Over it all was hung a board painted "The House of Enlightenment". It was a hot, dusty afternoon, and the taxi had run through several winding lanes. Seeing so much gaudy colour made Margayya's throat parched and thirsty; it also made him feel homesick. Before the car came to a halt the Inspector said: " I was able to trace this man through the post office. Don't be surprised by anything you may see or hear, we are going out to meet a madman, remember. He is a very wealthy man, gone mad. He owns a theatre, and his relations are managing it."

They got down. He knocked on the door. An attendant opened the door and showed the way. They went through several pillared halls. The pillars were of smooth granite, and the floors mosaic-covered. Potted ferns were kept here and there. Some parrots and miscellaneous birds were twittering in the cages hanging down from the ceiling. The house was so deep inside that the noises of the city came in from far off, completely muffled. The place was cool and shady. All along the walls of the corridors and passages and halls there were pictures of Gods in terrible shape and fury destroying the world. Margayya felt he was in an utterly strange world. The world of Vinayak Mudali Street, of his wife and brother, and Market Road, and banking, seemed to be distant and unreal. . . . The Inspector whispered to him: "Don't you feel that you are in a zoo? "

"Yes, yes," said Margayya, just to please him, although he did not know what it looked like inside a zoo. They were now in a large hall where a man sat on a divan, sur-rounded by cushions. He wore an ochre robe and had grown a beard. From two tall incense holders smoke was curling. The man had about him a heap of post-cards, a pen and a writing pad. He was writing furiously when they entered. He had an attendant fanning him, although there was an electric fan above. There were two seat-cushions along the wall. The man took no notice of the arrival of the visitors. The inspector whispered to Mar-gayya: "Take your seat there." They sat on the cushions and waited. The attendant bent over and whispered into the ear of the big man. He put away the pen, leaned back and looked at the inspector. The inspector salaamed. The other's face relaxed a little, and a smile hovered about it; but the next moment it became rigid again as he said:

" Who is that mortal next to you who does not seem to recognize us? Is it likely that we are invisible to his eyes? "

" Yes, that's so," said the Inspector. " That's the correct explanation."

" Oh, it never occurred to me. I can make myself seen. We often forget that we divine creatures are transparent, and that we cannot be seen."

" But it is easily remedied, if your holiness makes up his mind." The other shook his head in approval, then waved his arm, looked at Margayya, and asked: " Do you see me? "

The Inspector muttered: " Salute him."

" Yes," replied Margayya with a reverential salaam.

" Now, what is your business, mortal? "

The Inspector said: " He has come after his son Balu, about whom a card has emanated from here." He held up the card. " He wants to know in which world to look for him."

The other shook his head and said: " That I am not allowed to say. That only God can do. I am not God, but only God's agent. He ordered, ' Go and prepare the world for my coming '. That I am doing. I write every day to every King, Ruler, Viceroy, President and Minister in the world, that their boss is soon arriving, and let them get ready for it. Every day I write to President Roosevelt, Stalin, and Churchill, particularly." He indicated a big file of letters waiting to be posted.

The Inspector said: " That's fine—but we want to know the whereabouts of Balu. He is not a Maharaja or anything like that and it is enough for us to know in which world he is to be found. Will you please look up the necessary reference? "

" Is this his earthly father? "

" Yes," said the Inspector.

" Does he believe in Death? "

" He does not," replied the Inspector.

" I am very pleased about it. It's my mission in life to inform at least ten mortals about Death each day and educate them. People must learn to view death calmly."

"Of course, of course," said the Inspector and added: "Please look into your file."

The other took out a ponderous file, turned over its leaves, muttering "Balu . . . Balu . . . Son of . . . Malgudi . . ." Margayya could hardly believe his ears. He cried involuntarily: "How did you get my address?" The Inspector suppressed him with a gesture and said: "Where did you pick up this mortal's address?"

"How do I pick up George VI's address or Mahatma Gandhi's address?" he answered back. "Whenever anyone comes to me for charity, I will not give them an anna unless they give me their true address. Whenever anyone comes to me for employment in any of my businesses, I won't take him in unless he gives me his true address."

"How do you know it is his true address?"

"By writing a card to that address," the other said triumphantly. "You must not forget that there is God above me."

"Did this boy come to you for employment?"

"Didn't he?"

"Or for charity?"

"I don't believe in charity. Whenever anyone comes to me for charity, I give them employment."

"But when they come to you for employment——?"

"I give them charity," the other said.

"Where is this Balu?" persisted the Inspector.

"You may persist for a million years, but you will not get a reply unless God sanctions an answer."

"Hasn't he sanctioned it?" asked the Inspector.

"No," replied the madman.

"In that case we are going," said the Inspector rising. The Inspector walked away unceremoniously. Margayya hesitated for a moment at the door, and then followed the Inspector out. "What are we to make of it?" asked Margayya.

"Don't worry. Your son is living somewhere. We'll have to find that out. We will do it. Don't worry."

" How do you know that my son still lives? "

" Because I know this man. Every day he writes ten
death notices and sends them to the post. His servants
usually do not post them, but your one card must have
slipped through into the ordinary post."

" My misfortune is that he should have got at my
address! " Margayya wailed, suddenly realizing: "It's
three days since I went to my office. God knows what is
happening to my business. Probably this is the beginning
of the end——" he reflected ruefully.

The Inspector took Margayya to the Central Talkies that
evening. The Manager rose in his seat when the Inspector
entered his room. The police were a troublesome lot and it
was best to keep on good terms with them. The Manager
became elaborately fussy and cried: " What a pleasure!
It's ages since you came here, Mr. Inspector. Shall I order
coffee? The film is on now. Would you like to see it? " He
was as proud of the picture as if it were his own product.
Margayya sat in a chair, idly gazing on the pictures of
film stars hung on the walls in sepia print. A stale, sur-
charged tobacco smell pervaded the air and made
Margayya more bilious than ever. The Manager said:
" We are showing ——— on the 26th. You must definitely
send your children."

The Inspector waved off the invitation with a gentle
indifference and said: " We saw your boss sometime
ago——"

" Oh! How is he? "

" As usual, I suppose. How does he manage the business? "

" His son-in-law looks after everything. What he does
is—he comes round occasionally, sits through a show, notes
down the names of all the people he meets and goes—that
he does once in a while."

" Have you a new boy in your employment now? "

" Yes ... Yes ... We got one a few weeks ago. He seems
to be an educated boy."

" Is his name Balu? "

"Yes. That's it," said the Manager. "Why, anything wrong?"

"Is he about eighteen?" asked the Inspector, and gave a further description which the other accepted.

"What does he do?" asked Margayya interested.

"Well, miscellaneous things. Just now he is out with the sandwich boys. They will all come back before the evening show."

They had to wait there till the crowd for the evening show began to arrive at the ticket-window. A kettle-drum was heard approaching over the noise of the crowd. It came nearer and stopped, and now through the gate streamed in street-arabs wearing sandwich boards, on which colourful posters were stuck announcing: "*Krishna Leela*". The boys were ragged street-urchins with matted hair and sun-scorched complexions, their middles covered with loin-cloth and practically bearing on their bare bodies the sandwich frames. They put down their frames and gathered in front of the Manager's room along with the drummers and pipers. Presently Balu arrived, saying: "Payment only for three, sir; the rest dozed off under the trees." At which the rest started arguing furiously. "What injustice to get work out of us and cheat us! Hey, you are no——"

Over all this Balu's voice rose: "You won't be paid for just loafing." His voice thrilled Margayya. But he checked himself. He feared that he might make a scene, or that his son might start to run away out of sight once again, and then the Inspector and the others might blame him for spoiling the entire situation. So he edged away towards a corner of the room and turned his face towards the wall as Balu strode in. Balu came in saying: "Manager, sir, we went through the People's Park, Rundall's Road, and Elephant Gate, and returned this way—except for the three boys, the rest skulked away for a nap in Moore Market. You must teach them a lesson, sir."

Margayya could hold himself in check no more. He turned and observed that the boy wore a dirty dhoti, his cheeks were sunken, he was dark with wandering in the sun, and his hair was uncut. As he later explained to his relations, the moment he saw him he felt as if he had swallowed a live cinder. In this state he ran forward with a loud cry, some indistinct words coming out in a rush in which the only clear words were: " Is this spectacle my fate? Is it for this I prayed for your birth as my son? What has come over you? " His face was wet with tears. The boy was taken aback—so were the other two.

The Inspector had credited Margayya with greater self-possession. A crowd gathered at the door; the cinema-goers viewed this as a free show. The Inspector lost his temper at the sight of the crowd, and going up to the door, shouted: " Get out of this place." He stood at the doorway, and Balu felt that his retreat was cut off. He surrendered without a word.

§

The officer saw them off at the Egmore platform. Margayya gripped his arm and once again there were tears of gratitude in his eyes. He said: " You have been like a God to me. Tell me, if there is any way in which I can repay you, write to me. You know my address."

" Oh, yes. This is the first time I got at someone who was not a dacoit or a knave. I am glad to have done a good turn," said the Inspector. He told Balu: " Be a good son. Don't be a bother to your parents again. I have told the railway police to keep an eye on you." It was this part that Balu did not like, and later commented on after the Inspector went away.

" What can the railway police do? I'm not a thief. If I want to give them the slip there are a dozen ways."

The Inspector had got them comfortable seats in an end compartment which was not too crowded. All night Margayya plied his son with questions and tried to know what he had been doing with himself ever since his disappearance after the results, but the boy sullenly declared: " I won't speak of anything. Why couldn't you leave me alone? I was quite happy there."

" But . . . but . . . have you no affection, don't you want to see your mother, your——? "

" I don't want to see anybody."

" But my dear boy, do you know what it will mean to them to see you back in the flesh? Your mother broke down completely——"

" Why couldn't you have given me up for dead? I was quite happy, seeing pictures every day. I want to be in Madras. I like the place," he said, already feeling dull at the prospect of living in Malgudi. " What are you going to do with me? Make me read for exams I suppose? " he asked next.

" You need not go near books: you can do just as you please," said Margayya indulgently. He was filled with love for his son. He felt an indescribable pity as he saw the dirty, greasy dress and the famished appearance the boy had acquired. He became absolutely blind to all the dozen persons packed into the compartment. He hugged his shoulders and whispered: " You eat, rest, and grow fat— that is all you are expected to do, and take as much money as you like."

The boy seemed to accept this advice with a hundred per cent. literalness. As one supposed to be returned from the grave, he was treated with extraordinary consideration. His mother, he found, seemed to have become an entirely new person. She looked more youthful. A new flush appeared on her shallow cheeks. Her eyes had become very bright and sparkling. She became loquacious and puckish in her comments. She took the trouble to comb her hair with care and stuck jasmine strings in it. She seemed to feel that she was born anew into the world. She spoke lightheartedly and with a trembling joy in her voice. This was a revelation to Balu. He had never thought they attached so much importance to his person. He enjoyed it very much. His mother plied him with delicacies all the time. He had only to take a deep breath and look for his mother, and she at once asked: "What do you want, my boy?" Balu found that he had returned to a new home. Everything now was different. His father left him alone according to his promise. It was a very agreeable situation for all concerned—except Margayya's brother and family.

The moment Balu was brought back home, their position as the helpers of the family disappeared. It was a relationship essentially thriving on a crisis. The moment that the crisis was over, the two families fell apart; and they were once again reduced to the position of speculating from the other side of the wall what might be happening next door. Margayya's wife ceased to bother about them: Balu never knew that there had been a momentary friendliness during his absence. On the day he arrived with his father, when he stepped in and saw his uncle and the family in their central hall, he was speechless.

His uncle demanded: "What have you been doing with yourself? What is all this——?"

And his aunt and the children of the next house surrounded him and gaped at him. He felt abashed. He simply moved into the little room at the side and shut the door on the entire gathering. That was the signal; when he reopened the door, the house was cleared and the front door bolted. Margayya briefly announced to him: "They have all gone."

"Where?" Balu asked with interest.

"To their own house," Margayya said, and added: "What is their business here, anyway?"

His wife chimed in: "They probably wanted an excuse to plant themselves in here again!"

Margayya did not like to contradict her or say anything so utterly ungracious himself, although the moment he had secured his son, his first thought was to tell his brother's family, as diplomatically as his nature would permit, that they might go back to their house and resume their avocations. This he said very gently when the occasion came. As Balu shut himself into the small room, his brother wanted anxiously to know what had happened.

He said: "Did I not tell you to go to Madras, and then it would turn out to be good for you?"

Here is this fellow, Margayya reflected, rubbing in his own wisdom and judgment as usual. He hated in his brother the "Didn't I say so?" tone that he constantly adopted. It seemed to him a very irritating and petty habit of mind, and so he retorted sharply: "That's all right, nobody doubts your wisdom."

His brother ignored this sting and asked: "Well, where did you find him? What was he doing? Who wrote that card?"

Margayya lowered his voice and said in a whisper: "I will tell you all that later, when the boy is out of hearing. Now I had better attend to his wants." He moved towards the street door.

His brother took the hint: he cast a glance at his wife, who got up, herded the children together and started out, telling Margayya's wife: "I have so much to do at home —I think. . . . Anyway, let us thank God for his recovery," and marched out. The moment the door shut on them, Margayya's brother's wife ground her teeth and said: "Even if their house is on fire, let us not go near them again." It was a sentiment which was not approved by the last but one toddling beside her: "Why not, mother? It's so nice being in that house!"

"Now what has happened to you to make all this fuss?" her husband asked. There were tears in her eyes when she went up the steps of her own house. She said: "I only want you to have self-respect, that's all. After all that we have done for them these three days, baking and cooking for them night and day—five seers of rice gone for those ingrates——"

"After all, she was the only person in their house. You

have included the feeding of your own children," her husband said; which enraged her so much that she stabbed his cheeks with her fingers screaming: " Go and lick their feet for love of that wonderful brother of yours, you will do anything for him I am sure."

PART FOUR

BALU devoted himself to the art of cultivating leisure. He was never in any undue hurry to get out of bed. At about nine o'clock, his father came to his bedside and gently reminded him: "Had you not better get up before the coffee gets too stale?" Balu drank his morning coffee, demanded some tiffin, dressed himself, and left the house. He returned home at about one o'clock and sat down to his lunch. His mother waited for him interminably. He came home any time after one. Sometimes he came home very late. Even then he found his mother waiting.

"What are you waiting for, mother?" he asked. She never answered the question but went on to serve him his dinner. After dinner, he went up to the shop opposite, bought betel leaves and arecanut, chewed them with great satisfaction, and sat down on a dealwood box placed in front of the shop, watching the goings-on of the street for a while and smoking a cigarette, after making sure his mother was not watching. If he saw any elder of the house or of the next house coming out, he turned the cigarette into the hollow of his palm and gulped down the smoke. After this luxury, he suddenly got up, crossed the street, and went back to his house. He spread a towel on the granite floor, in the passage from the street, and, cooled by the afternoon breeze blowing in through the street door, was overcome with drowsiness and was soon asleep. He was left undisturbed. He woke from sleep only at five in the evening, and immediately demanded something to eat and drink, washed himself and combed his crop and went out. He returned home only after ten, when the whole town had gone to sleep. By this time his father had already come home and was fretting, bothering his wife to tell him where Balu had gone. He had got into the habit of feeling panicky if Balu absented himself too long from home. But the moment the door opened and Balu came in, he became absolutely docile and agreeable.

He said: "Oh, Balu has come!" with tremendous enthusiasm, and as he went in to change, asked with the utmost delicacy: "Where have you been?" avoiding to the best of his ability any suggestion of intimidation or effrontery.

The boy just said: "I've been here and there—what should I be doing at home?"

Six months of this life and the boy became unrecognizable: there were fat pads under his eyes; his chin was doubling, and his eyes seemed to shrink down to half their original size. Margayya wondered what to do with him. "Must do something so that he is able to grow up like other normal boys of his age—otherwise he will rust." He thought that the best solution would be to marry him. He sent out his emissaries, and very soon the results became evident. From far and wide horoscopes came in, and letters asking for his son's in return. Margayya carefully scrutinized the status of those who clamoured for his alliance. It was like the State Ministry scrutinizing the wedding proposals of a satellite Prince. The chief assistant in this business was his accountant Sastri. He had acquired a new status now as a match-maker. As he sat in his corner copying in his ledger, Markayya said from his seat: "Sastri, do you know anyone with a daughter?"

"Yes, sir," Sastri said, pleased to have an opportunity to look up from his ledger. "Yes, sir, quite a lot of inquiries have been coming my way, sir, for Balu——"

"Then why didn't you mention the matter to me?"

"You may be sure, sir, that when the right party comes they will be brought to you. Till then it does not seem to be very necessary to trouble you, sir."

"Quite right," said Margayya, pleased with his accoun-

180

tant and feeling his own eminence unquestioned and clearly placed. "You are right, Sastri—I'm very keen that if there is to be an alliance it must be with a family who have a sense of——"

"I know, sir, they must at least be your equal in status, sir."

"Status! Status!" Margayya laughed pleasantly. "I don't believe in it, Sastri . . . it's not right to talk of status and such things in these days. You know I'm a man who has had to work hard to make money and keep it. But I never for a moment feel that I am superior to anyone on earth. I feel that even the smallest child in the road is my equal in status."

"Very few there are, sir," said the other, "who are so wealthy and are so free from vanity or showiness. I have known people with only a tenth of what you possess, sir, but the way they——"

"How do you know it is only a tenth of what I have?" Margayya asked, his suspicions slightly roused: for he let the other keep only one set of accounts: the other set which gave a fuller picture of his financial position was always in his possession. Had this fellow been peeping into his private registers? The man gave a reassuring reply: "Any child in the town can say who it is if he is asked to name the richest man." It was very flattering and true, but Margayya hoped that the Income-tax people would not take the same view. Further development of this conversation was cut off because three clients from a far-off village came in asking: "Is this Margayya's?" At once Margayya and his assistant fell silent and became absorbed in their work. When anybody entered with that question on his lips, it meant that he was a new client, he had been sent in by one of Margayya's agents, and he would want ready cash before departing for the evening.

Margayya said: "Come in, come in, friends. May I ask who has sent you along?" They had come with the right recommendation. The three villagers came in timidly, tugging in their upper cloth. Margayya became very officious and showed them their seats on the mat: it was as if he had reserved for them special seats on fresh carpets and divans. He then said: "Will you have soda or coffee? Or would you care to chew betel leaves?" He turned to Sastri and said: "Send the boy down to fetch something for them: they have come a long distance. You came by bus?"

"Yes, paying a fare of twelve annas; and we want to catch the evening bus, if possible."

They went by the evening bus, but leaving their mortgage deed behind, and carrying in their pouches three hundred rupees, the first instalment of interest on what was already held at the source. The first instalment was the real wealth—whose possibilities of multiplication seemed to stretch to infinity. This was like the germinating point of a seed—capable of producing hundreds of such germinating points. Lend this margin again to the next man, as a petty loan, withholding a further first instalment; and take that again and lend it with a further instalment held up and so on . . . it was like the reflections in two opposite mirrors. You could really not see the end of it—it was a part of the mystic feeling that money engendered in Margayya, its concrete form lay about him in his iron safe in the shape of bonds, and gold bars, and currency notes, and distant arable lands, of which he had become the owner because the original loans could not be repaid, and also in the shape of houses and blocks of various sizes and shapes, which his way of buying interest had secured for him in the course of his business— through the machinery of 'distraint'. Many were those that had become crazed and unhappy when the courts made their orders, but Margayya never bothered about them, never saw them again. "It's all in the business," he said. "It's up to them to pay the dues and take back their houses. They forget that they asked for my help." People borrowed from him only under stress and when they could get no accommodation elsewhere. Margayya was the one man who lent easily. He made the least fuss about the formalities, but he charged interest in so many subtle ways and compounded it so deftly that the moment a man signed his bonds, he was more or less finished. He could never hope to regain his possessions—especially if he allowed a year or two to elapse.

There were debt relief laws and such things. But Margayya nullified their provisions because the men for whom the laws were made were enthusiastic collaborators in his scheme, and everything he did looked correct on paper. He acquired a lot of assets. But he lost no time in selling them and realizing their cash again, and stored it in an iron safe at home. "What am I to do with property?" he said. "I want only money, not brick and lime or mud," he reflected when he reconverted his attached property into cash. The only property he often dreamt of was the one at the foot of the Mempi hills, but somehow it was constantly slipping away: that fellow, Kanda, came again and again, but always managed to retain ownership of his lands.

Sastri turned up with quite a score of offers for Margayya's son. Margayya felt greatly flattered and puffed up with conceit. This was evidence that he had attained social importance. He had never thought that anyone of consequence would care to ally with his family. There was a family secret about his caste which stirred uneasily at the back of his mind. Though he and the rest were supposed to be of good caste now, if matters were pried into deeply enough they would find that his father's grandfather and his brothers maintained themselves as corpse-bearers. They were four brothers. The moment anyone died in the village, they came down and took charge of the business from that moment up to dissolving the ashes in the tank next day. They were known as "corpse brothers". It took two or three generations for the family to mitigate this reputation; and thereafter, they were known as agriculturists, owning and cultivating small parcels of land.

No one bothered about their origin, afterwards, except a great-aunt who let off steam when she was aroused by declaring: "It's written on their faces—where can it go, even if you allow a hundred years to elapse?"

It was Margayya's constant fear that when the time came to marry his son, people might say: "Oh, they are after all corpse-bearers, didn't you know?" But fortunately this fear was unfounded. At any rate, his financial reputation overshadowed anything else. Horoscopes and petitions poured in by every post. It produced a sense of well-being in Margayya, and a quiet feeling of greatness.

Sastri had done his part of the work efficiently. He had set aside all ledger work for the moment, and had written out scores of letters to men known to him within a radius of about two hundred miles. He was a compendium of likely parties with daughters to marry. He went out and saw in person quite a good many locally, as an ambassador. In all his correspondence and talk he described Margayya as the "Lord of Uncounted Lakhs" or as one who was "the richest in India"; and he spoke of Balu as an inheritor of all this wealth, and apprentice in his father's own business and a young man whose education was deliberately suspended because his father, having his own idea of education, was more keen on training the young fellow in business than letting him acquire useless degrees. Margayya scrutinized quite a file of applications and horoscopes. He rejected most of the proposals. They were from quite unworthy aspirants. Margayya felt, "Why should these people waste my time and their own? Are they blind? I have a certain position in life to keep up and I naturally want only alliances which can come up to that expectation."

Finally he picked up the horoscope of a girl who seemed to him desirable from every point of view. Her name was Brinda. She was seventeen years old. Her father in his first letter described her as being "extremely fair". He was a man who owned a tea-estate in Mempi Hills. At once it biased Margayya's mind in his favour. It was not a very large estate but yielded an income of ten thousand rupees a year. Margayya sent Sastri out to fetch an astrologer. There was one practising in the lane behind the Market Road. A man presently entered with beads at his throat and sacred ash on his forehead, wrapped in a red silk toga and dressed every inch for his part. There were a few of Margayya's clients waiting for him, and he had to dispose of them before he could attend to the astrologer. He seated the astrologer and made him wait for a few moments. The astrologer fretted at having to wait. He sat shifting uneasily in his seat, cleared his throat, and coughed once or twice in order to attract attention. Margayya looked up and understood. He interrupted himself in his work to tell the astologer: "Hey, Pandit, can't you remain at peace with yourself for a moment?" The astrologer was taken aback, but curbed his restlessness. Margayya disposed of his clients, looked up and said: "Come nearer, Pandit." The astrologer edged his way nearer.

By his manner and words, Margayya had now completely cowed the man. It seemed necessary as a first step to dictate to the planets what they should do. Margayya had made up his mind that he was going to take no nonsense from the planets, and that he was going to tell them how to dispose their position in order to meet his requirement: his requirement was the daughter of a man who owned tea estates in Mempi Hills, and he was consulting the astrologer purely as a formality. These were not days when he had to wait anxiously on a verdict of the stars: he could afford to ask for his own set of conditions and get them. He no longer believed that man was a victim of circumstances or fate—but that man was a creature who could make his own present and future, provided he worked hard and remained watchful. " The gold bars in the safe at home and the cash bundles and the bank pass-book are not sent down from heaven—they are a result of my own application. I need not have stayed at my desk for ten hours at a stretch and talked myself hoarse to all those clients of mine and taken all that risk on half-secured loans! . . . I could just have sat back and lost myself in contemplation——"

His mind sometimes pursued such a line of thought. But he at once realized that it was not always quite safe to think so and added the rider: "Of course Goddess Lakshmi or another will have to be propitiated from time to time. But we must also work and be able to keep correct accounts and pay for what we demand." This was no doubt a somewhat confusing and mixed-up philosophy of life, but that was how it was—and its immediate manifestation was to say to the astrologer, as he pushed before him his son's horoscope and the tea estate daughter's, "Pandit, see if you can match these horoscopes."

The Pandit put on his glasses and tilted the horoscopes towards the light at the door and studied them in silence.

Margayya watched his face and said: "What is your fee for your services?"

"Let my fee alone," the other said. "Let me do my work properly first."

Margayya said: "Well, probably I shall be able to add a couple of rupees to your usual charges . . . and if the alliance concludes successfully, well, of course, a lace dhoti and all honours for the pandit——"

"Give me a pencil and paper," the other said briefly.

The astrologer filled the sheet of paper with numbers and their derivatives, and worked up and down the page and on the back of it. He asked for another sheet of paper and worked up further figures. Margayya watched him anxiously. He said softly: "I want this alliance to go through. I shall appreciate it very much if you will work towards that objective. I can show my appreciation concretely if——"

The astrologer shook his head and muttered: "Impossible—you will have to find——"

"I don't want you to talk unnecessarily," Margayya said.

"The seventh and ninth houses in your son's horoscope

186

are . . . are not quite sound. The girl's marriage possibilities are the purest. The two horoscopes cannot match —they are like soap and oil."

"I have no faith in horoscopes personally——"

"Then you need not have gone to the extent of looking at these," the astrologer said.

Margayya felt angry. He asked finally: "Is there nothing that you can do?"

"Absolutely nothing. What can I do? Am I *Brahma*?"

Margayya could not trust himself to speak further. He called across the room: "Sastri——"

"Yes, sir."

"Give this Pandit a rupee and see him off."

"Yes, sir." Sastri proceeded to open a money bag.

The Pandit said : "A rupee! Am I a street-astrologer! My fee is usually——"

"I am not interested. My fee for such service as you do is just one rupee maximum. You will not get even that if you misbehave," said Margayya, and he shot out his hand and snatched back the horoscopes and the sheet of calculations. He looked for a moment at it to see if he could read anything. It was a maze of obscure calculations and figures. He thought of tearing it up, but remembering that he had paid for it, folded it neatly and put it into his personal desk. The astrologer got up loftily and walked towards the accountant, received his rupee with an air of resignation, and strode out without relaxing his looks.

Dr. Pal helped Margayya to find a different astrologer who re-arranged the stars of Balu to suit the circumstances. Margayya did not meet the astrologer in person. Dr. Pal took the task upon himself. He made several journeys between the astrologer and Margayya carrying the envelope containing the horoscopes, and finally came back one day with the astrologer's written report on saffron-tipped paper; the report said that the two horoscopes perfectly matched, with reasons adduced. Considering the mightiness of the task, the fee of seventy-five rupees which Dr. Pal said the astrologer charged was purely nominal.

Events then moved briskly. Dr. Pal's services became indispensable and constant. He saw Margayya through the preliminary negotations, the wedding celebraticns, and the culmination in a newspaper photo with Balu wearing tie and collar, his handsome bride at his side.

§

It was the third year of the war, and Margayya decided that the time was now ripe for starting a new line. He walked into Dr. Pal's Tourist Home and asked: "Doctor, how are you faring?"

"Not badly," said the Doctor.

Margayya observed the dust-laden table, the pen-holder which had not been moved, and the unwritten sheets of paper before him—unmistakable signs of dull business. Margayya settled in the chair and began: "Doctor, I think you ought to make more money."

"Why?"

"Just for your own good. I will show you a way, if you like."

"I'm quite contented with what I have."

"You are not, sir," said Margayya. "You forget I'm also in the same building as you are. Don't tell me that there are many fellows coming into your office to seek your assistance in tourism or whatever it may be——"

Dr. Pal became submissive: "I have tried one thing after another in life. You know I am a qualified Sociologist —one of the handful in this country——"

"Let us not talk of all that," said Margayya, not liking the idea of going back to the *Domestic Harmony* days. It was something which had gone clean out of his mind, except one copy of the book which he retained as a memento of his earlier days and which he kept locked up in his iron safe at home for fear that Balu might get at it. Fortunately, he felt, his daughter-in-law's father did not seem to have heard anything about his association with it. Otherwise he might never have gone through with the alliance—it was as risky as the ancestry of his corpse-bearing grandfathers. And so now he cut short Dr. Pal's reference to sociology and psychology as if it were dangerous talk, and said: "I want to do you a good turn."

"Why?" asked the Doctor.

"Because——" began Margayya, and was about to say, "you did me a good turn once by forcing on me your manuscript," but checked these words, and said, "Don't ask why. Because I have known you for a long while, and have seen you also—and I sincerely wish that you could make a little money and live comfortably——"

"Tourism," said Dr. Pal, "is a very honourable and paying proposition in the West, but here nobody cares. There is not a single person anywhere here who knows the history and archaeology of the country round about. Do you know that there are half a dozen different jungle-tribes to be found on the top of the Mempi Hills? All of them live, breed and die, in the jungles—but there are so many differences between them. No inter-marriage? My tourism does not confine itself to telling people, 'There is the river,' 'There is the valley,' 'Here is big game'—and pointing to a few ruined temples—that's not my idea of tourism; it's something different, something that's as good as education."

"But it hasn't been a paying line," said Margayya, growing impatient with his lecture. "For the moment, if you want a good income, listen to me. If I throw out a word about it, I am sure there will be dozens ready to take it up, but I want to give you the first chance because——" He once again narrowly avoided reference to *Domestic Harmony*, and said: "Because, because, I've been seeing you for quite a long while, and I would like to see you prosper."

There was another reason why Margayya wanted to help, which was also not mentioned. He found Dr. Pal hanging too much about his son's establishment at Lawley Road. Margayya gave one of the houses he had acquired to his son for setting up a family independently, although Margayya's wife did not much like the idea of living separated from him. But Margayya told her: "Think for a moment, my dear girl, Brinda comes from an up-to-date family, and already shows her superior training. Is she very comfortable in this house?"

His wife thought it over and agreed: "I don't think so. Balu has been saying that the new room you have put up on the terrace is not good enough. In her father's house she has four rooms, all her own." She added: "The girl hardly comes out of her room all day. I have to call her a dozen times before she will come downstairs for her meal. I hardly see anything of Balu either. He doesn't speak much. I'm probably not good enough for a modern girl like her."

"Tut! Tut!" Margayya said to her. "Don't get into the habits of a mother-in-law. I like the girl very much myself—if those two are happy, I think it's best they are left alone to manage their affairs in their own fashion. I have recently acquired a house in Lawley Extension. I think it best that they move off there."

"So far!" exclaimed the mother, horrified.

"It's not so far as you imagine . . . just half an hour by a *jutka*." He studied her face for a while and added: "Don't make a fuss. The boy is eighteen years old and he ought to look after himself. The girl will manage the household for him."

To Margayya's wife it seemed an unthinkable proposition. "They hardly know how to boil water or even to light an oven."

"They will learn everything," Margayya said. "And they can engage a cook if they want." He was adamant: "Sooner or later the boy will himself open the subject and ask for this and that. If he does that it will annoy me very much, and I will resist. I'd rather do things before he speaks—it'll look better. I will give him a house and a settlement. I want to see if that will make him think of doing something with his time."

His wife did not like the note of irony in his voice and

protested: "You have already forgotten what happened. I dread to think you have already started again believing you ought to improve him!"

Margayya's wife nearly broke down on the day Balu bundled up his clothes into a neat leather suit-case presented to him by his father-in-law, put them into a taxi and drove away with his young wife. Margayya's wife had spent a good part of an entire week in running up and down between Vinayak Mudali Street and Lawley Extension, arranging the bungalow at Lawley Extension for its new occupants. The girl prostrated at her mother-in-law's feet before taking leave of her.

Balu, a taciturn man, just said: "I'm going," got into the car, and sat down leaving space for his wife. Margayya's brother's family had crowded on the parapet of the next house. Margayya himself was away, for it had been a busy day for him at his office.

The house seemed to have become dull and lonely for Margayya's wife without her son. It reminded her of the days when he had gone away without telling anybody, but Margayya noticed no difference because his mind was busy formulating a new plan which was going to rocket him to undreamt of heights of financial success . . .

Margayya observed that after Balu settled in his new house, Dr. Pal became a constant visitor there. Whenever he went there, at the end of a day's work, he saw Dr. Pal settled comfortably on the hall sofa. He played cards with Balu and his wife. He also suspected that Dr. Pal constantly took cash from his son. Margayya did not like a man who could write *Domestic Harmony* to associate with young, impressionable minds; he would probably recite passages from it, talk over further projects with his son, and he couldn't say what Balu might or might not do under those circumstances. At any rate, it seemed imperative to wean his son away from Dr. Pal—and it seemed best to do it by employing Dr. Pal's hours usefully and so making it unnecessary for him to go to the youngster, at least for money.

Now Margayya told Dr. Pal: " You can make a thousand rupees a month easily if you will associate with me. After you have made some money it'll be much more feasible to try your tourism to your heart's content. Are you willing to try and do something? "

"Yes, definitely," said Dr. Pal. At which Margayya began a lecture on money conditions. The war had created a flood of inflated currency. All sorts of people were making money in all sorts of ways—some of it unaccounted or unaccountable.

" You know what the market has been! " said Margayya. " This is the time when I wish to attract deposits rather than lend. People have money and are looking for a place to put it—and I look to you to get me a few contacts. I will make it worth while. You know all kinds of people as a journalist, and you are the man for me."

" I will do my best," declared Dr. Pal enthusiastically, thinking: " At least next month I can pay the stores, instead of dodging; I am tired of dodging."

" I am tired of this tame business of lending to my rustic clients," Margayya said. "I want to do something better for a change. It does not mean I'm giving up my village clients. I shall continue to serve them as a sort of duty to them . . . but——"

Margayya's instinct was right in choosing Dr. Pal as his tout. He was a man who visited almost all the shopmen in the town every day. He knew the rice merchant in a certain back street who hoarded rice in a secret godown whose frontage was stuffed with innocent-looking rag and old paper collected for the paper mills, who sold rice at about a rupee for half a *seer* to needy people, and made an enormous quantity of money each day. Dr. Pal knew the man who supplied office glue to the army and hoarded enough cash by showing a joint stock firm with imaginary partners; another merchant who supplied screws in cartons only half-filled; the contractor who built huts and got enormous bills passed easily by bribing the Garrison Engineer. He was a rich man because his huts, meant to stand for three years, would stand only for a couple of months—till the bills were passed by the friendly Garrison Engineer! It was this margin that gave him real wealth. There were drug stockists who didn't show their stock, but bargained when it was a matter of life and death to a customer; there were military men with pensions, and go-betweens and busy-bodies who could secure contacts at New Delhi for a consideration, people who could manage export and import priority. All these people had a lot of money—the town was reeking with it. Only a part of it came out in income-tax returns, and the balance remained hidden in bundled-up currency notes in dark boxes—it was these that Margayya wanted to attract to his own stronghold. Besides these, people generally had a lot of cash these days. Margayya had decided that all the cash must go to him. He had a feeling that, though by ordinary standards he might be termed a man of wealth, yet the peak was still a long way off. He was like a fanatical mountaineer who sets his heart on reaching the summit of Everest. He might be standing on the highest peak. Yet he can never feel that he has really attained the highest . . .

The blanket man was Dr. Pal's first client. Dr. Pal sat in his shop amidst piles of dark blankets and lectured him so long that he expressed a desire to meet Margayya. Dr. Pal said: "I will see him first and speak to him. He is very reluctant to accept deposits. But I think my recommendation will work—wait until I see you again to-morrow."

The next day he came to the blanket shop and took the man along to meet Margayya at his office. Margayya effusively seated him on the mat, and went on with his work. He interrupted himself only for a moment to declare: "Still no light! As our landlord, you should look to our convenience."

"Certainly—I have ordered everything, it's coming," the other said in his routine manner. Dr. Pal said: "Our friend Guru Raj has some cash, and wants your advice as to what he should do——"

"He is himself an old businessman. Why does he need my advice?" said Margayya.

The blanket man said: "After all, you are an experienced banker. Your advice will be valuable." As he hesitated, Margayya threw a look at Dr. Pal and he got up and went away unobtrusively. Margayya drew nearer and in a confidential whisper asked: "Are you really serious about depositing your cash with me? I can offer you an interest of twenty per cent on your deposit which you can draw monthly." The blanket merchant gasped. "Twenty per cent? Did I hear you all right?"

"Yes, I said twenty per cent," said Margayya. "I know what I am talking about."

"The banks are offering only three per cent."

"I'm not concerned with them. I'm not a bank, but I can guarantee you twenty per cent."

"How do you manage it?"

"Well, that is my look-out," Margayya said. "I have a business which yields me more; I have investments which give me probably twenty-five per cent. I keep five per cent and turn over the twenty per cent to the depositor; after all," he said with a very virtuous look, "I am using your money. Unlike the banks and co-operative societies, I believe you are entitled to the larger share as the owner of money. You see, I have made enough money," he said with an air of sanctity. "I don't want more. I only want to be of help to people, that is all," he said vaguely.

At the end of his talk Guru Raj took out five thousand rupees in cash and placed them on the table. Margayya swept them into his desk and wrote out a receipt. "This is the receipt. Any time you want your money back, just take it to my accountant and collect your five thousand. But as long as you don't cash it, you can collect the interest on the first day of the month. As long as you do not withdraw the principal, you can draw the interest."

The blanket merchant went away with his head in the clouds. Twenty per cent! "I have to dispose of a hundred blankets a day if I have to make that money. How does this man manage?" On the following month when he went to Margayya's, the accountant gave him the cash. When he got this interest as a reality, the man was aghast and cried: "That man Margayya is a wizard. How does he manage it?"

Very soon the word "Wizard" came to be bandied about freely whenever anyone referred to Margayya. His methods were too complex for anyone to understand. The banks were puzzled. The deposits in their possession were all going. People speculated how the wizard did it. No one had any clear idea. Nor could they get any enlighten-ment from Sastri or Dr. Pal. Margayya assigned to them only portions of certain duties, and attended to all things personally, and they never had a full knowledge of what exactly he did. The whole town seemed to talk of nothing but this all day. People said that he underwrote shipments arriving at Madras Port or Bombay and made money; that he discounted bills of lading; that he paid interest on capital out of a sheer desire to impress. But the fact was there that he seemed to need new clients each day, and Dr. Pal had proved invaluable in this task. He had now earned for himself a second-hand Baby Austin, and brought into Margayya's at least a dozen new clients each day. Mar-gayya calculated: "If I get twenty thousand rupees deposit each day and pay fifteen in interest, I have still five thousand a day left in my hands as my own——"

PART FIVE

He might have been a movie celebrity. He could never take a few steps in the road without people gaping and pointing at him. It was now necessary for him to have a car, for it became a nuisance to walk in the roads. All sorts of people saluted him respectfully and stood aside while he passed. It made him feel very awkward. All sorts of people tried to make friends with him. All sorts of people tried to waylay him and explain their difficulties. One wanted help to get a daughter married, another to send his son to Madras for higher medical studies, a third applied for help to extricate his lands, or to buy rice for the next meal, and so on and so forth. In addition to this, public bodies seemed to have suddenly become aware of his existence—a Flood Relief Fund here, a Gandhi Fund there, Earthquake Relief for a far off country, Prevention of Cruelty to Animals, Promotion of Child Welfare, Education, and the War Fund: the most constant demand was from the War Fund of the local district authorities. People called on him at all sorts of places and all sorts of hours—in the street, at home, or in his office. Quite a flood of visitors waited for him. All applications for charity instead of rousing pity only angered Margayya: "What do they take me for? A Magic Pot? ... I do not work hard and wear myself out in order to give gifts. Who came to my help in those days when I was in difficulties?"

He had to barricade himself at home and in his office. At his office he had to move out of his original place and take another room and shut himself in. He left the disposal of his visitors and applicants to Dr. Pal, who just told people: "This is only a bank not a charity home," and sent away whoever came for cash. He was tactful where it was necessary, and diplomatic or downright rude where it was necessary. Sometimes he was visited by high Government officials who asked: " Well, what is your contribution to the War Fund? "

Dr. Pal said: " Our boss is a convinced Congressman. We don't believe that this is our war . . . unless the Congress High Command orders him to pay, he will never give a pie: he is a man of strict principles. Why should we contribute to a fund with which the British and U.S. fight their enemy—not our enemy; our enemy is Britain not Germany. When the Congress commands us to gather funds for fighting this enemy, you will see Margayya placing his entire wealth at the disposal of the country." Or he said: "Governor's War Fund! Nothing doing! Sir . . . somebody or other they've sent from England as our Governor pockets half the war fund he collects, isn't it a fact? If he takes twenty thousand in cash for the war fund, he takes a similar sum in kind, in the shape of a casket or something, for domestic consumption. Can you disprove it? Till you can do that you cannot expect Mr. Margayya to contribute anything. He is a man of strict principles." Or if it was a highly-placed police or Income-tax official who was making the request, Dr. Pal said: " Margayya has been thinking it over. You may rest assured he will send in his contribution very soon." And he advised Margayya to send off a cheque. "It will not do at all to get into disfavour with these folk—after all they will be using the money for defeating the Nazis." He also told Margayya: "You must have a car. You simply should not be seen in the streets any more: you have passed that stage. If you like a walk, go along the river, but don't walk in the streets." Margayya allowed the other to buy a car for him.

It was necessary for him to use a car also for another reason; at the end of a day, Margayya carried a huge bag of cash—notes of all denominations were in the old mail sack which he had picked up at an auction. " Very good

material," said Margayya of the sack, which came near
bursting when Margayya closed for the day. He now
worked far into the night with the aid of kerosene lamps.
The moment he reached home, he counted the notes again,
bundled them up in tidy little batches, the lovely five
rupee and ten rupee and that most handsome piece of paper
—the green hundred rupee note. He counted his cash over
and over again, and locked it up in his safe and shut the
door. It would be nearly midnight when he finished the
counting and rose to have his dinner. His wife waited for
him patiently and sat down for food after he had had his
meal. He hardly noticed that she waited for him: his
mind was fully occupied with various calculations. He
hardly spoke during dinner. If she asked: " Shall I
serve? " he merely answered back without looking up:
"Don't bother me. Do what you please: only don't bother
me." He ate very little—just the quantity that a boy of ten
would eat. It worried her secretly. She tried to improve
it by putting more rice and stuff on his plate, but he just
pushed it all aside, got up, and went back to work by the
lamp, for further additions. She never knew when he went
to bed, because even after she had finished all her work
and gone to bed, she still saw him bent over his registers.
She saw him with a drawn look and felt moved to say:
" Shouldn't you mind your health? "

" What's wrong with me? I'm all right. If you feel you
need anything, go ahead and buy it and do what you like.
Take any money you want. Only leave me alone."

She felt it would be best to leave him alone. He seemed
to have so little time left for rest that she concluded it
would be better not to encroach upon it with her own
comments. "Balu has only taken after his father—his
sullenness and silence," she concluded. It became a household where perfect silence reigned. She was only secretly
worried over his thin appearance and the dull weariness
about his eyes. She often wanted to ask him: " Why
should you work so hard? Haven't we enough? And what
are you aiming at? " But refrained from uttering it. She

knew it would only annoy him. Perfect silence reigned in the house.

In the course of time, at the end of a day he brought home not one bag, but quite a number of them. It was no longer possible to count the currency notes individually. He could only count and check up the bundles—and even that took him beyond midnight. For now his fame had spread far and wide and it was not only the deposits of well-to-do people that arrived at his counter, but also those of smaller tradesmen and clerks and workers—who brought in their life's savings. "If I have a hundred rupees, better hand it to Margayya, for he will give me twenty rupees per month for a lifetime. He is our saviour." Margayya accepted any deposit that came to him, however small it might be. He explained: "I like to make no difference between rich and poor in this business, which exists after all for serving society. We should not make distinctions."

"I heard," said Pal, "they are thinking of conferring on you a title for your services."

Margayya was really alarmed to hear it: "What for?"

"For doing the greatest Public Service. If you only found the time to go round and see the number of people who are happy and secure through your help. . . . There is talk in Government circles of giving you at least a Public Service medal."

In his home the large safe was filled up, and its door had to be forced in, and then the cupboards, the benches and tables, the space under the cot, and the corners. His wife could hardly pass into the small room to pick up a saree or towel: there were currency bundles stacked up a foot high all over the floor. Presently Margayya ordered her to transfer trunks and effects to the room upstairs. She patiently obeyed him. Very soon this room had also to be requisitioned: more sacks emptied themselves into the house every day.

"They have carried in five sacks today," said his brother in the next house.

200

"Do you really say all that is money?" asked his wife excitedly.

And then they heard Margayya going upstairs and a kerosene light burned far into the night. His brother's family would have given anything to know what Margayya was doing up there so late. His brother's wife strained her ears against a small crack in the wall and heard Margayya say to his wife: "You will have to clear out of the upstairs room too."

"Where shall I put my trunks?"

"Keep them in the store room for the present."

"Is it a safe place? I have some gold jewellery."

"Oh, there are more valuable things for me to keep in the rooms. Don't make a fuss."

"All right," she said docilely.

"Only till I build a vault somewhere," he said, feeling that he ought to be a little more mollifying. "I must have a strong-room built somewhere: I wish I could find the time to attend to it."

§

It was about seven in the evening. The lights had not been lit yet. Margayya's eyes pained him and he felt weak and weary. He had been skipping his morning food these days because he had lost the taste for it: he drank a cup of diluted butter-milk, kept himself on a few cups of coffee throughout the day and had his food only at night after closing his cash. "With work ahead, I have no patience for food." He went to his office almost as soon as he got up from bed: he washed and changed and rushed off, and returned home at indefinite hours. He said to his wife: "Opening the office is in my hands, but the closing is in the hands of other people." He had to cut out even his snuff—the one thing he liked and still enjoyed. Dr. Subbu of the Reliance Medical Hall, one of his investors, advised Margayya to give up snuff. He consulted him with regard to a persistent pain at the back of his head, which kept him sleepless at night. The doctor examined him when he came over to collect his interest.

He said: "Probably your snuff irritates the optic nerves. Why don't you stop snuff? Anyway, come over to my clinic for a thorough examination. We want to see you kept in the fittest condition possible, you know." He laughed like many other doctors of his kind at his own joke.

Margayya gave up snuff with a resolute will, and felt better for it. It was not quite so easy to give it up, but he said to himself: "If I do not sleep at night properly, I might mess up my calculations and then God knows what will happen." He had mitigated his headache, but a sort of dizziness perpetually hung about his head.

Dr. Subbu said when he visited him next: "Why don't you take a holiday at Kodaikanal Hills? It'll do you good. Can't you afford a holiday?"

Margayya shook his head sadly: "Not possible in this life. I'm tied up too much with various things——" He figured himself as being in the centre of a tangled skein. "If I move even slightly," he began, but merely said: "I cannot afford to move even slightly this way or that."

His accountant, Sastri, was bundling up currency, stuffing it into mail sacks, and preparing statements. All his customers had left. Margayya felt ill. He sat in his room with his head resting on his arms. He called out: "Sastri, hurry up with your stuff."

"Yes, sir," said Sastri from his corner. "Your son is here to see you, sir." The door opened and Balu entered and took his seat opposite him.

"Balu, come in," Margayya said, feeling happy at the sight of his son. "It must be more than two weeks since I saw you. How is your family?"

"Baby has some stomach trouble and is crying."

"Must be teething, I suppose. Take your mother there and show her the child. She will be able to do something: she understands these things better."

"You never come to our house. I took Brinda to see mother today——"

"Oh! That's good . . . otherwise . . . I wish I could go over to your house. . . . Well, when the pressure here lessens, I suppose I shall . . . I am virtually a prisoner here. Your cook is all right, I suppose."

"Yes, but he is sometimes very impertinent. I want to send him away, but Brinda is too patient. She spoils him."

"Don't quarrel with her. Leave these things to her. She is right."

Now the common topics of conversation seemed to be over. There was a moment's silence. Balu sat moving a pebble on Margayya's desk as a paper-weight.

"Why don't you buy a better paper-weight and a good table and chair instead of squatting like this on the ground, father?" asked Balu.

He merely replied: "I don't need all those luxuries." He locked up his desk and made preparations to start out, calling: "Sastri, is the statement ready?"

"Almost, sir," replied Sastri, giving his customary reply.

"I want to talk to you seriously, father," said Balu nervously.

Margayya looked at his face apprehensively before saying: "I am not quite well today. Tomorrow I will come to your house."

"No, I must speak to you now. You have got to listen to me," said Balu authoritatively.

"Oh!" said Margayya. "Wait a minute then." He quickly passed out of the room, went over to Sastri and whispered: "Don't bring in the cash bags yet," returned to his seat, and settled down. He sat looking at his son fixedly, without saying anything.

The boy sat biting his nails for a moment. He did not know how to begin. His voice shook as he said: "Father . . . I . . . I want more money."

"Oh!" Margayya said, with a feeling of relief. "I thought as much. Why do you hesitate? How much do you want?"

The boy felt encouraged by his kindness. He brightened up. Still he felt hesitant to answer the question. The father encouraged him: " Come on, Balu, speak boldly. I always like a fellow who talks freely and openly and boldly. Have I refused you anything so far? "

The boy preferred to ignore this question: " I . . . I want to ask you something. . . . I want more money——"

" That is all right," replied Margayya irritably. " I've told you I'll give it you. How much do you want? "

" It depends. It depends on . . . what you have . . . I have no idea what you have. How can I say? "

" What do you mean? I do not understand you," said Margayya, feeling puzzled. " If you cannot talk clearly, you had better see me again some other time. I am not quite well," he said sharply. He liked to have things clear cut as in interest calculations: vague indefinite talk annoyed him. He got up saying: " I wish to go home and lie down. Come with me if you like."

" No, I can't talk to you there. Mother will be there. I don't like to talk before her."

Margayya called out: " Sastri, get the car ready," and made a move towards the door. The boy sprang up and blocked the door, with arms spread out. " You must let me talk to you——"

Margayya did not like scenes in his office. He threw a look at Sastri, but he was engrossed in his accounts. Margayya went back to his seat calmly and sat down. He was completely bewildered. This was the first time he found his son so talkative—it was a revelation to him. The boy, though not docile, was always taciturn and quiet and never so aggressive. He asked for money, which was granted, and yet what happened? He had said, " It depends on how much you have "! Margayya could hardly believe his ears. He sat in his seat and patiently waited. He felt weak and fatigued. He wanted so much to lie down.

Margayya struck a match and lit the dim kerosene lamp. He resigned himself to whatever might be coming. The boy said: "I want to speak to you about something very serious."

Margayya suppressed the annoyance that was coming over him. He felt afraid to be angry. Probably his son had taken to drinking: he sniffed the air to find if it was confirmed by his breath. He found himself clutching the ruler on his table—but relaxed his hold at the thought, "After all, it's Balu——" It seemed to be an unworthy move to make. He let go his hold on the ruler and waited. The boy still would not open his lips. Margayya felt exasperated. He pulled out his watch and said: "It's about seven o'clock. If you do not speak before the clock hand points to seven-five, I will go. I will knock you down and walk out if necessary." He felt relieved after delivering this threat. He felt his authority re-established: "The boy cannot have it all his own way," he told himself. He placed the watch on his desk dramatically, turning it towards Balu.

Balu fidgetted for a moment with his eyes fixed on the clock and then said: " I want a share of the property—my share of the property."

"What property?" asked Margayya.

"Well, I mean, my share of the property—our ancestral property."

"H'm—I see. Why? Why do you want it?"

"Because I have attained my majority. You know it as well as I do. I am nineteen and entitled to my own share of the property."

"What property?" asked Margayya.

"Ancestral property," the boy answered.

At this Margayya put his hand into his pocket, brought out a half-rupee coin, placed it on the table, pushed it over, and said: "There it is, take it—that's exactly half of what your grandfather left in cash: take it and give me a receipt.'

The boy picked it up and looked at it: " Is this all the movable and immovable property? "

" What movable and immovable property . . . movable? "

Margayya lost his temper on hearing it, lost his head completely : "Movable! Immovable! You want me to give you a list, is that it? Here it is: this is, this is what it was, listen," and he described in coarse terms the movable and immovable properties possessed by his worthy ancestors: he was filled with chagrin at the memory of the travails he had gone through with his brother before the partition of their single house, the trip to the courts, the hours of waiting on the old lawyer's bench, the Court Commission visiting their house and so on and so forth. He remembered how miserable he had felt, wondering where his wife was going to cook the next meal and where they were to put the youngster down to sleep, while the legal proceedings were going on and they hung on to his brother's house uncertainly. Those miseries could not be understood by the boy even if explained to him. He felt sorry. He said softly: "Boy, let us go home now and discuss it. It's all right. This is not the right time to talk of all those things."

"No," said the boy. "Don't try to dodge me."

"Where did you pick up all this language?"

"I'm old enough to know the world," retorted the boy. "If you don't give me an immediate account, I will go to court."

"Very well—go ahead, I have nothing more to say." Margayya got up and tried to move out. The boy once again sprang up, spread out his arms and blocked the door. Margayya slapped his face, crying: "Get out of the way, you swine." The boy burst into tears, and sobbed. Margayya looked at his face and was moved. There were tears in his eyes too. He put his arm around the boy and said: "You are being misled by someone, probably a lawyer, who wants an occupation. Don't listen to such people. Here I am, your father, ready to do anything for you: only ask what you want."

"I want a share of your property——"

"Idiot! What obstinacy is this! What property is there?"

"I know how much you have made. I am entitled to half of it."

"How do you make that out?"

"Because it is multiplied out of grandfather's property and I am entitled to half by right."

"I have given you a house to live in, I give you three hundred rupees a month for your expenditure. Well, if you want it, ask for more, I will probably increase it to four hundred."

The boy shook his head. "I want nothing of it. I want my share."

"And why?" asked Margayya.

"I want to buy——" He stopped short, changed his mind and merely said: "I want it for various things."

Margayya said in a mollifying manner: "All that I have is yours, my boy. Everything that I have will come to you: who else is there? To whom can I pass these on after my time?"

"After your time! When is that?"

"Are you asking when I am going to die?"

The boy looked abashed: "I am not saying that, but I cannot wait. I want my share urgently."

"Pray, what is the urgency, may I ask?" said Margayya cynically. "Do you think that I ought to drink poison and clear the way for your enjoyment?" The boy did not know how to answer. Margayya could no longer keep standing. He pushed the boy aside and walked out. He told the accountant: "Put the bags and the statement into the car." He got into the car and drove off, leaving his son standing on the steps of the bank.

Margayya felt restless. After closing his accounts, putting away the cash, and bolting down his food, he told his wife: "I am going out for a moment. Close the door."

"At this hour?" she asked, but he had gone. She turned in with resignation.

His driver had locked the car and gone home. Outside

the stars were sparkling in the sky, and the streets were deserted and silent. Margayya had to walk the entire way —it was some months since he had walked—and he felt exhilarated by the exercise today. "I have perhaps been too severe," he told himself. "I must investigate what his troubles are more sympathetically. Probably he is genuinely hard up. Perhaps I might take him into business and see that he has a better income and standing." He wondered if the boy would be surprised to see him there at that hour. "This is the only time I can spare," he told himself. "If the morning rush starts. . . . He must also be fairly annoyed that I have not been seeing the grandson. Young parents think the world exists in order to take an interest in a new born child," he reflected philosophically. "When Balu was born, we cut off relations who didn't come and stand over the crib and say admiring things about him. All the same, he had no business to upset me—I have not been feeling well. He should have had more sense. Share of the property! The damned fool." The recollection of this made him so angry that he stopped and almost turned to go back home. "What right has that fool to make me walk to him at this hour? It is sheer nonsense, why should I go there?" he asked himself suddenly. "Share of the property! Accursed fool! What share—I gave him the right answer." He chuckled at the memory of his vulgar repartee. "Anyway, there is no other time when I can meet him and speak to him—might as well get through it and see what ails him. I will make him a proposition to join me in business. That is the thing to do. It is ages since I saw Brinda—nice girl——"

He came to Lawley Road. It was about one o'clock. He stood before number 17, at Fourth Cross Road, a small villa with a bluebell creeper over the gatepost and a mesh-covered verandah. He stood outside and admired the house: "Got this practically for a song—less than two thousand rupees. If that fool of a fellow could not pay the interest even after two years, the fault is not mine if it falls in my lap—the fruit can only fall on the palm of him who holds up his hands for it." As he opened the little wooden gate and entered, he saw no light in the house: "Probably the boy has slept," he reflected. He was hesitating whether to turn back and go. But the gate had creaked; a verandah light was now switched on and the bolt of the front door was being drawn back.

"Who is there?" asked Brinda's voice from inside.

Margayya called out, "Brinda," to disclose himself. Brinda had just risen from bed; she looked sleepy and rather tired. She was a very elegant girl. Looking at her Margayya thought, "What a fortunate thing to have secured this daughter-in-law. If those fool astrologers had had their way!" He climbed the steps.

"You have come walking at this hour?" his daughter-in-law asked. Her voice was soft and musical.

Margayya said: "I couldn't find any other time. How is the baby?" He walked in and stood looking at the little fellow sleeping on his mother's bed. He gently touched his cheek.

The girl demurely said: "He wouldn't sleep and gets up at the slightest sound."

"Why should you not let him stay awake?" asked Margayya.

"He gives us no peace. He wants to be carried about all the time," she answered. She was showing him the utmost respect as an elder.

He admired her for it—her tone of courtesy, her soft movement and elegance. "God bless her!" he told himself. "Yes, Balu used to be troublesome too when he was a baby. Where is Balu?" he asked, noticing the vacant bed beside hers.

She hesitated ever so slightly before answering briefly: "He has not yet come home." Her face became serious when she said that.

"Where has he gone?" Margayya asked.

She still hesitated. She merely bit her lips. Margayya sensed something was wrong. He persisted, and she merely replied: "He has gone to a cinema," with an effort.

"A cinema! So late as this! How can he leave you and the child alone and go away like this?" There was so much genuine sympathy in his voice that the girl was affected by it and burst into tears. Margayya was totally at a loss to know what to do now. This was a new situation for him, and he did not know what to say. He said to her: "Why don't you sit down? Why do you keep standing?"

She wouldn't sit down out of respect for her father-in-law. But he was able to persuade her. She rallied and said: "I wanted to come and see you. Every day this happens: he comes home every day at two o'clock. If I ask him, he . . . he . . . I'm afraid of him."

And then it came out bit by bit. Dr. Pal was his constant companion They gathered in a house and played cards—it was the house of a man who called himself a theatrical agent. She had learnt from their servant that there were a lot of girls also in the building. Pal had something or other to do with these people, and picked Balu up in his car. They sat there continuously playing cards till midnight. They chewed tobacco and betel leaves, sometimes they drank also, and men and women were very free, and all of them dropped down wherever they sat and slept and became sick when they drank too much—it was a revolting description that she gave: all learnt from the servant who worked in the house, the uncle of the girl who looked after the baby. Brinda also said that Balu seemed to be thinking of becoming a partner in their business. In fact he always explained to his wife that it was business that kept him out late. "If I speak . . . he threatens to drive me out. It's that Pal. . . . Can't you do something to keep him away?"

"How long has this been going on?"

"For months——"

"Why didn't you tell us?"

"I was afraid. Even now, please don't tell him that I have said anything."

Margayya brooded over it darkly. He now seemed to understand why his son was asking for a partition. "Dr.

Pal! Dr. Pal! What shall I do with him?" he reflected. He was torn between caution and an impossible rage. God knew where it would lead if he alienated Pal's sympathies: the fellow might do anything. He decided, within a fraction of a moment, that the thing to do was to separate his son from Pal without making a fuss about it, and then deal with his son separately. He would have to tempt Pal to go out of town—probably on the pretext of a contact outside; but if he went there and . . . Margayya found he was in terror of him. The only element that kept people from being terrified of each other was trust—the moment it was lost, people became nightmares to each other; this seemed to be truly his problem, that he could neither keep the fellow in sight nor let him go out of sight. But anyway he had better move with the utmost caution. The daughter-in-law patiently sat in a chair and watched his face. He told her with a great deal of tenderness: "You go in and sleep, my child. I will go home, and I will see about this tomorrow. Don't worry about anything. I will set your husband right. You lock the door now; look after the baby. Tell me if you need anything. Don't be afraid. I will send your mother-in-law to see you tomorrow morning." He got up and left. The girl bolted the verandah door and put out the light.

As he was closing the wicket gate behind him, Dr. Pal's Baby Austin drew up. The moment the rattling of its engine was heard the verandah light was switched on again and the bolt was drawn with a pat. At the same moment, Balu got down from the car. He leaned his elbow on the door and whispered something to Dr. Pal, at which Dr. Pal burst into a laugh and giggling sounds emanated from the back seat of the car. They did not notice Margayya's presence. Margayya could not restrain himself any longer. He was conscious of a desperation that impelled him on. All his caution and discretion were swept aside. He dashed to the other door of the car near the driving seat, thrust his arm in, got Pal by the scruff of his coat and dragged him out as Balu on the other side was saying: "Good night! " Nobody was prepared for it: and Dr. Pal staggered out. The moment he was out of the car, Margayya took off one of his sandals and hit him with it; he kept hitting out with such tremendous power and frequency that Pal could hardly protect himself. He was blinded by pain, and blood oozed from the cuts on his face. The girls within the car screamed: Balu came over and demanded: " What has come over you, father? "

Margayya turned on him, put his fingers around his neck and gave him a push towards the gate with: " Get out of my way, you little idiot! " Balu staggered and hit his head on the gatepost.

His wife came down the verandah steps with the cry: " Oh, are you hurt? What has happened? "

He rushed towards her asking: " When did this father of mine come here? " Meanwhile the child had been awakened by the hubbub and started howling and Brinda turned and ran back into the house. Balu followed her blindly in.

Meanwhile, the two girls in the back seat of the car cried out: " Help ! Help! "

Margayya put his head in and ordered: " Shut up, you whores! " He felt overpowered by the scent of powder filling the inside of the car. " Who are you?" he demanded. They at once became silent, and his tone became more menacing: " Who are you? " he thundered. His voice woke up a couple of street dogs and they started barking: which again woke up Balu's child so that it shouted more than ever.

The girls said: " We belong to . . . the theatre——"

" The theatre! Why don't you say what you really are! If you are seen again anywhere——"

The rest they could not hear, because Dr. Pal wriggled himself free, and suddenly dashed into the car, started it, and was off. He looked back and remarked: " You miserable miser, who cannot share your goods with your own son—all right——"

The red rear light of the car receded and vanished

around a bend. Margayya hesitated on the road for a moment to decide whether he should follow his son into the house. But he saw his son bolt the verandah door, and put out the light. "Good! Good! It is a good sign. He is a good son that trembles and runs away from his father," he said to himself, and turned homeward.

Later in life Margayya often speculated what would have become of him if he had started back home after speaking to his daughter-in-law a little earlier and missed Dr. Pal's Austin that night, or if he had remained in the shadows and had allowed Pal to go off after dropping Balu, whom he might probably have tackled with more circumspection and diplomacy: he might even have shared his property with him as he demanded: that would have saved him at least the rest of it—and prevented the doctor from doing what he did.

Dr. Pal went straight to a police station and recorded an immediate complaint of assault. The two actresses and Balu were his witnesses. Next morning he went round with plaster on his face to his various customers and businessmen. His first visit was to the blanket merchant. He took Balu along with him in the car. The blanket merchant was the first to ask: "What has happened to your face, Doctor?"

The doctor looked sad and said: "I am an academic man, and I should not have associated with businessmen——"

"Can't you tell me what happened?" the blanket merchant persisted.

The doctor just shook his head and said: "No, I can't—better leave things alone. It was my mistake to have associated with all sorts of folks, and I ought to blame only myself . . . I'm paying for it."

"Don't say so, sir. We have the greatest respect for you——"

"Business people have money, and they can help me

to set up my Psychological Clinic—that was my chief interest: that would have been of the greatest benefit to them: nowadays psychological wear and tear has the highest incidence among businessmen: theirs is a life of the utmost strain. I thought I might be of some help to the business community more than to anyone else—and what is the result? "

"No, sir, you must not speak like that. We have the greatest regard for you. But business life is becoming difficult with so many controls and permit forms to be filled up for all sorts of things. You have no idea how many obstacles a businessman has to face before he can get through anything in the Government——"

After this the doctor drew his attention again to the plaster over his cheeks. The merchant asked: "You have not yet told me where you got it? "

Dr. Pal lowered his voice to a whisper and said: "You will not believe me! Margayya assaulted me last night near his son's house."

"What! Why? "

"How can I say? He is somewhat queer these days. His son went up to him with some request and was slapped in the face. Later, I had to see him. Things are probably not going smoothly there."

"Ah! " exclaimed the merchant.

He was the first to meet Margayya at his house that morning. "I want to take back my deposit. There is a marriage proposal likely to shape out——" He grinned awkwardly, nervously, and held out the receipt issued by Margayya.

"My accountant has all the figures," began Margayya.

The blanket merchant cringed: "It's urgent. I've to find immediate cash."

"You have already drawn interest on it? "

"Yes . . . yes . . . But I want the principal."

"Oh, yes, certainly," said Margayya, and went into the small room and came out with a bundle of currency.

"You are a clever rogue! You have earned so much

214

interest and are now getting your capital! Very clever, very clever," Margayya said light-heartedly, which pleased the blanket merchant tremendously as he counted the cash and went out. This was the starting point. Margayya could not leave for his office. One after another they came with their receipts. Margayya returned their cash without a murmur. The street became congested with people converging on his house; people hung about his steps and windows. He bolted the front door and dealt with them through the window.

Margayya's wife looked panic stricken: "What has happened? Why so many people?"

"They are wanting their money back, that's all."

"What are you going to do?"

"Well, give it back, that's all."

"You have not eaten this whole day."

"I have no taste for food." He felt very weak and still could not stomach the thought of food. His eyes smarted with scrutinizing so many receipts. His wrist pained him with the counting of notes. He wished he could get his accountant by his side. He saw him through the window, struggling to approach the house in the midst of the crowd. But he could not come nearer. Some persons recognized the accountant, and turned upon him. Margayya saw them manhandling the old man.

"I knew nothing about it. I swear. I still know nothing about it," he was crying.

"My life's savings gone! I am a beggar today!" one of them shouted into the ears of the old man.

They were pulling him here and there. His spectacles were broken and his turban torn. A policeman came into the crowd and took away the old man.

By about four o'clock all the cash in the house was gone. All the mail sacks lay about empty and slack; yet peeping through the window, Margayya saw seas and seas of human heads stretching to the horizon, human faces at their most terrifying. The babble of the crowd was deafening. Luckily for him the front door of the house was at least a century old and made of thick timber, and could stand the battering by a hundred hands. People jammed the passage and windows and shouted menacingly. There seemed to be only one theme for all the cries: "My money! My money gone! All my savings gone——"

Margayya could sit up no longer. He just flung himself down on the floor beside the window. No air could come in. There were terrifying faces all around and the babble of voices; and over it all came the cry of an ice-cream pedlar: "Ice Cream! Ice Cream for thirst!" as his bell tinkled.

Margayya's wife was scared by the siege and at the condition of her husband. She bent over him and asked: "What shall I do? Oh, what shall I do?"

"Call my brother," said Margayya.

She ran to the backyard. Very soon Margayya's elder brother climbed the lavatory wall and the parapet of the well, jumped into the backyard and was in a minute by his side.

"Brother, what is this. What has come over you?"

"I'm tired . . . Please send for the police . . . Hurry up, otherwise they will mob this house: they will kill us, they will set it on fire, they will——"

"Do you still owe all of them money?"

"To all of them and many more unseen; more will come tomorrow. More and more of them . . . Get me the police to save us now and bring a lawyer. I am filing insolvency at once."

"Insolvency! Think of your family reputation!"

"No other way out, none whatever."

The brother, ever a man for a crisis, stood thinking. The hubbub outside was increasing every moment.

"The flood is outside," Margayya said. "It will wipe us out. Please, please run——" He felt too weak with his effort and lay still with his eyes closed.

His brother ran to his sister-in-law standing at the door sobbing. "Quick, give him something——"

"There is no milk in the house. The milkman could not

216

come in. There is nothing in the house. We have been
shut up here since the morning."

"Oh, is that so?" He rushed away, and returned soon
carrying a vessel full of coffee, and something to eat. He
seemed to be enjoying the situation. He said excitedly:
"Now, try and give him something. I tried to see if there
was a regular meal next door—but it was not available:
your sister-in-law will send you food presently. She has
just started cooking." He bustled round spreading his
utensils about. "Give him something at once. I will go
and get the police to guard us. I will also get a lawyer. I
will do everything to exempt this house at least from the
schedule. This is inalienable property. They cannot
attach this." His talk was full of technicalities. He rushed
off to the backyard and then on to his task.

The tide rolled back in about three or four months. Days
of attending courts, lawyers, inventories and so on and so
forth. Margayya felt that he had lost all right to personal
life.

He relaxed completely. He lay on a mat with his eyes
closed, his wife in the kitchen. A jutka stopped outside,
and in marched his son followed by his wife, carrying the
infant on her arm. The jutka man brought in a couple of
trunks and beds and placed them in the hall. Margayya
clutched the baby to his bosom. His daughter-in-law went
into the kitchen. Balu stood about uncertainly. Margayya
did not speak to him for a long time. The boy stood in the
passage undecided what he should do, his shirt unbuttoned
at the throat. A feeling of pity overcame Margayya. The
boy had lost some of the look of confidence that he wore
before—the radiance that shone on his face when there
was money in the background. Money was like a gem
which radiated subdued light all round. The boy looked
just dull and puzzled. Margayya kept looking at him so
long that he felt he had to explain: so he just said: "I
have come away—they have attached the house."

"With the furniture and all the other things?" Margayya asked. "I was expecting it——"

"It was difficult to come out even with our clothes and Brinda's jewellery. They demanded a list."

"I was expecting it. Come here, Balu."

Balu approached him and sat beside him. Margayya put his arm round him: "You see that box there. I have managed to get it out again." He pointed to a corner where his old knobby trunk was kept. "Its contents are intact as I left them years ago—a pen and an ink bottle. You asked for my property. There it is, take it: have an early meal tomorrow and go to the banyan tree in front of the Co-operative Bank. I hope the tree is still there. Go there, that is all I can say: and anything may happen thereafter. Well, what do you say? I am showing you a way. Will you follow it?"

The boy stood ruminating. He was looking crushed: "How can I go and sit there? What will people think?"

"Very well then, if you are not going, I am going on with it, as soon as I am able to leave this bed," said Margayya. "Now get the youngster here. I will play with him. Life has been too dull without him in this house."